IN AMERICA'S WAR AGAINST TERRORISM, THERE'S ONLY ONE ARMY—

CODY'S ARMY

JOHN CODY. A former Princetonian seasoned in Vietnam combat, he's the CIA's most amazing "mission impossible" man— and sworn to fight terrorism by any means necessary.

HAWKEYE HAWKINS. The tough, wisecracking Texan, he's one of the most daring men Cody took fire with in Vietnam.

RUFE MURPHY. The black giant whose exploits as a daredevil pilot became a legend, he saves a special hell for terrorists.

RICHARD CAINE. Booted out of England's crack antiterrorist strike force for insubordination, he's the world's greatest demolitions expert—and one of the bravest men alive.

Also by Jim Case

CODY'S ARMY: ASSAULT INTO LIBYA

Forthcoming from
WARNER BOOKS

Cody's ARMY

BY JIM CASE

WARNER BOOKS

A Warner Communications Company

WARNER BOOKS EDITION

Warner Books, Inc.
666 Fifth Avenue
New York, N.Y. 10103

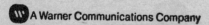 A Warner Communications Company

Printed in the United States of America
First Printing: July, 1986
10 9 8 7 6 5 4 3 2 1

CHAPTER
ONE

John Cody went into a low combat crouch just short of the tree line, his M-16 held up and ready in firing position, his eyes scanning the semidarkness ahead. He raised his left hand in a gesture that halted the five-man column behind him in the muggy, predawn gloom.

The sticky closeness of rugged jungle terrain murmured with the incessant chatter of birds and insects.

Four of the men behind Cody assumed a loose defensive formation, assault rifles aimed outward at different angles, probing the night for any sign of human movement.

The jungle sounds continued undisturbed around them.

Cody was a big, tautly muscled man, clad in camou fatigues and loaded for bear: in addition to the M-16 head weapon, he wore a Browning 9mm hi-power holstered at his hip. The military webbing strapped across his chest bore an assortment of grenades, a wire garrote, pouches with spare ammunition, and a combat knife sheathed at midchest for quick cross-draw. His hands and face, smeared with a cosmetic blackface goo, rendered him practically invisible, one with the night.

Lopez detached himself from his four men and scrambled forward to crouch beside Cody at the tree line. He, like his men, wore camou fatigues considerably shabbier than Cody's, and their M-16s were the only weapons they carried.

He and Cody gazed out across the fifty-yard clearing separating their position from ten-foot-high stone walls of the mission and country church.

A half moon shimmered in a cloudless sky, offering enough illumination for Cody to see the white stucco bell tower rising in the night from behind the walls.

Two Soviet-made Jeep-like vehicles with government markings sat parked near the arched entrance of the mission, an armored Soviet-built recon vehicle next to them.

Two Sandinista sentries leaned nonchalantly against the armored vehicle, their backs to Cody and Lopez, their AK-47 assault rifles propped against one of the Jeeps.

Cody saw the red pinpoints of two cigarettes in the gloom across the clearing.

"Get your men ready," he instructed Lopez in a low whisper. "We're moving in."

"Is it not as I told you *Señor* Gorman?" The contra's hushed reply quavered with pride and eagerness. "They expect nothing!"

"Yeah, it looks that way," Cody grunted. "Move it. Let's go."

"As you say."

Lopez crept back to his men, leaving Cody alone to refocus his attention on the mission objective.

The scent of cooking drifted through the heavy air to tantalize Cody's nostrils.

The government army patrol that had spent the past two nights inside this mission would be waking, stirring, he knew, and the only time to hit was *now,* in that period just before dawn when the security of any such position is universally at its weakest, when the night-shift sentries have grown bored with their lonely post, and careless.

In a high-risk situation, a commander would change his guard often enough to keep them fresh, but Cody figured the men those vehicles belonged to would be sleepy-eyed and more or less easy pickings for the hard hit that was now heartbeats away from going down.

The mission was situated on a single-lane dirt road that disappeared into the shroud of night in either direction.

They were less than fifteen kilometers north of San Jose de Bocay, but Cody's group had taken more than two hours to arrive at this spot; night driving was slow along the chaotic mountainscape, and extreme caution was necessary when traveling day or night through this harsh region. The mangrove swamps and cotton or coffee farms that were nominally under government control by day belonged to whomever had the strongest firepower after the sun went down.

Gorman and Snider, the two company contacts for this band of contras, had remained back with the van one kilometer behind.

The contra unit separated, Lopez silently signaling two of them further down the tree line away from Cody's left flank while the other two antigovernment guerillas jogged off and out of sight in the opposite direction—with barely a sound except for their muted footfalls and the soft sigh of branches and fronds being eased aside as they withdrew.

Lopez returned to crouch beside Cody.

"We are ready."

The contra stank heavily of b.o. and garlic. Scars from shrapnel wounds marked his throat and forehead.

Cody had little liking for the man or for any of the contras: a ragtag collection of scavenging mountain bandits who took money and weapons from the CIA to wage a guerilla war, supposedly for ideological reasons against a revolution they felt had betrayed them. Cody had no love for Marxists, but could discern little difference between the Sandinista strongmen running things from Managua and these unshaven, grubby opportunists, most of them ex-Somozan thugs who had most likely been robbing and pillaging the campesinos before the company decided to exploit them.

The Central Intelligence Agency had seen fit to utilize these "guerillas" to fight the spread of communism in Central America; to hopefully contain the situation from ever reaching proportions that would require U.S. military intervention.

Cody worked for the CIA.

He thumbed a bead of sweat away from his left eyelid and glanced sideways at Lopez.

"In and to the right of the chapel building?"

Lopez nodded.

"The classroom. It is where the nuns have been kept since the soldiers arrived. They are interrogated there during the day and forced to sleep on the floor during the night."

"I want you and your men to move in the instant I take out those sentries," Cody instructed. "No noise. Just get us those Jeeps and that armored job and get ready to start the engines as soon as you see me. I'll have the nuns with me."

Lopez shrugged in an offhand manner.

"Do not worry yourself so, my *yanqui* friend. All will go as you wish."

"Sure, it will," Cody growled.

He moved out, traveling low and fast, bee-lining across the clearing, then along the wall of the mission, advancing on the two sentries from their blind side.

Cody had been at this sort of thing for a long time, utilizing infiltration and combat skills taught him courtesy of Uncle Sam's Marine Corps and honed to a razor's edge during three tours of combat duty with the Special Forces in Vietnam. There he had commanded a covert "hit-and-git" hard strike force intended to neutralize important enemy targets, both military and civilian, and, more than a few times, behind enemy lines, pulling off success after success when there had seemed no chance for success, and usually with no mention made in official files.

During that time he had begun working with the CIA, and after the U.S. pullout he continued, even after his official military discharge, handling difficult jobs for the Company that took him from Ireland to Iran, from Libya to El Salvador.

He drew the missions that were considered impossible, or maybe just too damn dirty, except for someone with his skills and track record; dangerous, lonely work, but the only kind Cody could imagine for himself.

He came up on the two sentries.

They were not aware of his presence and wouldn't be until the killing began.

He had slung his rifle by its strap across his right shoulder so it could be swung around instantly if necessary, but at this point it was essential to keep the hit quiet.

Within moments all hell would break loose, but he had to get inside first and he had to free up these vehicles for Lopez and his men.

He unsheathed his combat knife with his right fist and snaked his left arm around the throat of the closest sentry.

The young soldier's cigarette dropped from his lips as he was yanked backward off his feet by the soundless, nearly invisible apparition that buried the knife to the hilt from behind just below the sentry's rib cage.

Cody's left hand clamped over his victim's face to silence the death gasp. He withdrew the blade from the body, stepping clear from it as it sagged, turning his attention to the second soldier, whose eyes had widened into white orbs of terror at the sight of his comrade's collapsing to the ground, the apparition coming at him next.

This sentry started to track his AK-47 around into firing position, started to open his mouth to yell a warning to those inside the walls.

Cody executed a martial-arts snap kick that ripped the rifle from the sentry's grip and, before the man could step back or react in any way, he moved in with a smooth continuation of the kick and slashed backhand up and outward with the knife's heavy blade—slicing open the guard's throat from ear to ear. He swung away from the spurting geysers of the severed jugulars.

The sentry became a dancing dead man, toppling backward against the nearest Jeep, then flopping forward flat onto his face, where he did not move, his dead hands clasped around his throat in a vain attempt to stem the blood flooding from between his fingers to twinkle blackly across the moonlit ground.

Silently.

Silent killing was another of Cody's specialities.

He faded back against the deeper shadows at the base

of the wall and paused just long enough to eyeball Lopez and the inky figures of the four others, jogging toward the vehicles from several points along the tree line across the clearing.

He moved out before they reached him, sheathing the combat knife, swinging his M-16 back around into firing position. He light-footed across the distance separating him from the archway set in the center of the south wall of the mission.

As he advanced, the scent grew stronger of someone boiling cabbage soup.

The day started early in Nicaragua, as in all of Central America, because of the heat, which was already oppressive.

He had been summoned from a secret base in Honduras, where he had been assigned to train some contra leaders in the more refined techniques of "soft" penetration and "hard" hit. The mountain bandits sent to him for shaping up had been lousy students, drunk most of the time and not particularly bright. So he had welcomed the hurry-up summons from Gorman's station in San Jose de Bocay.

Four American Roman Catholic nuns were being held prisoner, under "house arrest," within the walls of this mission, where they had been serving their church for the past eighteen months. The Sisters were being held here for interrogation by a unit of the Sandinista army battalion and charged with engaging contras in this region, according to Gorman.

The Nicaraguan regime was understandably sensitive in its dealings with the Church, since eighty percent of the Nicaraguan population was Roman Catholic. So this "preliminary questioning" was taking place here under extreme low profile over the past two days. It was for the men on the scene to decide if there was anything to suspicions that the Sisters were aiding and abetting the contras.

This situation had been brought to Gorman's attention by Lopez, the CIA's liaison with the regional contra network.

Gorman had reiterated the gravity of the situation to Cody as they had ridden in the van together to within hoofing distance of the mission.

"The kicker is that the boss nun at that mission, a

Sister Mary Francine, has been up to everything those Sandinistas think she's been up to. Managua made a massive fuck-up when they first took on the contras up here. They relocated nearly seventy-thousand peasants to keep them from being, uh, 'co-opted by the counterrevolutionaries,' is, I think, how they put it. They weren't too nice about it. A lot of the people who originally welcomed the new government lost their enthusiasm in a hurry when they saw their homes and land burning and were forced to move at gunpoint, and that brought about exactly what the government was afraid of. That mission has served as a contact point for all kinds of things the government isn't too happy with, and if they do get those nuns to talk—and they will if they decide there is something to what they've heard—well, then, the Company can just kiss off two years of damn hard work.''

Snider, Gorman's partner, had tacked on almost as an afterthought, ''And of course we want to pull those nuns out of that situation in any event.''

Cody reflected on that for a moment as he reached the archway to the mission. He froze with his back to the outside wall, his finger circled around the M-16's trigger. He watched Lopez and his contra team reach the vehicles.

He had been hustled into the country for a rendevous with the Company men, and Lopez and this crew, and had been brought here directly. His superiors in Honduras had told him that they needed one of the Company's specialists in this kind of thing and the nearest specialist had been Cody.

There was no time whatsoever to spare.

This was day three coming up of the soldiers questioning these nuns; it would surely be the day they would decide whether or not to leave the Sisters alone or take them to their headquarters for a more thorough ''interrogation''—which would be the last anyone ever heard of the nuns, period.

That was the way things happened in Nicaragua. Life was even cheaper than it had been before the revolution. Atrocity was the order of the day for both sides. For their part, the contras were unable and unwilling to care for captured troops and informers in their mobile hit-and-run campaigns against both the government and civilians sympathetic to the government. At the same time, the high command in Managua had intensified its military sweeps through cities and countryside with brutal repression backed up by the muscle of Soviet arms unloading almost daily at the port of Corinto. In a country the size of Alabama, population: three million, it was brother against brother; a bloodbath threatening to spill over Nicaragua's borders and growing worse day by day.

And here I am, right squat in the middle of another dirty little war, thought Cody, and he wondered what the tightness in his gut was trying to tell him. It could have been the people he had to work with or maybe he had just been around this track one goddamn time too many.

He told himself this was no time for such thoughts.

He glanced over at Lopez and gave the contra a thumbs-up sign that Lopez did not acknowledge or return. Then, taking a deep breath, Cody pushed himself away from the wall and went around and through the archway and into the mission courtyard, his M-16 up in both fists, ready to deliver.

CHAPTER
TWO

He could see why the military vehicles had been parked outside. It was more than just a show of force to impress and intimidate the locals.

The tiny courtyard of the mission was simply too confined a space in which to park or maneuver vehicles with any effectiveness in the event of an attack.

A long structure that Cody had been told was the nuns' living quarters, which had been taken over by the seven remaining troopers Lopez claimed were stationed here, was ahead and to his left, beside an area where a tethered donkey munched contentedly from a hay-filled cart.

Next to a chicken coop, a man in fatigues stood in the gloom, over a field stove, his back to Cody, preparing the soup Cody had smelled.

Directly ahead of Cody, next to the living quarters, was the chapel with the bell tower he had seen from outside the walls.

Next to a playground, where a children's swing set and slide clustered in the silver moonlight, to Cody's right as he came through the front gateway, keeping to the deep shadows, stood the wooden structure that would be the classroom where the nuns slept by night and were questioned by day, again according to Lopez's information.

He double-timed along the inside of the wall toward the rear of the classroom building.

A single light shone from the living quarters across the compound.

There would be one, possibly two, men stationed to keep an eye on the nuns.

The other three would be over in the nuns' living quarters; the noncoms and officer probably already stirring, beginning another day.

Movement from the building over there caught his attention before Cody could reach the rear wall of the classroom structure, to put the classroom building between himself and those living quarters.

He froze in a kneeling position at the base of the wall, M-16 swiveled in the direction of the front door of that building across the courtyard.

The front door had opened and a government soldier emerged onto the porch. He did not look in Cody's direction, and if he had, probably would not have discerned the blackfaced penetration specialist poised there, ready to open fire if need be.

Cody held his fire.

The trooper stood on the front porch and urinated into the dirt, then yawned, stretched, farted, turned and disappeared back into that building.

Another light went on over there.

A glance at the eastern sky showed the first pink traces of the coming dawn.

This mission courtyard would be humming with activity within a matter of minutes.

Cody cursed again the delays that had beset his small group on their way here. The rough country roads had tortured their van as Lopez had steered at a crawl past the scorched hulks of trucks ambushed by contras. A pin had sheared in the clutch linkage, which one of Lopez's men had replaced with a nail. Cody would have much preferred to stage this rescue in the dead of the night, when all but the sentries would be sound asleep and there would have been a good chance of making it inside, silently taking out the sentries and making it out of there with the Sisters, without any of the officers or noncoms finding out about it until morning. But the time element was something he had no control over.

He quit his position, hurrying to the back door of the classroom building. He paused with his back to the wall of the building and reached down to try the door handle.

It turned under his careful twist.

He used the barrel of his M-16 to nudge the wooden panel open a couple of inches, enough for him to get something of a look inside the one-room school building.

A kerosene lamp cast the room in a warm, golden glow.

He did not see the nuns, but he did see one soldier—no more than a kid, like most of those serving on both sides in this nation's civil strife—seated behind a desk at the front of the classroom, in front of a blackboard.

The soldier had tilted his chair back against the wall and had nodded off, his AK-47 straddled across his lap.

Cody figured it one of three ways.

Either the Sisters had taken advantage of their guard nodding off and had already taken flight. Or they passively remained captive somewhere inside the room, out of Cody's line of vision; this was possible, since there was much of the room he could not see from behind the two-inch space he had prodded the door open. Or the nuns were here and staying put because of a second sentry that Cody also could not see.

He stepped back so he was facing the door, gripped his shoulder-strapped M-16 with his right fist, and again unlimbered the combat knife. He delivered one mighty kick that slammed the flimsy piece of wood off its hinges, awakening the kid behind the desk long enough for him to push himself forward away from the wall, righting his chair, springing up like a jack-in-the-box, starting to track his AK at the figure in the doorway.

Cody flung the combat knife with his right hand and went into a forward diving roll into that room in the same motion even as the big blade whistled across the length of the room to bury itself in the young soldier's heart, driving him backward against the blackboard, a look of shock and pain frozen into a death rictus across his boyish features. Then his body pitched forward like a falling piece of timber behind the desk.

Cody came out of his roll in a kneeling crouch, whipping his M-16 in a wide circle to take in the sight of the four nuns where they sat along the floor against the wall to his left—and the soldier who had been sitting half-awake across from them, against a connecting wall, who now tried to leap to his feet. He went right back down under the force of Cody, who launched himself upon this sentry, bearing the guy down to the wooden floor beneath him, bringing the wire garrote from his belt in a two-handed wrapping around of the soldier's throat. Cody placed a knee on the man's chest and began to strangle him to death.

The soldier realized what was happening and hammered frantic survival blows that rained ineffectually upon Cody's unflinching chest and face.

The nuns became aware of what was happening, too, even if this rude awakening and the shock of sudden death before their eyes left them time to grasp nothing else.

Cody heard whimpers of dismay and a plea to stop from that direction, but he did not stop, knowing he had no other choice, given the odds against them getting out of here alive if his presence was detected. But he made it fast as he could; one savage jerk broke the soldier's neck with a dry snap, and the struggle ended.

He let the dead body rest and rewound the garrote, replacing it on his belt, turning from what he had done. He retrieved his knife, then glanced out the window to see that the small sounds which had seemed so loud in here, two men dying, had not been loud enough to be heard by those across the way. Then he turned for the first time to face the nuns, four women in their twenties.

Two of the Sisters could not take their eyes from the corpse of the strangled man.

The body made flatulent sounds as gas escaped. The dead man's face, twisted toward the ceiling, was purple in the glow of the kerosene lamp. His tongue protruded like an obscene, rotting sausage.

Cody ignored the look in the eyes of the one Sister who stared at him. He rushed over to the back door, motioning for the four to follow.

"Get a move on, Sisters. We don't have a hell of a lot of time."

The one who had been staring at him asked, with a nod to the two dead men, "Was . . . that absolutely necessary?"

"Sister Mary Francine?" he asked her, recalling the name Gorman had given him of the nun who led this pack and worked most closely with the antirevolutionary forces.

She nodded. "Yes, I'm Sister Mary Francine, but—"

"No buts or we're all dead. I came here for you."

This time she nodded briskly, a new look in her eyes.

"You're right." She turned to the other three, who were now paying somewhat more attention to this man who had brought death into their midst. "Come, we must leave here," she instructed them. "We have no choice, if we are to continue our work."

The other three nodded, following their leader. The four of them filed past Cody, out of the door and into the darkness, all of them avoiding glancing his way, as if they ultimately understood the necessity of what he had done but could not look with thanks into the eyes of the one who had cold-bloodedly murdered two youngsters.

Cody knew how they felt.

He started out after them when the front door of the classroom building opened inward at the opposite end of the spacious room.

The government soldier who had been working the field stove across the compound filled that doorway and started to speak something to the two men he expected to find in here. When he saw their corpses, which took all of about three seconds, he also spotted Cody and the nuns heading through the opposite doorway.

The soldier blurted something loudly even as he grabbed for his holstered sidearm.

Cody had no choice. He pulled off a three-round burst from the M-16, the assault rifle bucking in his grip, ejecting smoking spent shell casings, stabbing hot smoke and fire across the length of the room, the pounding reports, almost deafening, reverberating in the confines of the small building.

The soldier went into a spasming death-jig backward out through the doorway and into the courtyard, his ruptured back belching out blood and destroyed flesh as he took all three heavy projectiles across the upper chest.

Cody spun from that sight to join the nuns out back of the building, where they huddled in a group, watching him with staring eyes wide with apprehension and horror. He moved around them.

"This way," he urged.

They followed with alacrity.

He reached the corner of the classroom structure and peered around the corner at the living-quarters building across the courtyard.

Shouts and a sense of movement rippled through the half-light from over there.

The ridges and undulating terrain of the surrounding mountains were etched in stark relief against the warming horizon to the east, a dreamy half-light illuminating the mission in these final moments before dawn.

It was seventy feet or so to the front gate, by Cody's estimation. They would have to try for it. He hoped Lopez had the good sense to have his men cranking up those vehicles out there for a fast getaway now that this had blown to shit, but he could not hear any engine sounds outside the mission walls.

The tightening intensified in his gut; he expected something was about to go real wrong.

He blocked that thought, hurling himself away from his cover before anyone could show himself from the building across the way. He motioned for Sister Mary Francine and the other young missionaries to rush along after him, which they did.

He turned to them.

"There are people waiting outside the gate," he urged. "Hurry!"

Sister Mary Francine eyed him with new concern.

"What about you?"

He liked her for that. She was a fighter.

Two soldiers appeared on the run from the building across the way, gripping assault rifles, galloping toward the classroom building, not yet spotting Cody and the nuns because of the angle and the dawning half-light.

"I'm right behind you," Cody grunted to the nuns. "Just a couple of things to take care of. Now *go!*"

The head Sister followed his instructions, indicating for the other three to rush along with her toward the archway.

They had made it halfway there when their movement caught the attention of the two soldiers who had almost reached the front of the classroom building and the dead soldier sprawled there.

Cody had hoped to hold off on the fireworks until the Sisters had made it clear of the courtyard, then possibly withdraw himself without detection.

That changed when one of the soldiers yelled to the other and they both swung their weapons around toward the nuns, who did make it to and through the arched entrance to the mission courtyard.

The soldier to Cody's left triggered off a burst from his AK-47 that sent a line of ricocheting projectiles whining off the wall right beside the archway and just after the nuns had passed through it.

The soldier to Cody's right aimed at Cody.

Cody triggered a wide figure-eight burst intended to take out both of these goons of the state, but the one on the right saw it coming and leaped sideways.

The soldier who had been firing on the nuns started to readjust his line of fire toward Cody but a half-dozen of Cody's projectiles slammed the guy and sent him quivering into a backfall, haloed in a crimson spray.

The other soldier got Cody in his sights and fired, but Cody saw it coming with an eyeblink of time to pitch himself to the ground. The hail of bullets slashed the air where he had been standing an instant earlier.

He supported his aim with both of his elbows to the ground and pulled off a burst that melded with the clatter of the AK.

The soldier was lifted backward off his feet, as if

pushed by some giant invisible hand under the impact of the slugs that pierced and stitched his chest. The guy was a corpse before he hit the ground, but his dead finger remained curled around his rifle's trigger for the few seconds it took him to topple, spraying bullets into the sky.

Cody rolled onto his side, spotting the movement of two figures appearing in the front door of the living-quarters building.

The Sandinista officers who saw Cody and what he had done leaped back inside, hurried along by the noisy burst Cody flung after them, and a moment later both officers knocked out the glass of windows flanking either side of the door to commence firing at where Cody had been. But by that time Cody had scuttled away from the center of the small courtyard and gained the side of the building from which the two Nicaraguan officers were hosing down the courtyard with steady streams of automatic fire, fire that crackled like surreal strobelights in the lifting gloom.

He slinked around the corner of the building and started edging along its face even as the rifle muzzles spat death from the two busted-out windows, the army officers unable to see Cody. He kept himself against the wall and eased in inch by inch toward the window nearest him, reaching across his chest to pluck one of his grenades off his webbing.

He wondered where the hell Lopez and his bunch were, now that he could use some backup.

Just as he got to within two feet of the nearest window, the twin streams of auto-fire from inside the building ceased. The officers must have decided to reload, or were trying to get a bearing on what they were firing at, or both.

He kept his right index finger curled around the M-16's trigger. He lifted the grenade with his left hand and clamped his teeth about the grenade's pin, biting the damn thing free, drawing his arm back for a backhanded pitch through the window.

At that moment, a woman screamed from outside the wall of the mission.

The the sound was swallowed up by the angry chatter of several yammering automatic weapons.

Cody lobbed the grenade in through the shattered window and pulled back.

A thunderclap detonated inside the building, throwing the remaining glass from the window along with chunks of wood and one of the Sandinista officers who had pitched out partway through the nearest window, the back of his head a bubbly murk like warm strawberry jelly.

The door burst open again and the other officer reeled out in a cloud of billowing smoke from inside, stunned, injured, trying to get his bearings.

Cody heard the machine-gun fire from outside the mission taper off to nothing. He fed this goon a head shot that burst the guy's skull into a million bloody bits like an exploding melon; then he whirled and rushed for the archway, slapping a fresh magazine into the M-16.

He hoofed to a stop just short of the archway, pausing to ease one eye and the snout of his rifle around the corner for a look-see, not knowing what to expect, thinking that possibly some additional Sandinista troops had closed in on the contras and—

It wasn't that.

It was a scene from Hell.

It had been less than twenty seconds since the gunfire from outside the walls had ceased. Gunsmoke hung heavy in the air like a cloud.

The first soft rays of the new day revealed Enrique Lopez and his four contras standing to one side of one of the Soviet Jeep-like vehicles, the men all in the process of plunking fresh clips into their rifles, and none of the men were looking away from the gut-wrenching sight of what they had obviously just done.

The four nuns must have been instructed to hurriedly board one of the vehicles

Then Lopez had ordered his men to open fire at point-blank range.

Three of the women had been tossed into wretched positions of sudden, violent death upon the floor of the open vehicle, which was pockmarked with dozens of bullet indentations and the blood of the dead women who had been literally chopped into stringy, gory pieces by the close-in barrage of automatic fire.

Sister Mary Francine had been tossed bodily out of the far side of the Jeep by the impact of the bullets, her corpse a gruesome ruin that palpitated like the others in the throes of postdeath tremors.

The horrible, overly sweet stink of violent death wafted through the air like a tangible thing.

Cody had trouble believing his eyes, but he gave none of that away.

He had long ago lost count of the dead bodies he had seen; of the horrors he had witnessed, and perpetrated. It kept him up nights if he thought too much about it, but he did not lose his head in its presence.

He crossed over to where the contras had fallen in loosely behind Lopez, who regarded Cody as if nothing in the world was wrong. Lopez tossed a glance over Cody's shoulder, through the archway.

"All I have been told about the great John Cody in action is true, it would seem, *Señor*. There were . . . no survivors?"

Cody answered with one last, long look at the destroyed, ghastly remains of what, less than a minute ago, had been four living, breathing, vital human beings, then he looked back at Lopez.

"No survivors."

The contra discerned something in his eyes.

"You did know what was to happen, did you not, *Señor*? I thought Gorman—"

"Let's get back to Gorman," said Cody.

Lopez nodded to that with a grin that was half nerves, half relief.

"In any event, *Señor,* you helped us much, the way you handled those Sandinista swine. It is for the good of our cause, after all."

"Let's get back to Gorman."

Cody turned from the sight and trudged off, back across the clearing, toward the tree line, the way they had come.

He did not look back.

*   *   *

It was daylight when he and the five contras reached the
waiting van.

A sluggish morning mist hugged the surrounding
mountains except for the mile-high volcano, San Cristobal,
which puffed a white semaphore into the hot, white sky in
the distance.

Gorman and Snider had been sitting on the front
bumper of the van, watching the spot where Cody emerged
at the front of the column, the contras trudging along behind
him.

A circle of smoked cigarette butts around the front of
the van told Cody that the Company men had not had an
easy wait.

They stood as he and the contras approached them.

Gorman was a broad-shouldered, mean-faced guy.

Snider was as average as they come in appearance, and
seemed extremely nervous.

Gorman eyed Cody across a distance of some twenty
feet.

Cody had halted at that spot as the contras continued
their approach to the van.

Gorman studied Cody just standing there, not advancing with the others.

"I, uh, guess I owe you an explanation, John," was all
the bastard said.

"I guess you do."

Cody let nothing show in his expression or voice.

"It, uh, had to be this way, John."

"Did it? Tell me about it."

"Aw, hell, Cody, I didn't give the goddamn order,
y'know. I *follow* orders. You know how hard it is, getting
our people funded down here. I, uh, guess it was figured
that a few martyrs were needed. It will look like the
Sandinistas did that back there. You and Lopez's boys got
there to take them out, but too late."

Cody nodded.

"Too late," he echoed, a low, dangerous growl, and
this time some of what he had been carrying inside since the

mission must have come to the surface because Gorman got a worried look on his face and stepped back.

"Anti-Nicaraguan sentiments will be fanned to a blind hatred," Gorman went on. "That's what we need, if we want to serve America's interests. Getting money out of a tight-assed Congress will be a cinch now."

"And that's why those four women lost their lives?" Cody asked. "I just want to be sure, Jack. We murdered those women because it was our *job*?"

He could not help the rising inflection on that last word.

Gorman heard it too. So did Snider, behind and to Gorman's left. And so did the contras, who started to turn toward the confrontation with mild amusement.

Gorman tried to chuckle, but it came out a sour, grating sneer.

"Hey, Cody, I thought they were sending me a pro. You're not one of these dopes who still believes in right and wrong, are you?"

"I guess I am," Cody replied in a bare whisper.

He pulled up the M-16 he had been holding and opened fire.

CHAPTER
THREE

Fourteen Months Later . . .

He could tell instinctively that the first three human beings he had seen in more than a month meant trouble.

He had been about to set out to check his traps after breakfast, after his first drink of the day. The whiskey had felt as good as ever burning his throat to release that first glow of warmth in his gut that meant the day was really beginning.

Cody had almost come to enjoy the short stretch of time during the preparation and eating of his breakfast, before that first drink.

The scent of the pines and the crisp bite of the Canadian mountain air packed an almost painful nip that was strong enough to wake a man with a clear head no matter how much he'd put away the night before. Morning was a time when the world was nothing but Cody in his cabin on top of his mountain, alone up there in a clean world that had barely changed since Time began.

Times like those, he felt almost glad to be alive.

Then, if he had not awakened with them, the images would surface from the subconscious to torture him, and there he would be once again, standing outside that country mission near San Jose de Bocay, staring down at what remained of four women of the cloth; staring down at their pulverized corpses twisted in palpitating attitudes of death, what was left of their faces registering expressions that cried pain and surprise, and the glazed eyes of the corpse that was a Sister named Mary Francine.

That's when Cody always reached for the bottle and began the drinking that would last all day and into the night until loss of consciousness granted refuge from grief and pain.

He was pulling down and checking the heavy duty Weatherby Mark V bolt-action .460 Magnum hunting rifle from its rack above the fireplace. He always toted the big Weatherby and an Army issue Colt .45 automatic holstered at his right hip. A wide-blade, double-edged hunting knife was sheathed at his left hip.

Old habits die hard.

He had started out of the cabin, when the buzzer sounding stridently across the room stopped him in his tracks. He wheeled around and crossed to the electronic control panel, where he flicked off the alarm warning mechanism and activated the three closed-circuit television screens located there.

The twelve-inch screens winked and shimmered to life, the center one picking up a late model station wagon as it bounced along the narrow, rutted, steep incline through the rugged pine forest that was Cody's 100-acre corner of the world.

That placed them one half-mile southwest of the cabin, no more than two or three minutes away.

He flicked off the system, exiting the cabin at a run toward the high ground thirty yards from the structure's back door.

A few months from now, later in the year, he would have expected them. Hunters had ventured up the road as far as his cabin on several occasions during the preceding hunting season, despite the posted No Hunting and No Trespassing signs.

He paused well into the dense, towering tree trunks.

On those previous occasions, he had pulled back to this spot to watch and wait, and those hunters had realized the road dead-ended on private property and had steered their vehicles around and retraced their route away from his cabin site.

These weren't hunters, he knew. The time of year, and a quiver of foreboding that reached down inside him and squeezed, told him so.

He remained standing, his back to the direction of the cabin, pressed against the trunk of a pine that had to be eighteen inches in diameter. He held the Weatherby perpendicular to his body and twisted around the trunk just far enough to peer down into the clearing around his cabin.

The sigh of a cool breeze through the towering pines, and the earthy tang of nature enveloped him and he allowed himself to become one with the living, breathing wilderness around him.

He was at home here.

He knew those in the vehicle would not be, and that was his one advantage. They would be pros, he was somehow certain, as skilled in the art of tracking and killing as he was.

The station wagon halted. He heard the driver kill the engine.

A brief pause, then three men debarked to stand near each other but not clustered, two of them toting hunting rifles.

Cody recognized the one in the middle. The one without the rifle; the agent in charge. The one who lifted his hands to his mouth to magnify his voice and shouted.

"Cody!"

Cody did not move, maintaining his position, his rising combat senses probing the thickly wooded wilderness around him in all directions for any sign of danger, but the only other presence he could detect was the trio down there by the cabin.

Yeah, he recognized their leader all right. He'd known Lund all the way back to Nam, and had been on friendly terms with Pete right up until Cody's abrupt leave from government service.

The last time he had seen Pete, Lund had headed the CIA's assassination unit.

Cody rapidly considered his options. He had hoped they never would find him but had somehow always known they would if they really wanted to. A man cannot hide from the Central Intelligence Agency of the United States of America any more than he can hide from his own past.

He had taken every conceivable step to conceal his ownership of this land, and since leaving the Company under the cloud of what had happened in Nicaragua, he had not left his property line since arriving here except for a monthly sixty-mile round-trip down to the crossroads country store at the base of the mountain, the nearest outpost of civilization.

He had remembered, from his long-ago days at Princeton, Plato's dictum that "the unexamined life is not worth living." Well, he'd given himself a life with nothing to do but survive up here mountain-man style the year around, alone with the wilderness and his past, with nothing more than the solitude and time to examine the life he'd led, but he could find no good in his life that could ever balance the scales for what he had been a part of on that last mission into Nicaragua; the atrocity that drove him to this Canadian mountaintop.

Technically, of course, the massacre of those nuns had not been his fault, but such knowledge did little to erase the stark mental images of the bloodied, fresh corpses of Sister Mary Francine and the other three women at that little country mission.

He had spent his time up here prowling this no-man's land, hunting, trapping, trying to somehow make sense of the ungraspable; of what was done and lost forever. He spent his nights hitting the bottle too damn hard but he had never let self-pity or guilt dull responses and reflexes and a soldier's sixth sense earned in the hellgrounds of the world prior to his "retirement."

Lund stopped calling out his name from the clearing by the cabin, he and the two men with him standing in their loose cluster down there, gazing off in various directions toward the walls of pine that lined the ridges around the cabin.

Cody noted that the two guys with Lund had their rifles aimed at the ground, not in firing position.

He made his decision.

A hawk chose that moment to soar into the clearing, riding the air currents high beneath the cobalt-blue sky.

Cody left his concealment, not with any sudden rushing movement, but, rather, assuming an easy gait as he purposefully made himself visible to the others, as if he were coming upon the cabin, returning with no prior realization that Lund and his two pals were down there.

He had to keep himself visible several moments longer than he intended because Pete had his eyes skyward, watching the hawk.

Then one of the other men spotted him, shouting something that swung around the attention of Lund and the other man, and they all saw him then, which is what he had waited for.

He whirled, lunging back into the shadowy interior of the half-lit world at the base of the pines that made the mountains a carpet of crisp green.

Lund shouted something at him from below back there but he could not discern the words.

He heard nothing but his own footfalls along the rocky trail that had been here when he bought this property. He did throw one look over his shoulder to make sure Lund and the others were after him.

They were, the Company men hoofing up the incline in hot pursuit.

He poured on the steam, his legs pumping, following the trail for several yards to where it dipped beneath the lip of a wrinkle in the terrain, losing him from the line of vision of the men dashing after him.

They had not opened fire on him, and that decided him on what to do next.

He jogged a dozen more long paces, then darted to his left, positioning himself behind another tree trunk amid a thick growth of conifers that would effectively block him from sight of the men giving chase; the reason he had chosen this exact spot fourteen months ago when he had gone about securing his hideaway.

His erstwhile employers were the least of his worries, he had known all along. A man made enemies working for the Company and the many Cody had made would hardly be expected to give up the chase to even up old scores just because he had declared himself out of the game.

So far, no one from his past had managed to track him down.

Until now.

They came over the ridge at the dead-heat gallop, Lund in the middle, the rifle toters evenly spaced from each other, not bunched together.

Lund topped the lip of the ridge and Cody saw he toted a snub-nosed .38 revolver, as the three charged along the trail coming past where Cody knelt in the milliseconds it took before the three Company men had time to pull up with the realization that they had lost sight of him.

The first man trotted by his place of concealment, the one in the lead, starting to slow when he realized Cody was not up ahead on the trail as they must have expected him to be.

Lund and the third man slowed their pace.

Cody waited until Lund was where he wanted him, then he leaned forward to a taut length of clear rope and he severed that rope with one swift cut, causing the trap to be sprung.

The loop of the nearly invisible line snapped around Lund's ankles while the tree limb it was attached to sprung up, released by the line severed by Cody, the loop tightening into a knot around Lund's ankles and whisking him upward, head-over-heels upside down, the .38 flipping from his fingers.

Too caught by surprise to even emit a shout of alarm before he was dangling upside-down like bagged game ready to be skinned, Lund ended up with the top of his head five feet from the ground.

Cody bounded out from cover, the knife already unsheathed, the Weatherby swinging around in a punching arc, used as a club.

The first man, in front of Lund, came around with a snarling oath at the commotion of Lund being hoisted topsy-turvy, but the guy walked into the sharp smack of the Weatherby's ventilated rubber recoil pad buttplate across his right temple. His knees buckled and he went down.

Cody pulled the Weatherby around, down into firing position on the third man before the first had fully collapsed upon the ground.

Lund swung lazily back and forth, a human pendulum, cursing vividly, attempting to pull himself up and around, reaching up toward the knotted line around his ankles, but he could not bend himself back up far enough.

The third man had his rifle nearly around in target acquisition, but abruptly ceased all movement like a robot with its juice cut when he found himself looking into the Weatherby's muzzle.

This one know weapons, thought Cody. He'll recognize the rifle aimed at his heart. He'll know the Weatherby fires a five-hundred-grain bullet that achieves the highest velocity of any bullet in the world. He'll know what such a bullet would do to his chest if he made the slightest wrong move.

"Drop it," Cody instructed. "You don't have to die."

The man dropped it.

Lund continued swaying back and forth, not giving up the impossible task of trying to free himself.

"Cody, damn you, you rotten goddamn sonofabitch. Let me the hell down from here!"

Cody did not take his eyes or the Weatherby's muzzle away from the bead drawn on the third man's heart.

"Handgun, too."

Lund shouted, "Cody, for chrissake—"

"Shut up, Pete."

He watched the other man reach under his jacket and ever so gently remove a .44 Magnum from concealed shoulder leather. The man held the pistol by his fingertips, away from his body, and let it drop.

An owl hooted from a tree somewhere nearby.

Cody motioned with the rifle, directing the man to stand near where the unconscious figure of the first one lay sprawled.

"Over there."

The agent obeyed, his hands raised, his mouth a worried, tight gash across a nervous face.

Lund gave up struggling.

"Jesus H., Cody, what the hell is this? Let me down, damn you—"

Cody kept his peripheral vision on the agent standing with upraised hands next to his unconscious pal. He lowered the Weatherby so the snout of the muzzle nudged Lund's nostrils none too gently, like the cold kiss of death.

"You've been behind a desk too long, Pete. You bozos were too easy. How did you find me?"

"How the hell should I know?" Lund bristled. "I didn't find you. I was told where you were and I came, and this is the kind of a goddamn welcome I get!"

Cody could not hold back a grin that was tight around the edges; the first grin he remembered cracking since he'd come here.

"You've still got your balls, Pete, I'll say that for you." He applied a degree of pressure and the Weatherby's muzzle nudged Lund's nose not quite so gently. "What makes you think I won't blow your Company head off for coming up here after me?"

"Hey, hey, relax, John." Lund's voice took on a shading of panic that had not been there before. "*Relax!* I'm not with the old unit anymore. They gave me a new job."

Cody stepped back, removing the end of the Weatherby's barrel from Lund's nose, pulling the rifle away.

"I came up here because I don't want any part of you people, or of anyone else. I want you and these two clowns off my land or I will blow your heads off and I'll take real good care of what's left of you and no one will ever pin it on me. And when they send the next team, I'll be ready for them, too."

"There won't be any teams," Lund insisted from his upside-down position. His swaying had stopped when he ceased struggling. "For godsakes, cut me down from here so we can talk, will you?"

Cody mulled that over for a few seconds. He reached

another decision. His right hand flashed across his chest and the knife blade glinted.

The length of line stringing Lund up was snicked in two.

Lund plummeted head-first down five feet to the ground, emitting a full-bodied *thump* and a full-throated yowl that lifted high above the treetops.

"In a nutshell," Lund said, some time later, "the U.S. government has decided to do something about its inability to cope with international terrorism; an inability that has reached crisis proportions."

Cody and Lund sat at the table in the center of the one-room cabin, Lund nursing with a makeshift ice pack the bruise on his forehead, Cody nursing a glass of scotch.

The two Company agents Lund had brought with him loitered out front of the cabin near the station wagon, the one having regained consciousness, and he and the other having both been given their weapons back. Neither had tried to conceal their open resentment of Cody when Lund had instructed them to wait by the station wagon and keep their eyes open.

Cody did not give much of a goddamn. He was not even sure why he was sitting here right now, listening to Lund.

"I'm all finished working for you people, Pete. No more."

"I've tuned and greased one hell of a sweet machine," Lund continued, as if he hadn't heard. "And it's all on orders right from the top and I am talking the Man, John. The Oval Office. I've been given a free hand. I've got the thing organized. I just need the right people, and it's ready to happen. I want you in on it from the start—you'll run the show, and you'll take orders only from me."

Cody returned Lund's level stare across the table.

"You go to Hell, Pete. You and the Man."

Lund pretended not to hear that, either.

"I've fought every step of the way to bring you back in." A trace of a grin crinkled the Fed's grim expression. "They had to give in, in the end. Every time they put all the specs they wanted into the computers, your name kept spitting back out at them from the top of every list of those best qualified to head such a unit.''

"Must be a real dirty jobs unit, huh, Pete? Dirtier than Nicaragua?''

Lund sighed.

"You won't let that one drop, will you?''

"Let it drop?'' Cody echoed quietly. "You weren't down there. You didn't see four women with their guts splattered out all over the goddamn—''

"Okay, okay,'' Lund countered uncomfortably, "but you did something about that, didn't you?''

"All except for Gorman,'' Cody nodded. "He's still working for you, I'll bet, isn't he? If he'd been a little slower while I took care of the rest of those scum, he'd be dead meat now, too.''

"There weren't any reprisals against you, were there, John? You took out Snider. You took out Lopez and those other contras. It took Gorman six months to recover from the wound where one of your bullets grazed him where he wasn't protected by that vest. We deeply regret what happened and we cleaned house. The public never found out about what happened to those nuns. Dammit, John, you've been working for the Company since Nam. You know the left hand never knows what the—''

"I've heard all of that,'' Cody growled. "And I know the field agent who ordered that massacre bought the farm himself two weeks later in Grenada. That's why *I* didn't take any more reprisals.''

"You were back at Langley being processed out when that happened,'' Lund nodded. "That's the only thing that stopped you from taking the fall for that one, and they would have terminated you if they'd thought you were behind that. As it was, they traced it to the Cubans.''

"And now they want me back.''

"*I* want you back,'' Lund corrected. "I wish I could be as sure about the President. I think he realizes you're the man for the job, but he thinks of it more as the evil to fight evil. General Johnson is still the Man's principle advisor on covert military operations, and you know what a by-the-booker he is. I don't think the general ever quite got over what you did down there in Nicaragua, and he's got the Man's ear, too. He seems to think you're a wild card: that you can't be trusted.''

"Maybe he's right. Have you thought of that?''

Lund emitted an exasperated sound.

"You are the sanest man I have ever known. And the meanest, and the most bullheaded. You're the man for this unit I've been authorized to form, can't you see that? The computers say so, I say so, and you know it's so.

"You will be given carte blanch to assemble, prepare and command an elite four-man commando unit intended to strike quick and hard in a crisis situation.''

"The Army has Delta Force for that!''

Lund shook his head.

"Your unit will be strictly off the record, right from the git-go. You will operate ruthlessly, if necessary, to fight back as dirty as it gets with only one objective: your team goes in when delicacy or timing preclude use of standard military response like that of Delta Force; situations where a visible U.S. military response would endanger American security.''

Lund paused; then, studying Cody closely, "Well, that's my pitch. That's why I've come here. What do you say?''

Cody pushed back from the table, stood and walked over to the cabin's window, where he gazed out at the two agents by the station wagon, but he was not really looking at them, or thinking about them.

"You made the trip for nothing, Pete. There was a time when I thought there was a good fight worth fighting. No more.''

He somehow found himself wondering about those words the moment he spoke them.

Lund snorted angrily.

"I may be taking my life in my hands saying this to a berserk guy like yourself, but you are one disgusting sight, do you know that? All alone up here in your little world while the real world is going to hell because there aren't enough good men to fight what you call the good fight. Let me show you something. Come here.''

Cody went back over to stand next to where Lund sat at the table.

Lund reached into an inner pocket and withdrew an envelope from which he extracted a sheaf of six-by-ten-inch glossies, stark black-and-white wire service photos. He slapped them down on the tabletop one at a time, spreading them out for Cody to see, punctuating the slap of each grisly photo on the table with a curtly spoken caption.

Slap. A shot of dead human beings in casual civilian attire; dead human beings—men, women and children—sprawled in what looked in the black-and-white photo like spreading pools of black oil, in front of a baggage-claim area.

''Rome airport. Two months ago. Four terrorists walked in with concealed automatic weapons and opened fire; the four of them were killed, too, but not before they did this, and notes on their bodies claimed that this was just the beginning.''

Slap. Tables and chairs overturned, decorated with inanimate remains only halfway identifiable as human.

''Bomb planted in a London restaurant. No one's really sure about this one, believe it or not. The IRA and the Libyans both claimed responsibility. The sick bastards actually fight over claiming atrocities like these as their own.''

Slap. No bodies this time, only the charred, smoldering remains of a structure that had just finished burning to the ground.

''A children's hospital in El Salvadore. Twenty-seven dead.''

Lund spread the remaining seven or eight pictures out across the table in front of him, indicating with an angry wave of his hand what Cody could see was more of the same.

''This is from the last twelve months, and it's only a sample. *This* is what is happening, John. Can't you see what you're doing? You're giving *them* the edge. You're helping *them* to get away with these kinds of things by not being out there doing something instead of wallowing up here in self-pity for a tragedy that wasn't your fault. I know you've been through Hell and it was the Company's fault, but damn it, John, there's more Hell to come and the lines are being drawn. We aren't perfect, God knows, and that means we need men like you all the more, don't you see that? Come back, John. We need you. The whole blessed country needs all the men like you it can find at a time like this.''

Cody set down the glass of scotch he had not touched since Lund began his pitch. He knew why he had allowed himself to sit and listen to an old friend who had come so far for something that mattered.

Lund was absolutely right.

"If I had to narrow it down to only three men in the world I'd want to take into combat with me, you know who they'd be.''

An ear-to-ear grin split briefly the Fed's face, then he got serious and very businesslike again, scooping up the pictures, returning them to the manila envelope.

"I figured they'd be the same three we went through Nam with when you anchored your team there and I was the guy who handed you your assignments. Kind of brings back old times, doesn't it, Sarge?''

"Where are they, Pete?''

"I had the three of them tracked down," said Lund, "and they may be our next problem. They're all three kind of unreachable.''

"Last I heard, Caine was SAS.''

"Was," Lund acknowledged. "They gave him the boot about a year ago. Who knows why; no one talks in that outfit. And guess who he tied up with when he went looking for a job?''

The glint in his eye gave Cody the clue.

"You saying I won't have to make that many stops to round up the old team?''

"I mean just that. Caine and Hawkins teamed up to work a bounty-hunter scam out of south Texas." Lund saw the question marks *that* must have brought and chuckled. "Don't ask me. Hawkeye says the pickings for fugitive bond-jumpers is overripe down there and Richard seems to agree. They've got a very profitable business going for themselves.''

Hawkeye Hawkins. A Charles-Bronson-goes-Panhandle sort of guy; a coarse, wiseacre Texan who was one of the best fighting men Cody had ever taken fire with.

Richard Caine had been attached to Cody's team in Vietnam and Cody knew of no better demolitions expert in the world than the dour, hard-as-nails Englishman.

He experienced a renewal of some life force within him which his sorrow over the fate of those nuns—for all mankind—had dammed up for too long, he now realized.

The lines were being drawn, Pete had said.

Damn right.

''And Rufe?''

Rufe Murphy. The black giant and best buddy who had piloted Cody's unit in and out of more hot LZs in Nam than any grunts had a right to survive.

Lund lost some of his enthusiasm.

''Uh, now there we could run into a real problem.''

''Let's hear it.''

''Rufe's been running a one-man charter helicopter service in Mississippi, but at the moment he's in a jail cell awaiting trial.''

''On what charge?''

''Grand theft, auto.''

''Anything to it?''

''Hell, no. You know Rufe. He was banging the mayor's wife.''

''The mayor's white?''

Lund nodded.

''And so's the wife. And I think that cancels out your third choice. It's like I said, John: Hawkins, Caine, Murphy. . . . unreachable, all of them.''

''I'll reach 'em,'' Cody growled. He picked up the tumbler of scotch and pitched it into the fireplace, where it shattered ceremoniously; the closing of one chapter in his life, the beginning of another. With no looking back. He grabbed up the Weatherby, which was all he intended to take with him that he wasn't carrying, and started toward the cabin doorway. "Let's go, Pete. Let's do it."

Lund hurried to catch up, murmuring to himself. "Well, all goddamn right. Here we go again!"

CHAPTER
FOUR

The road appeared to stretch into infinity in either direction across the lean, sun-burnt desert lands fissured here and there by an empty riverbed with nothing else on the horizon except the occasional buttes—rosy pink now in the minutes after sunset. The western sky was a warm red, with wispy traces of scudding clouds just beginning to take on a purple hue.

The only sign of life in the desert was the overworked engine whine of a four-wheel-drive vehicle eating up the two-lane blacktop from Chihuahua, eighty kilometers to the south, toward the U.S. border crossing at Presidio, Texas, sixty kilometers to the north.

Hawkeye Hawkins had his eyes pasted to the rearview mirror.

"Reckon this rodeo is about to pump into high gear," he drawled over his shoulder to Richard Caine, in the back seat with a third man. "Looks like some of Ruiz's boys have found out the boss man ain't among them."

Caine, a sturdy, flat-muscled, handsome man, applied pressure to the 9mm Beretta he held pressed against Jesus Ruiz's temple.

"That best not be your crew, El Gato. If any shooting starts, lad, you're going to catch the second shot fired."

Ruiz, who had been dubbed The Cat by drug agents on both sides of the border for his ability to walk away from death every time it came looking for him, appeared, in his silk shirt and pressed slacks, cool as a guy out for a Sunday jaunt, or maybe on his way to drop in on some border-town police chief with the month's payoff.

"Certainly those are my men," he purred with barely the trace of an accent, his pencil-line moustache curved upward at the ends with his smile. "And you will not kill me, gringos. If I die, you most certainly will die. I suggest you pull this vehicle over at once and allow me to rejoin my friends, or I am afraid—"

Caine rapped Ruiz sharply in the mouth with the butt of the Beretta.

"Shut the fuck up," he said quietly.

Ruiz lost some of his composure, his hands flying to his mouth with a yip of pain. He spat out red-specked pieces of teeth, cussing hotly in Spanish.

"Oh-oh," said Hawkins. "Trouble up ahead too, if I read this right." Caine looked over Hawkeye's shoulder, out the front windshield at what the Texan behind the wheel saw: a Jeep coming fast at them, growing from a dot on the horizon. A look over his shoulder told him the same kind of vehicle, behind, was gaining, too.

"Trouble is right," the Brit grumbled. "I thought this was going to be one of those easy ones, mate. I thought this whole bloody bounty-hunter business was supposed to be a piece of cake."

"There you go again," Hawkins sighed, scanning either side of the road they roared down without slacking speed. "Always griping about a little hard work. You got to earn your pay once in a while."

Caine's eyes followed Hawkeye's.

"That high ground to the right," he said as if reading the Texan's mind. "Those rocks. We can make them if we're lucky."

"Luck's got nothing to do with it, pard," Hawkeye growled. "Hold onto your tea bags."

He palmed the wheel. The four-wheel-drive vehicle bulleted off the blacktop toward an outcrop of rock at the base of an incline toward one of the buttes, perhaps a quarter-klick away.

The vehicles closing in on them veered off the highway the moment those drivers ascertained what Hawkeye was up to and began speeding in from different angles about one-half a kilometer behind, clouds of dust spiraling up behind all three vehicles as the four-wheel-drive led the pack toward the base of the butte.

Ruiz watched his men closing in from behind.

"You have no chance, *Señors*," he gurgled between broken teeth. Crimson spittle stained his shirt. "You are outnumbered. The Jeeps will be in radio contact with others—"

"You just don't take a hint, do you, hairbag," Caine sighed. He whapped Ruiz across the temple with the butt of the Beretta.

El Gato's eyes rolled back in his head, and he slid to the floor of the backseat of the bouncing vehicle.

"Now maybe we'll have some peace and quiet," said Hawkeye, glancing back out their vehicle's rear window at the two Jeeps closing in fast from different directions. "At least for a minute or two," he added.

Felipe Gallegos set down the hand-held transceiver after having summoned reinforcements from the hacienda. He held onto the frame of the Jeep to keep from being tossed from the vehicle as the driver kept the accelerator pressed to the floorboard. His rifle rode between his legs, aimed up and out, and the three men in the back held on too as the Jeep bounced along off the road in pursuit of that four-wheel-drive vehicle up ahead. It was like riding a bucking bronco, but Gallegos, as the man in charge of security at *Casa* Ruiz, thought far more about what El Gato would do to him when this was over than the danger of being thrown from this vehicle, or of having to deal with the bounty hunters who had the boss.

The two men could be nothing else, Gallegos reasoned

as he cast a glance at the other vehicle, commanded by Sanchez, closing in.

Bounty hunters.

They were the ones you had to fear, and somehow they had gotten to Jesus during the siesta and Gallegos had not learned of it until the four-wheel-drive vehicle was seen racing away with a handcuffed Jesus Ruiz already in it.

Up ahead, the vehicle reached the cluster of rock where the bare ground began its incline to become one of the sporadic buttes dotting the region.

It could be worse, Gallegos told himself. At least we will get El Gato from them. We outnumber them right now ten-to-two, and it will be twenty-five-to-two when the others arrive shortly. The gringos would be promised safe passage. They would release Jesus. They would, of course, be slain, their bodies left to the buzzards and the jackals.

Gallegos looked behind, to the west. The light of the western sky was fading but they still had another forty minutes of light. Enough time, yes. And this would teach the boss to stay on this side of the border, Gallegos hoped, where El Gato would not run the danger of having any more warrants sworn for his arrest in the States, which would bring more men like the two who had him now.

He saw the four-wheel-drive skid to a stop and the two men alight from it.

Where was the boss?

The bounty hunters moved to one side of the car and pulled out what looked to Gallegos from this distance like a rolled-up rug. Then as the two Jeep-loads of men closed in to within several hundred yards of that rock cluster, he saw with something of a shock that it was the boss!

El Gato's body landed roughly on the ground, and one of the men grabbed the unconscious Ruiz where the handcuffs linked his hands and dragged Jesus behind the rocks.

The boss is going to be real pissed now, thought Gallegos, and the only way to get off El Gato's shit list would be to fill those two gringo bastards so full of holes that the buzzards and jackals wouldn't even bother with what was left.

*   *   *

Hawkins dragged an unconscious Ruiz roughly across the rocky ground to behind the cluster of boulders, where a shelf of level land, surrounded by brownish-green, bunchy shrubs, allowed him to look from higher ground down upon the converging Jeeps full of gunmen—rifles poking into the air from each bouncing, speeding vehicle like antenna on some strange desert predator.

He dumped Ruiz against one of the boulders and turned to stretch flat across the ground, unholstering the .44 Magnum he wore leathered cross-draw fashion on his left hip.

He called to Caine, "Better get a hotfoot on, limey. This here gunfight's about to commence."

Caine spun from the back of the four-wheel-drive. He gripped an M1 match rifle equipped with a rifle grenade attachment and fitted with a Startron infrared telescopic sight. He shouldered a pack loaded heavy with grenades and ammo.

"Had to fetch the peashooter," he called back, jogging toward the boulders on the higher ground. "How's sleeping beauty?"

Hawkeye turned from eyeing the oncoming jeeps, now some five hundred yards out and zeroing in side by side.

Jesus Ruiz groaned and mumbled something groggily and started to open his eyes and sit up.

Hawkeye leaned over and cracked the drug dealer behind the right ear with the butt of the .44.

Ruiz settled back against the rock to resume snoring fitfully.

"A tad worse for the wear but still sawin' 'em off," he replied as Caine joined him. "Looks like we could be boxed in this time, Richard, old chap."

The Brit bellied out beside Hawkins, supporting himself on his elbows, sighting in on one of the Jeeps through the M1's sniper scope.

"Let's see what some heavy artillery buys us, shall we?"

He sighted in on the Jeep of gunmen roaring in on the left, flicked the selector switch, and triggered, the M1's report cracking in the open desert air, the recoil jerking his body.

The Jeep on the right blossomed into a forward-moving rolling fireball intensified when the Jeep's gas tank went as it turned end-over-end, tossing flaming bodies this way and that.

"Not bad shooting," Hawkeye commented, "for a limey."

Gallegos could not believe his eyes. A heartbeat earlier the Jeep with Manuel and the four others had been racing along side-by-side with his own vehicle, perhaps two yards away, toward the gringo bastards behind those rocks where they held Jesus.

And then—the explosion out of nowhere, death shrieks swallowed up into the ball of flame and now the earth behind his Jeep littered with human and metal debris, aflame and lifeless.

"To the left, to the left!" he screamed at his driver. "The other side of those rocks!"

The driver careened the Jeep into a two-wheel turn that nearly tumbled every man out of the Jeep, as the vehicle dashed toward the same butte before which the bounty hunters had sought cover, the Jeep heading toward their blind side; the far side of the rising butte.

Gallegos worriedly eyed the horizon behind them but could not as yet discern any sign of the three Jeeps full of men that should at this moment be racing here in response to his radio summons.

The hacienda was no more that ten kilometers from here, so they would be here soon, and then—

His thoughts were interrupted by another heaving explosion rocking the earth, one of the grenades fired by the gringo detonating a shower of earth upon the racing Jeep, a near-miss.

Then they made it to behind the butte, disappearing from the line of vision of the two who had Ruiz on that high ground of boulders.

"Stop here!" Gallegos ordered.

The driver obeyed, flooring the brake pedal, swinging the Jeep around in a 180-degree turn.

Gallegos wondered what he should do. He had never

doubted the gringo's expertise in these matters even before seeing his amigos in the next Jeep getting blown to pieces. El Gato's hacienda was a veritable desert fortress, and yet these bounty hunters had somehow penetrated his defense perimeter and gotten away with the boss.

Then he saw the three Jeeps full of rifle-toting men turn off the highway, coming high speed in this direction. He recognized the vehicles and laughed. He hopped from the Jeep.

"Come, muchachos! The gringos will have their hands and eyes full with those who approach." He started hurrying up the incline, gesturing for them to follow, which they did. "We shall outflank the gringos, kill them, save El Gato and the glory will be ours. Let's go!"

The eastern sky yielded to the purple of oncoming night, the western horizon's warm red becoming the bleak gray of dusk.

Caine lowered the M1, having viewed the oncoming Jeeps through the scope.

"Fifteen men," he informed Hawkeye coolly. "They'll be in range soon."

Hawkins shifted to scan in another direction, into the failing light of an ending day, at the spot where the first Jeep had disappeared behind the butte.

"It's them other boys got me worried. Maybe we oughta wake up sleeping beauty," he nodded toward Ruiz. "He might make a better bartering chip awake than asleep."

"My guess is he'll just go back to telling us how we're going to get killed," Caine muttered, "just before we get killed. But yeah, give him a few slaps. It's about the only chance we've got short of standing these blighters off until we run out of ammunition."

He turned his attention to the nearing vehicles, waiting for them to come into range.

Hawkeye started over toward Ruiz. Movement caught his peripheral vision among some creosote, higher up behind them. He whirled, the Magnum pulling around with him, just as four weapons opened fire from various points along that higher ground.

He snarled, "*Son of a fucking bitch!*" and then started pulling off rounds from the .44, realizing as he did so that the unseen riflemen from the Jeep were purposely firing high, over their heads, so as not to hit their boss.

Caine rolled onto his back, his M1 opened up on full auto, spraying the leafy shrubbery with a steady rain of lead that momentarily silenced the other gunfire.

Hawkeye reached down and grabbed the unconscious Ruiz as he had before, pulling the disheveled guy around to the other side of the rocks, where Caine had moved to give cover fire.

This side of the cluster of rocks left them exposed to those reinforcements bumping in about a quarter-klick away.

Caine ceased firing to reload, the echoes of the gunfire echoing away to nothing.

"*Señors*, you are surrounded. Throw down your guns. All we want is El Gato! I, Felipe Gallegos, assure you you will not be harmed—"

Hawkeye aimed across the rock at the source of the sound and fired.

He was rewarded with a death grunt, and one dead Felipe Gallegos toppled into view and somersaulted down the hill until a big rock stopped him.

While the other riflemen up there resumed an automatic fusillade down upon Hawkins' and Caine's position, the air filled with the crackle of their weapons, the whistling of projectiles coming too close and ricocheting, and now the engine sounds of the Jeeps from their rear.

The Texan looked sideways at the Englishman, there where they knelt beneath the cluster of boulders. "Uh, y'know, tea bag, maybe you're right; maybe it is time we gave up this bounty hunting."

Caine aimed the big M1 around on the approaching Jeeps.

"Maybe it's bloody well time to die," he grunted, raising the scope to his eye.

He pulled the rubberized eyepiece away as a sudden new sound boomed into the montage of war in the desert; the unmistakable *choppa-choppa-choppa* of a helicopter rotoring in low and fast from the north—at the moment blocked from sight by the butte.

Then the chopper thrust into view; a big single-engine jet-turbine Bell Ulti-D "Huey" boasting, Caine's trained eye spotted at a glance, 40mm cannons and 5.56mm machine guns mounted externally on turrets, the cannons stabbing geysering explosions that loudly chomped up the earth behind the high-ground ridge as the warbird flew by low overhead.

Two bodies flew out, hurled under the impact of the flesh-eating detonations.

The third Mexican drug hood charged blindly out into the clearing to escape and walked into a round from Hawkeye's .44 that messily lifted off a quarter of his skull and whatever brains went with it.

The Huey continued out, banking gracefully above the three Jeeps that were slowing down in confusion.

Hawkins wheeled around to watch the sight and so did Caine.

"Now who the hell could that be?"

"I don't know," muttered the Brit, raising the sighting scope back to his eye, "but I damn well intend to give him some help."

Cody worked the Huey's controls, easing the chopper around into a strafing run at the Jeeps on the ground as the drivers tried to separate—but not fast enough.

The gunship zoomed by overhead, its miniguns yammering now, the lines of pounding bullets pulverizing the desert floor, tracking across two of the filled-to-capacity Jeeps, brutally pulping most of the men in one vehicle, the parallel line of slugs crossing the other vehicle's gas tank, blowing it to smithereens in an orange-red blast that lit up the ascending shroud of night settling across the desert.

At that instant, Richard Caine sent off a grenade from his and Hawkeye's position over by the rocks, and the remaining Jeep full of Mexican hoods caught another on-the-money hit that banged that moving vehicle off the ground—flying shrapnel devastating the passengers into bloody ruins, flung into the air, not moving after they landed across the ground.

Cody pulled up the Huey, easing the warbird into a landing approach toward a level patch of ground near where Hawkins and Caine now stood erect.

He felt a grin and a good feeling coursed through him as he set the chopper down, creating a mini dust storm caused by the backwash of the rotors. He had wondered what kind of shape Hawkeye and Richard would be in when he found them; wondered if they would still have that sharp combat edge he remembered from ten years ago in Vietnam when they had fought together.

Ten years could be a long time. A lot could have changed.

But these two men, he now knew, had not changed.

Perhaps men like Caine and Hawkins never changed, because they had found perfection of mind, body, and spirit in what they did, in being tested by a harsh world, and they would not give that up to anything but infirmity or death.

He touched the Huey down on terra firma and cut the engine to idle, wondering what Caine and Hawkins would think of an offer from the last man on Earth they could have expected to see.

The Huey soared through the night at three-thousand feet above an ocean of black nothing, bearing northwesterly toward El Paso from where Jesus Ruiz, El Gato, had jumped bail after the DEA had managed to bust him.

Ruiz had regained consciousness. He was trussed up for delivery against the rear bulkhead and appeared to have lost all stomach for trying to reason these gringos out of taking him back to the law. One look at what was left of his gang after he came to on the ground just before lift-off had convinced the drug boss that the curtain had come down on this act. He sat back there, apprehensively watching the three up front as if fearful that they might decide on a whim to stroll back and pitch him out.

Cody had just finished calling in their flight plan and ETA to El Paso, relaying the message from Hawkins and

Caine to be passed on to the authorities that they were
bringing in a bail-jumping fugitive, Class A.

He had obtained the Huey through Pete Lund's connections after Lund's inquiries had tracked down the approximate whereabouts and intentions of the Caine and Hawkins
partnership.

He had briefed the two on what he wanted of them
before the take-off from that desert kill ground in Mexico,
after a warm round of bear hugs and high-fives. He had
seen close up that his first impression of the two—that they
had not changed a whit since their old combat days together—
was correct, but he still was not sure what their response
would be to his offer.

Hawkins and Caine had been discussing the proposition
between themselves, as he had suggested, and in the pilot's
seat he had not been able to hear them due to the all-
enveloping rumble of the chopper's engine.

At last the two came back to him, shouting to be heard.

"Well, we kicked it around, Sarge," Hawkeye yelled
at his ear.

"And?"

The Texan grinned.

"Well, I woulda said no a couple hours ago, but the
way me and the limey here look at it, I reckon we owe ya
one. You want to put the old team together and Uncle
Sugar's paying good; hell yeah, we'll sign up for the fun."

Caine leaned forward, adding, "I would have said no a
couple of hours ago too, because I'd forgotten what it's like
to be in a fight with you, Cody. We were too good a unit to
never work again."

"Question," shouted Hawkeye. "You told us about
Pete. What about Rufe?"

Caine nodded.

"Where is he? He's not—"

"No, but right now he probably wishes he was," Cody
told them.

And he told them about Rufe Murphy's predicament,
and what they would have to do about it.

CHAPTER
FIVE

Athens, from its crown on the Acropolis hill, spreads across an arid plain in a network of old buildings and circuitous streets that give way to wide modern boulevards and squares.

Omonis Square, with its *bouzouki* music in the air and sidewalks lined with *tavernas* where the men sit sipping thick black coffee and conversing animatedly, is the home of Athens' three major department stores, but has about it a rabble-filled, hustle-bustle atmosphere closer to that of the nearby marketplace of the old town—where the country people come to buy, sell and socialize—than to the swankier tourist environs of Kolonaki Square or the Athens Hilton.

Christus Imports was on Caningos Street, a narrow, relatively quiet thoroughfare two blocks east of the square; an area of some small businesses but primarily residential, which is why Anton Christus had chosen it.

Christus felt a cool chill of premonition touch the base of his spine despite the intense dry heat of midafternoon as he resealed the blond wooden box intended for Farouk Hassan's people: the Uzis, ammunition enough to stand off an army, hand grenades, pistols, and daggers. He looked around the empty loading dock inside the garage.

No on had come in while he had been making the final check of the shipment.

He slammed shut the back doors of the van. He had waited until his workers were gone on their daily afternoon break before making sure everything was as it should be. Most of them knew nothing of his reputation as Athens' leading black-market arms dealer.

Now all that remained was the wait on word from the PLGF.

He glimpsed his dark reflection for a moment in the smoked glass of the van's back doors. His Gallic features, inherited from his mother and as out of place as ever atop the stocky Greek body, wore a pinched, high-strung expression that he tried to erase by consciously telling himself to relax. He always got this way when dealing with the Palestine Liberation Guerrilla Force.

He heard the phone back in his office ring once, and a moment later Apodaka, his driver and the only man in his employ who knew about and assisted with his "second business," stuck his head out the office doorway at the far end of the dock.

"For you, Anton."

He hurried to take the call.

"Hello?"

"We are ready," said a voice that he recognized at once as belonging to Ali Hassan, Farouk's younger brother and one of the PLGF, Ali's voice somehow deeper in resonance than Farouk's. "So are we," he replied curtly. "Where? When?"

"Right now. We will be parked facing west just east of the corner where Pireos connects with Ermou."

"But that is too near the Acropolis," Christus protested. "There will be tourists, crowds all around us."

"And hundreds going about their daily chores," Ali Hassan countered tersely. "We will be lost in the crowd. No one will pay attention to laborers transferring a box from one van to another."

"I don't like it."

"These are Farouk's orders," Ali replied with utter finality. "We leave for there now. We will meet you there in exactly one half-hour."

The receiver clicked and Anton's ear was filled with the irritating purr of the dial tone.

He slammed the receiver onto its base angrily.

"Filthy swine—" he started to say, then he remembered Apodaka's presence and turned to find the driver staring back at him expectantly from the doorway. "Well, don't just stand there, get the truck started," he barked peevishly. "We're on our way to earn more blood money."

"There they are," said Rallis the moment he saw the van emerge from the garage of Christus Imports. "After them."

Detective Giorgios gunned the unmarked police car to life and waited.

The van, with Apodaka driving and Christus in the passenger seat, turned left into the baking sunlight of Caningo Street, heading away from the police car.

Giorgios slipped the car into gear and pulled into the moderate flow of economy cars and bicycles clogging the street.

One of the two detectives in the backseat leaned forward.

"Think this is it?" he asked Rallis.

"If it's not," Giorgios answered for his superior, "it is the first move they've made all day."

Chief Inspector Constantine Rallis, of the Special Affairs branch of the Athens police department, felt the stirring air through the open windows dry the patina of sweat coating his face.

They had been staking out Christus's place for two long, hot days, ever since the PLGF informant had contacted Rallis.

Rallis still did not know the informant's name; it had been but a voice on a telephone two days earlier, but since Rallis was the one who had drawn the assignment of breaking up the terrorist cells, which appeared more and more to make Athens their home base for launching terrorist attacks in the area, he had some time ago reached the decision that he needed all the help he could get, including terrorist informants like the one whose "information" had brought him and the three other men to Caningo Street.

He had risen through the ranks during his fifteen years with the department—due for the most part to his tenacity and skill as a policeman and his record for bringing to a successful conclusion nearly every assignment handed to him—but this terrorist business was something else again. He had learned that the hard way; typical criminals were invariably apprehended because their greed or lust got the better of them and a betrayed woman or a double-crossed accomplice would eventually come forward or be tracked down to supply the pieces of the puzzle.

That was hardly the case with terrorists; their religious beliefs and zeal for their cause generally canceled out their taking up with loose women who would talk. Nor did greed enter the equation, he had come to learn. These were killers who committed their crimes for their people and their faith, not for their pocketbooks, and that kind of motivation was most difficult to crack with standard police operating procedures. There had been some arrests, but nothing of consequence. There had been too little to go on.

That was until the phone call; the whispering voice telling Rallis only that "something very big" was about to happen—a PLGF initiative, is how the caller had put it—the anonymous informant claiming that even he did not know the details. The only information he furnished was that the weapons and armaments for such an operation were to be obtained within the next day or so from Anton Christus, and that had been enough for Rallis to set up this stakeout; for he and his men to perspire profusely in their car across from Christus Imports, waiting, waiting, waiting.

He had begun to grow more than a bit skeptical by the middle of this second day. The police knew about Christus, certainly, though knowing and proving were two distinctly different kettles of fish.

Christus had come to police attention several times, relating to both drug and weapons smuggling, and had been under surveillance from time to time, though not by Rallis's unit, but nothing had ever come from it. The importer was as careful as he was rumored to be successful in the black-market underworld and so far he had not spent one night in jail, though Rallis knew of several underworld murders that could be laid at his doorstep, probably carried out by his henchmen, but much as this present supposed opportunity to close Christus's career once and for all appealed to him, it actually paled to insignificance next to the real reason he had put himself on the front line on this stakeout when he could have been safely riding it out behind his desk at Headquarters.

A chance at closing in on the Palestine Liberation Guerrilla Force meant a chance to arrest Farouk Hassan and his unit. the prime movers of the PLGF, and that, Rallis knew, would be just the ticket to make his superiors overlook his practically nonexistent progress thus far in tracking down and rooting out the terrorist cells known to be operating in this city.

The Greek government had its antiterrorist division, of course, but they had been of little help to Rallis since they really knew little more than he did, and in any event you could not expect a government agency to be overly cooperative with a unit with a similar function at the local level.

He had come to the conclusion that hunting terrorists was like hunting shadows. They had no set base of operations, being constantly on the move, totally mobile, and generally the participants of any action—like the Rome or Vienna airport massacres, converged on a city from different points of origin—generally traveling on Syrian or Iraqui passports, sometimes days, sometimes only hours, before the action was to commence. You did not know what they were up to until the guns opened fire and the innocent went screaming and dying with blood splashing everything in sight.

Rallis noted the van up ahead picking up speed, unable to travel very fast but weaving more between the hubbub of vehicles, bicycles and pedestrians.

"Don't lose them," he rasped at the driver.

Detective Giorgios steered through an opening in the traffic where a tourist bus was loading near Omonia Square.

"I won't, Inspector. Do you really think Christus will lead us to al Hussan?"

"He'd better," growled Rallis. "This is the only lead we've got."

As far as he could tell from the skimpy dossier on the PLGF, Farouk Hassan *was* the Palestinian Liberation Guerrilla Force; a wily, ruthless mass-murderer whose rage was fueled by memories of the humiliations his own people had suffered over the years.

As the unmarked police car threaded through the traffic, Giorgios staying back far enough so as not to crowd the van up ahead and yet always keeping the van in sight, Rallis reflected on the kind of man he hoped to apprehend this day.

Hassan had been born about the time of Israel's war of independence, and the boy's family had been forced from their home in Galilee to settle in the yarmouk refugee camp near Damascus. Hassan's dossier had informed Rallis that even as a boy, little Farouk had loved to play hide and seek, staying hidden long after everyone had ceased searching for him.

Farouk had gone on to attend Damascus University, where he received a degree in Arabic literature, though much of his time had also been spent consuming and absorbing the works of Marx, Lenin, and Mao, which had resulted in a prominent role in student politics.

He took a job for a short time as a schoolteacher, but it had not been long before Hassan had signed up as a foot soldier in the Palestinian struggle, at first assigned to hunting recruits in the Palestinian camps in Jordan, and receiving his first taste of combat during King Hussein's Black September war on the PLO in 1970. Up to this point, Rallis knew Hassan's b.g. had been not very different from thousands of other young men of Palestinian descent in the Mideast, but his interest had perked when he'd read about Hassan being sent to the Soviet Union for training as a battalion commander, after which Farouk had commanded a topflight combat unit along Beirut's Green Line until the early 1980s when a group of disenchanted guerrillas broke away from the PLO to form the PLGF, and Farouk had gone along to sign on as their operations chief and secretary-general.

Since then, Farouk Hassan had left his mark on the pages of Mideast history with a list of terror atrocities that had an effectiveness unrivaled in their design to attract world media attention instantly and completely.

It was rumored, but not substantiated, that Farouk's younger brother, Ali, had lately joined the ranks of the PLGF's strategists.

To Rallis, these were enemies worth the effort it would take to catch them.

The van with Christus and Apodaka, one block ahead, turned onto Pireos after leaving the Square, traveling southwest.

Rallis wondered if this would prove to be what the Americans called a wild goose chase, but for some reason he did not think so. Athens is a compact city nestled on the sea, its central area small, and he knew it would not be long before the van's destination became apparent if their destination was somewhere in Athens, as he was sure it would be.

"Radio the other units," he instructed Giorgios. "Tell them to stand by and to be ready for anything."

Tahia Ahmed, sitting on the floor of the back of the van, said sternly to the new man, "Najib, you must stop your fidgeting." She turned to the man behind the steering wheel of the parked vehicle. "Ali, tell him to relax. He will draw attention to us the minute we step out of the van, the way he's shaking."

Najib Yaqub, rail thin with a harsh, thin-lipped visage, lost some of his nervous demeanor, glaring at her.

"Mind your tongue, woman. I—"

Ali Hassan turned sideways in the front seat to look back at Yaqub, who sat with his back against the opposite side of the inside of the van from Tahia.

"She's right, Najib. I know this is your first mission for the organization, so—"

"You are not such a battle-hardened veteran yourself, Ali," Najib bristled.

"I have enough experience to have been placed in charge of this operation," Hassan snapped. "I forgive your loose tongue and account it to a case of nerves on your first assignment. We all experience that the first time. Allah will grant you strength when the time comes.''

Najib lowered his eyes contritely.

"Of course, Ali, I spoke out of turn. It would perhaps ease my mind, though, to know more about what I am a part of.''

Hallah al Molky snorted from where he sat in the passenger seat, an Ingram MAC-10 submachine gun resting on his lap beneath view of passersby on the sidewalks.

"Have you not been told, Najib? This is how we operate, and we would have it no other way. You and I arrived in Athens this morning from Damascus. Ali and Tahia arrived here this morning from Istanbul. We pick up these weapons from Christus, as you've been told, then Ali drives us to where his brother is staying and after we connect with Farouk and Abdel, *then* the four of us learn why we have been brought to Athens, and not a moment before. You had your chance to back out long ago.'' Hallah turned his attention to watching the busy street scene outside. "You'll be making me nervous before you're done.''

Tahia Ahmed chuckled good-naturedly.

"That would be a change, seeing our young hotblood Hallah nervous. You wish the action had already begun, don't you, Hallah?''

Al Molky, slightly built, not out of his teens, said in a man's voice, without hesitation, "I live to slay the enemies of Allah and our people.''

"As do we all,'' nodded Ali. He wore a Beretta in a concealed shoulder holster. He glanced at his wristwatch, then back out through the windshield at where Pireos street merged with Ermou at the foot of the Acropolis hill, near where a dozen or more workmen labored near their vehicles, vans like this one, apparently on some sort of restoration project by the *Agora*, the original marketplace where Socrates met with his students; where vehicular traffic had to wind its way through workmen and a human ocean of tourists and throngs of peddlers and street merchants, the air a lively human babble.

"Christus should be here by now.''

No one answered him.

Ali and Hallah kept watching the street for some sign of the Greek arms dealer's vehicle, while Najib only stared down as if in contemplation of the floor of the van.

Tahia moved to kneel, looking out the back windows of the van, watching down the crowded street in either direction with the thought that the Greek arms dealer might choose not to follow the orders Ali had telephoned a short time before. She gripped a 9mm Czech-made pistol. She suddenly wished very much that it was this time yesterday and that she and Ali were still back at that hotel in Istanbul, in bed, making love.

Tahia loved Ali Hassan as much as she loved the cause to which she had dedicated her life; a love that had unexpectedly made of life a precious thing, something it had not been for her before she had met him, and she found herself wondering if, at this moment, he was thinking of her as she thought of him.

Hallah's excited laugh interrupted her reverie.

"There they are! Christus may be late but by Allah he has not let us down."

Tahia watched a commercial van glide from the opposite oncoming lane of traffic and ease to a stop, its rear end several feet behind the back of their van.

"Everyone out," ordered Ali. "Farouk has already taken care of the payment. We pick up what Christus has for us and get away as quickly as possible. Act naturally, but keep your eyes open." He added as they began debarking from the van, "There is always the chance of trouble."

Rallis unholstered his pistol from its shoulder holster when he saw the van up ahead, the one that read Christus Imports on the side, pulling up back-to-back with a van parked at the curb amid the flow of crawling motor traffic and tourists.

"This is it," he hissed.

The two detectives in the backseat unholstered their pistols.

"Gutsy bastards," one of them said. "We can't very well turn the Acropolis hill into a shooting gallery."

"We can't let them get away, either," the other man in back pointed out with no enthusiasm.

"What should we do, Inspector?" Giorgios asked from behind the steering wheel.

A half block ahead, Christus and Apodaka were debarking from their van, while three young Arab men and an Arab woman stepped from the van that had been parked, waiting.

"We can't very well let them escape, either. Pull in, fast. Get ready, men. This won't be easy. I'll radio in backup. If we can just get the drop on them close up by surprise, we may be able to keep the lid on."

He did not think he sounded very convincing.

Giorgios floored the car's accelerator when a break in the crowd parted and sent the police vehicle zipping forward to close the distance on the two vans.

Rallis reached for the dashboard transceiver to broadcast to the backup units to close in, a rage coursing through him that had nothing to do with his job of closing in on criminals.

He hated these terrorist vermin for desecrating this sacred place that stood as a monument to the glory and genius of men; a shrine to lovers of beauty for more than 2,500 years: the Parthenon, the finest building of the ancient world; the Theater of Dionysus, dating to the fourth century B.C., where were first presented the plays of Sophocles and Euripides; the Temple of Athena Nike. All of it desecrated by animals who dealt in the slaughter of innocent civilians.

Rallis and the three men in the car rocked backward under the forward momentum as the unmarked vehicle barreled forward.

"*Police!*" snarled Apodaka, and he pawed for his shoulder holster beneath his jacket.

Tahia and Ali had reached into the back of Anton Christus's van as Christus held one of the doors back for them. Tahia and Ali's eyes had connected once across the box as they reached to take opposite ends of it in order to slide out the weapons and ammunition, but she had not been able to read what she saw in the brief look that passed between her and this man she loved so much.

Then everything fell apart as Christus's driver cried the alarm.

She and Ali spun away from the truck, the box of weapons and ammo temporarily forgotten, reaching for their weapons.

Christus, and Hallah and Najib, who had been holding open the back door of the other van, did the same.

A sedan screeched to a stop, its tires shrieking on the pavement, nosed in toward the scene of these "laborers" transferring one box of "tools" from one of their trucks to another, the four doors of the sedan flapping open even before the car had braked to a full halt, four men from inside spilling out with pistols in their hands.

The one who had to be in charge, an older man who hopped out from the front passenger seat, started to shout, "Stop where you are, all of you! You're under—"

Apodaka pulled off the first shot.

The policemen scattered for cover behind the open doors of their car.

Ali cleared his Beretta of its leather and fired a round that caught one of the men in the chest.

The policeman, who had jumped from one of the back doors of the car, flew into a wide-armed backward fall to the pavement.

Screams of hysteria and surprise erupted from the touristy crowd that began scrambling in every direction for the nearest cover.

The policeman from the opposite rear side of the car, and the plainclothesman who had been driving, returned Apodaka's fire at the same time, and so Tahia could not tell whose bullets sent Christus's driver slamming backward into the side of the van, projectiles coring his body, splashing his guts across the lettering that read Christus Imports.

Christus dodged behind the van, undercover.

Tahia saw the policeman she had guessed to be in command raised his pistol on Ali. She started to bring her own weapon up and shouted a warning to Ali at the same time.

The policeman fired a single shot that drilled Ali through the stomach, jackknifing Ali al-Hassan to the ground, where he spasmed into a fetal ball.

"Oh *no*!" Tahia shrieked. "*No*!"

She rushed over to Ali's side while Hallah stepped forward, his Ingram MAC-10 tracking toward the police car.

"Get him in the van!" the youth screamed at her. "We've got to get out of here! Najib, help her!"

Hallah triggered a nonstop burst from the Ingram MAC-10, the automatic fire spewing wildly at the police care and beyond.

The police car's windshield shattered under the fusillade that pockmarked the frame of the car and began toppling people across the street among the wildly scattering crowd of pedestrians.

Tahia and Najib scrambled to each lift one of Ali's arms around them, tugging the wounded man between them toward the back of their van. Tahia caught one glimpse of the gruesome horror that was her lover's abdominal area. She averted her eyes with a small shriek, fighting off panic while one small part of her mind kept telling her no, no, this was not happening, though the noisy chatter of Hallah's MAC-10 spraying everything in sight was a fearsome reminder that yes, the world had gone crazy around her.

She and Najib lowered Ali onto his back upon the floor of the van, then she turned to Hallah, yelling, "He's in . . . let's go!"

Najib jumped into the back of the van, slamming shut his side of the back doors, pressing himself to the floor of the van, a look of naked fear across his face.

Tahia crouched and pulled her door most of the way shut with one hand. Steadying herself, she opened fire with her pistol on the police car.

Hallah ran to the driver's seat, hopped into the idling vehicle and upshifted so abruptly that Tahia was almost pitched out of the van, but she kept on firing.

The police, who had not shown themselves from behind their cover during the twenty seconds or so that Hallah had them pinned down, now realized that the incoming fire was from a weapon of less firepower, and the three surviving cops showed themselves at the same moment that Tahia's pistol clicked on empty.

Projectiles pierced the back-door windows, zinging high through the van.

She slammed shut her side of the van's back door as the vehicle sailed away from there. She threw herself across Ali, who lay on his back, tremoring with terrible shudders, holding his stomach wound. His blood smeared her.

With everything happening, she forced herself to keep in mind what was most important of all.

"Ali . . . dearest," she whispered close to his ear. "Tell us where to go . . . where is Farouk?"

She placed her ear close to his red-specked mouth and listened as he told her. She realized tears were pouring from her eyes, down her cheeks. She cried out the address to Hallah as the police gunfire from behind them died down.

She placed her arms around Ali as the van rocketed away and then hugged her lover to her, knowing he was dying; knowing that the tears and the killing would not stop.

Pandemonium reigned, the air filled with the moaning of the dying and the civilian survivors, the street at the foot of the Acropolis hill dotted with bodies, the sirens of squad cars arriving too late, noisy above everything else in the white heat of midday.

Rallis went over behind the Christus Imports van to where the surviving detective from the backseat of the unmarked car had Christus under cover on the side of the van where Christus had remained during the shooting.

Rallis saw the van with the terrorists picking up speed as it tore away down the street.

Christus saw the look in Rallis's eyes.

"I'm not armed!" the importer screamed.

"Where are they going?" Rallis demanded.

"I don't know, I swear I don't know!"

Rallis had not time to believe or disbelieve that.

He charged to the police car where Giorgios stood from examining the fallen policeman.

"Dead, sir."

"After them," snarled Rallis, throwing himself into the passenger seat.

Giorgios jumped in behind the steering wheel, and tires screeched a burning rubber cloud behind the unmarked car as he piloted them away from there in hot pursuit.

Rallis hurriedly reloaded his pistol as Giorgios rounded
the corner from Ermou Street onto Pireos, heading back into
the downtown district, the street ahead of them well cleared
by the crowds that had scurried for cover. Rallis saw the van
up ahead, at about a block and a half lead, traveling fast.

At first, back there when they had screamed to a halt,
surprising these terrorists in the obvious act of picking up
weapons, Rallis had thought he'd been lucky enough to
catch Farouk Hassan right at the beginning, but the man
who had killed one of his detectives, who Rallis had
plugged through the stomach, was a younger edition of the
Most Wanted Terrorist in the World. That would make him
Ali al-Hassan.

If Rallis was right, the speeding van they were chasing
could lead him and Giorgios straight to the heart of Farouk
al-Hassan's headquarters.

CHAPTER
SIX

"**A**re we being followed?" Tahia demanded of Hallah from the rear of the van.

She cursed the quaver she heard in her own voice, the fear and rising sense of panic she also heard there. She looked down at Ali, whose head she cradled in her lap, and her fear caused her to tremor and she realized she feared not so much for herself but for this man she held, the one she loved, dying before her eyes.

Hallah steered the van smoothly through the narrow, winding backstreet toward the Athens waterfront district. The youth kept the van well below the legal speed limit, as he had since racing them away from the Acropolis hill area, having taken a zigzag course ever deeper into the city. He glanced in the rearview mirror, then chanced a look over his shoulder into the van's interior, where Tahia held Ali.

"I think we'll make it. How is he, Tahia?"

Dark gore bubbled out of the bullet hole in Ali's stomach. Tahia had peeled back Ali's shirt and jacket and tried to stop the flow of blood with a cloth, but to little avail.

Ali rasped out in pain.

"D-don't concern yourself with me," he gasped. "Just get us to Farouk."

He winced, spasming in agony across the floor of the van, but he did not cry out.

Tahia pressed the wound harder with the cloth, but the flow of blood continued to puddle beneath them.

"Ali, you must be still. We will get you medical attention."

He reached his arm over his head to touch her face, a trembling finger wiping away a tear from her cheek.

"It . . . is too late for me, Tahia. You and the others must continue the mission without me . . ."

"Don't say that!" she cried out. "Please, Ali, you must live. We need you. The movement, the cause, needs you . . . *I* need you . . ."

Najib Yaqub turned from where he rode in the passenger seat. He had been watching his own outside rearview mirror for any sign of pursuit. He gripped his pistol in his lap. "Continue the mission?" he echoed. "We cannot continue! Not after what happened tonight. Not after"— he nodded to Ali —"*this*."

Hallah snickered derisively. He steered the van around another corner, slacking off their speed even more as he guided the vehicle down a somewhat wider, secondary residential street on the edge of the waterfront warehouse district.

"You speak as a coward." The youth's countenance glistened with perspiration despite the night's dry coolness, and his eyes glinted with the excitement of all that had happened. "All is in readiness. Too much has gone into this. We can not turn back now."

"Hallah is right," rasped Ali raggedly. "There can be no turning back from . . . the course we have set for ourselves. I . . . only wish Allah had not ordained . . . this—"

Tahia looked up from him, speaking to all three of the men.

"What could have happened back there? What went wrong?"

Najib stared with anger at the teenager steering the van.

"You were a fool to open fire like you did, Hallah."

"I got us out of there, didn't I?" the youth retorted. "And I would not hurl accusations, Najib. I did not let others do my fighting for me."

The man in the passenger seat looked away uncomfortably.

"I wonder what Farouk will have to say to all this," he mumbled, more to himself than to the others.

"We're about to find out," said Hallah.

He braked, guiding the van into a narrow alleyway between two two-level structures.

The building on the left appeared uninhibited except for a slight motion that came from a curtain, on the second level, being parted slightly behind a window, and then the shade was dropped back into place.

Ali Hassan groaned aloud for the first time since receiving his wound, lurching his head fitfully in Tahia's lap. He began coughing. Hemorrhaging blood burbled from his nostrils and from the corners of his mouth.

Abdel Khaled turned from the window, dropping the shade back into place where he had parted it a fraction of an inch to peer out and down into the alleyway.

"They have returned," he told Farouk Hassan.

Hassan looked up from completing the reassembly of a Uzi SMG he had dismantled and cleaned upon the table at which he sat.

He knew his second-in-command to be fearless and committed to their shared cause, but he had never fully trusted Khaled. Abdel had learned to enjoy the brutality, the killing, too much. He had become a sadist, and it showed in his eyes, even now. Farouk wished again that he had his brother as his right-hand man, but Khaled would never give up his power and influence except in death, and so he and Farouk worked together.

"You see, Abdel, you were wrong."

"Perhaps." Hassan glowered. "And yet I say again, we have more to fear than what the authorities may do to us."

"You mean Kaddoumi? I told you, I will have no more

of this talk. Our cause is splintered enough as it is by differences among us.''

''I must speak what is in my heart,'' Khaled insisted evenly. ''Majed Kaddoumi has placed a traitor among us, and if it is the authorities to whom the traitor, whoever he is, informs, can it make any difference?''

''Majed is a moderate in the Palestinian cause,'' countered Farouk. ''He is not our enemy. He would not plot our undoing.''

''I hope you are right,'' Khaled conceded. ''If you are wrong, Farouk, then everything—today, the operation, *everything*—is at risk.''

They heard a clatter and voices from the bottom of the stairway outside the closed door of this room, this room that had served as their station during the three days since they had arrived in Athens to make final preparations for what was to happen later this day—if all went according to plan.

''Do not worry, Abdel,'' Farouk assured the other. ''Flight 766 from Athens *will* be hijacked this morning. Blood *will* flow. Allah's will be done.''

At that moment the door burst inward as if flung by a battering ram, startling both men, who had not expected such an entrance.

They whirled toward the doorway, Farouk bringing up the reassembled Uzi, holding his fire.

Tahia and Hallah rushed in bearing Ali between them, one of Ali's arms draped over each of them as they supported him into the room while Najib held the door open.

Farouk's heart leaped into his throat and he could not speak for a moment as he realized with shock that his brother was badly wounded and bleeding.

''What's this?'' Abdel demanded. ''What has gone wrong?''

Farouk rushed toward his brother.

Rallis told his driver to brake the unmarked police car to the curb across the street and three buildings away from where the van had disappeared into the alleyway at midblock.

They had followed the van without detection all the way from the Acropolis.

Or so it seemed.

Giorgios, seated beside him, seemed to read his mind.

"It could be a trap, Inspector. I've a feeling it may take more to fool these boys than tracking them from a distance without being spotted. They could be suckering us in."

Rallis nodded to the dash radio, not taking his eyes from the entrance of that alley.

"Call in backup. I don't want them jumping our net this time. This time we've got them, the Hassan brothers and Khaled and all the rest. Call the others in, and hurry."

Giorgios obeyed, breathily summoning assistance from the other unmarked cars that had more or less accompanied Rallis and Giorgios, assisting in tailing the van by picking up the track while Rallis and Giorgios had shifted over a few blocks parallel before resuming the track for his final distance.

When the van began its approach to this seedy waterfront area district, Rallis had felt certain he was tracking these rats directly to their hole.

He only wished he knew what it was that he was so hot on the trail of.

The world's most wanted terrorist gang, yes. But what were they up to?

Whatever it was, he hoped it would end here, in the next few minutes when they closed in.

Something told him time was already running out.

Giorgios replaced the mike hookup to the dash radio. "They'll be here in two minutes."

Rallis unholstered his pistol and unlatched his door. "We can't wait that long."

Giorgios unleathered his pistol, but he looked uncertain.

"We don't know how many are in there, Inspector."

"And they're dealing with a wounded man," Rallis grunted. "They'll be confused, upset. We've got surprise working for us. Come on. Something's in the wind and it won't wait."

Giorgios left the car with him. Together, the two of them darted across the inky shadows of the street.

*   *   *

Tahia did not know which hurt the most, watching Ali die right before her eyes or seeing the agony in Farouk's expression as he helped her and Hallah carry Ali to the couch.

Ali coughed again and more pink bubbles burst at the corners of his mouth.

"A . . . trap," he gasped unevenly to Farouk. "The police . . . waiting for us—"

His voice tapered off and he doubled over into a fit of convulsive, death-rattle coughing.

Farouk, perched on the arm of the couch with an arm around his brother, looked at the others in frustration and anger.

"Trap?" he repeated. "Who would do such a thing?"

Abdel remained standing back somewhat, with an air of cool, removed detachment as if observing the scene with only mild interest. Tahia, though, could see that his eyes were marble cold, reptilian, and calculating as ever.

"Only the six of us knew of the rendevous with Christus," he noted without inflection, gazing from face to face of those around the wounded man.

"My brother is above suspicion," snapped Farouk. "As am I, as are you, Abdel; as should we all be."

Ali forced himself to speak from the couch, a weakening gurgle. He gripped his brother's arm.

"Tahia," he rasped to his brother. "She is . . . of us."

"And that is good enough for me," nodded Farouk to Abdel.

Tahia felt she must say something, when she sensed Farouk and Abdel centering their speculative glare on Hallah and Najib.

"Halla fought valiantly," she told them. "We would all be dead or in police custody if not for Hallah."

Hallah remained standing on the far side of the couch from Abdel and Farouk. The youth stood with is back straight, returning their glare, his fingertips lingering near the front of his open jacket and the .38 pistol holstered there.

"Thanks, Tahia," he said, "but I can take care of myself. I'm not your traitor, may Allah damn your eyes," he snarled at Farouk and Abdel, "and I'll kill the man who says I am."

"Relax, my headstrong young one," Abdel purred smoothly. "No, you are not the informer among us."

His eyes turned to Najib, who pulled back from the couch as the eyes of everyone there, including the wounded man, fell upon him.

"*No*, it was not I!" Najib cried out, his voice rising with each word. "I could not have led the police anywhere! I have never been to this house before right now, you know this to be true!"

Farouk nodded slowly, picking up the chain of accusation.

"Which is why the police did not close in on us here," he intoned grimly. "You did know the arms pickup. They intended to force Ali to tell where we were."

"No, I tell you, *no!*" Najib's cry became a pleading whine. "It was not I! I am loyal!"

"It could be no other way," Abdel glowered with an air of finality. He reached toward a shoulder-holstered pistol beneath his jacket, his gaze centered unblinkingly on Najib. "We have been dealing with Christus for years. He did not cross us. This is your first mission, Najib. You have made it your last."

Najib saw what was coming and knew there was no place to run. He stumbled back a few paces until his back was against the wall and the whine in his throat climbed into a scream. "Please, no . . . Allah forgive me . . . I'm *sorry!*"

Abdel yanked out his pistol, attaining a straight-armed target acquisition with one smooth motion as he triggered a round from a West German 9mm P-38 that cored Najib Yaqub's forehead, splashing brains, blood, and skull fragments mural-like across the wall behind him.

Khaled holstered his pistol before Yaqub's body collapsed to a messy heap in the corner.

"I would have preferred his death to be more befitting a traitor," Abdel commented almost conversationally. "That is, particularly slow and humiliating, but . . . ," he shrugged slightly, " . . . we have no time to spare."

Tahia tore her eyes from the sight of Najib's gory

corpse, now shivering as if from an intense chill. She felt faint. Reality was unraveling all about her.

There came shouting, then automatic gunfire from downstairs, at the door to the alleyway.

Khaled unholstered his pistol again.

"Police," he snapped above the clatter of weapons from below.

A three-man defense team had been set up on the building's first level.

Hallah crossed to the door of the room and slammed it shut; then he tilted a wooden chair against the door handle.

"That won't hold the swine for long," he breathed.

Tahia could tell he was enjoying himself like a boy playing at a game.

Abdel moved to a throw rug across the room before an archway. He kicked the rug aside to reveal a trapdoor. He knelt and flipped the door open.

"Let's go," he snarled. "We can still carry out the mission! We will have less firepower, the weapons we carry now, but we can still take over an airplane. We cannot turn back now."

Tahia rushed to the couch to join Farouk in starting to help Ali to his feet.

"We'll make it," she breathed fiercely in Ali's ear as she came to him, some of his blood smearing across her cheek.

Ali shook his head weakly.

"No . . . no, leave me . . . I'm finished anyway . . . I can hold them off . . . give me my gun, that's all I ask . . . I'll die as a warrior should . . ."

"*No*!" Tahia shrieked. "Farouk," she beseeched, "tell him he must come with us."

Farouk shook his head, no, solemnly. He pressed his lips to his brother's forehead once, holding Ali tightly to him, then he pulled away from his brother and stood.

"No, Ali is right." He took Tahia by the arm and brought her to her feet. "Come. Abdel is right, too. The mission must come first. You know that, Tahia. There is no other way for us.'

The gunfire ceased from outside and downstairs.

Tahia knew what she had to do, much as it hurt to do it.

She placed Ali's Beretta in his limp right hand.

"Farewell, my love," she whispered softly, "until Paradise."

Rallis poked his head cautiously around the bullet-riddled doorway.

The bit of burnt cordite irritated his eyes and nostrils as he gazed in on the sight of three bodies sprawled in and around a narrow companionway with an archway leading to the darkened ground floor of this house.

A stairway reached up to the second level and a trail of glistening pools of blood showed in an unbroken trail up those stairs to a closed door at the top. Giorgios, looking nervous and scared, joined Rallis just outside the doorway.

"Cover me," Rallis instructed.

He left his cover and started up the stairs hurriedly, his eyes and pistol scanning the hazy shadows.

Abdel closed the trapdoor after them, cutting off all light except for a finger of penlight which he pointed ahead of them. He and Tahia and Farouk hustled down the narrow stairs of the hidden passageway.

"This house is owned by our organization," Abdel explained to Tahia's unasked question. "This passageway will take us to a basement connected to the building next door."

Tahia's heart hammered against her rib cage.

They ran down the steps, their rapid breathing and footfalls seemingly magnified inside her ears by the nearly suffocating closeness of the walls and the low ceiling of this passageway.

Then sounds of gunfire could be heard popping off with a removed, distant sound from behind several walls away, and each report stabbed like a burning knife into Tahia's guts. She stopped.

"We must go back! Oh, Ali—"

Farouk grabbed her arm, urging her onward.

"Ali does what he must. So must we. *Hurry*, Tahia. We fight on *for* Ali. Nothing must stop us!"

The words of her lover's brother ignited something inside Tahia that overcame the sorrow she felt.

"And *nothing* will stop us," she told Farouk.

The gunfire from upstairs stopped.

Abdel was so far ahead, he was not in sight.

Tahia choked back the sobs and tears she wanted to unleash. She and Farouk hurried to catch up with Abdel, to get away from there.

Rallis stood up from the floor of the room, cautious and slow even though he had convinced himself in the preceding heartbeats that he was alone in this second-floor level of the house except for two dead men, a wafting haze of gunsmoke, and the receded echoes of the brief, blistering exchange of gunfire that came after he had kicked in the door of the room while bullets had zipped out at him from inside. Barely missing him, the ammo had been fired by the man he had recognized instantly as Ali Hassan.

The terrorist had appeared moments from death, propping himself up on a couch, firing at Rallis; and some of Hassan's bullets might have scored their mark, Rallis realized, except for the pain blurring Ali's vision.

Now, Ali Hassan was dead, as dead as the second man sprawled in the far corner of the room, who took a bit more scrutiny, because much of his face was blown away, before Rallis was sure that this was most likely the informant who had brought Rallis into this in the first place; the man's treachery had obviously been discovered and was rewarded by the others before they fled.

Rallis heard voices and activity from the bottom of the stairs. He crossed to see Giorgios being joined down there by others in police uniform, the men moving with extreme caution as they commenced searching the first-floor level of this house.

"Have the neighborhood cordoned off," Rallis instructed from the top of the stairs.

Giorgios looked relieved that he had survived this firefight.

"What of the others?"

"Gone, except for two," Rallis grunted. "There must

be a hidden passage somewhere in this building. We'll find it, but I fear we've lost them.''

Giorgios nodded and went back outside as the others saw to the cleanup below.

Rallis stepped back into the room, holstering his pistol. All of this killing, he told himself, all of this work, and only two dead terrorists to show for it.

He cursed no one in particular and everyone and everything in general.

He could hear some of the other men coming upstairs to join him. He began feeling along the walls for the exit the terrorists must have used.

Today was a failure and he knew nothing could change that. The terrorist unit commanded by Farouk Hassan and Abdel Khaled was running free with their weapons and their hate and their coldbloodedness, and that meant trouble for someone, somewhere, very soon.

Farouk Hassan's terrorist team had been blocked from attaining the weaponry they preferred, but his reading of Farouk told Rallis that the terrorists would continue with their mission, whatever it was, despite the loss of Najib and Farouk's own brother. Standard terrorist procedure meant that the men downstairs, the security unit, were local Athens people supplied only as a precaution. The core of Hassan's force was now minus two, but Rallis had no doubt Farouk would continue.

Rallis knew it was out of his hands now.

There was nothing more he could do.

It would happen soon—whatever *it* proved to be—and then he would learn about it along with the rest of the world when the media blazed headlines of another atrocity, and more spilled innocent blood . . .

CHAPTER
SEVEN

The little town where Rufe Murphy was being held, pending his trial, was a sleepy burg of two streets and one stoplight, snoozing under sultry, humid summer sunshine in the hills of northern Mississippi, a short distance east of the rich, dark, cotton-growing soil of the alluvial plain, known as the Delta, of the Yazoo and Mississippi Rivers.

The one-horse, ramshackle town practically reeked of backwoods poverty, though it reeked far more of the sawmill plant located just outside of town, near the town's only inhabitable-looking motel, where Cody, Hawkins and Caine checked in—as "traveling salesmen," as Cody told the clerk—before heading out, off to pound shoe leather and learn what they could under the guise of "market research" at the businesses lining the town's main street.

Cody had no intention of breaking Rufe out of this redneck jail with weapons blazing. They would find another way.

Caine and Hawkins found an elderly citizen named Old Joe sitting on a bench in a little park dead center of the town square. They had been at their assigned task for two hours and were both dripping sweat in the seemingly airless heat, when they moved through a line of parked cars, over to where the old man sat, looking up at them as if they were Russian invaders, his left jaw lumped up.

After staring at the two strangers for a moment, the oldster picked up a small milk carton on the bench beside him, spat into it and part of the lump in his cheek disappeared.

"You fellas want something or you just trying to give me some shade?"

"We'd like to talk to you," Caine smiled cordially, "if you don't mind?"

"Suppose not. We going to talk about women? That's one of my favorites. Or is this going to be how's the weather and such?"

"Neither," said Hawkeye, and he sat on the old man's left while Caine sat on his right.

"I know you boys?"

"No, but we talked to a fella over at the drug store," Hawkins told him, "and he told us some things but he said you were the one to talk to; said if we wanted to know something and hear it straight, you were the one."

Caine took his wallet out, unlimbered it and produced a fifty-dollar bill which he held in the palm of his hand and pushed toward Old Joe.

"I seen one of them before," the oldtimer noted dryly. "Once. About nineteen-fifty, I think."

"It's yours if you'll answer a few questions," Caine said.

Old Joe's ears perked at the British accent. He looked quizzically at Hawkeye.

"What's wrong with your talker? He a Yankee?"

"English," Caine growled, "and bleeding proud of it."

"Bleeding," Old Joe snorted. "What kind of a gawldang word is *bleeding*?"

"Foreign," Hawkins chuckled. "Look, we came over here because the guy over at the drugstore said you could tell us some things about the sheriff."

Old Joe nodded.

"He's an asshole. Now do I get my fifty?"

"Not quite," Hawkins grinned. "We've roundabouted

our questions to everyone else, but we won't to you. We know from what we've heard that you don't like the sheriff any. We get the feeling no one in this town does, but they aren't saying so. We don't care for him either, oldtimer, and we intend to do a little something about it.''

"Like what?"

"Depends on what you tell us," Caine put in. "What's he like?"

"Crooked as a dog's hind leg, for one," Old Joe snapped. "Gamble on anything. I mean anything. He once bet on how long a racehorse would piss. The sheriff won. Reckon the only thing you can say for him, he gambles good.

"Y'all heard right. I don't like that fat fuck worth a damn. He's one of them there southern sheriffs gives southerners a bad name. They ain't all like that, course, but Braddock is. Only reason he's in office a'tall is he got the right asses greased. Knows who's poking who, that sorta thing. Wiley in some ways, I reckon, but a damn ignoramus in others."

"Would you like to see him get his?" Hawkeye asked.

The old man considered that.

"Well, now, I ain't out to hurt no one, not even a shithole like that bastard."

"Not physically," Caine explained. "Just . . . embarrassed."

"Maybe put in a position to be kicked out of office," Hawkeye added.

"Now you're talking," Old Joe nodded. "Him and his deputy beat up a nephew of mine a few years back for nothing more than a taillight out. My nephew, he ain't been right in the head since. Yeah, I'd like to see high-and-mighty Braddock get his. But you knew that, didn't you?"

"We talked around some, like I said," Hawkins conceded.

"I think it's the gambling part that has potential," Caine prodded "Maybe we should talk some more about that . . ."

Cody listened to what Hawkins and Caine had to say.

It was just after lunch. The odor from the sawmill plant

came through the shut motel windows and filled the room, the processing of those trees not too unlike the aroma of decaying bodies.

"Gambler, huh?" Cody considered that after Caine and Hawkeye finished their report. "That's what most of the folks I talked to about the sheriff got around to mentioning sooner or later, too."

"Old Joe in the park told us that one time Braddock poured gasoline over a possum, flipped a match at it, and he and a deputy bet on how long the little critter would burn. It'd be a real pleasure sticking it to a creep who'd do something like that," said Hawkeye.

"Then Braddock's compulsive gambling is the angle we use?" Caine asked.

"That's the angle," Cody nodded.

"Ideas?" asked Hawkeye.

Cody did not respond immediately.

The only sounds for the next minute or so were the air conditioner humming and the whining and whizzing of cars outside.

After a short while, Cody said, "Y'know, the same thing, shall we say, that got our man Rufe into his jail cell just might get him out."

Hawkeye studied Cody quizzically.

"I don't get you, Sarge."

Caine was studying him too.

"Nor I," he added, "but I will say, mate, that that grin you're wearing calls to mind the proverbial cat that has just swallowed the canary."

Cody, not losing the grin, turned to Hawkins.

"Hawkeye, that southern accent of yours is going to come in handy for a change, but you're going to have to play this one easy. Don't get anyone suspicious. Say you're some sort of termite specialist or something. Just find some way to call around to the sheriffs' offices in the neighboring counties; find out the sheriffs' names. We'll need a name or two."

"Gotcha," Hawkins nodded. "Sort of."

"What have you got in mind, John?" Caine asked.

"Something that could work," Cody explained. "And

I'll guarantee you Rufe will like it so much he'll want to
marry the idea. So Braddock'll gamble on anything, eh?
Okay then, here's what we're going to do . . .''

Rufe Murphy, six-foot-two and two hundred and sixty
pounds of restless black muscle, sat on the lumpy jail-cell
mattress and contemplated his small universe; the one
into which he had been hurled due to his never-ending
quest for pussy.

Pussy.

It was that simple.

Here he sat in a cell eight feet wide and eight feet
deep, sharing it with a drunk, because he could not make
the big head override the urgings of the little head. Now, a
good, cool distance from the passion that had sent him here,
he decided it had not been at all wise to bang the mayor's
wife. He should've stayed busy with his chopper and his
charter services.

True, she had wanted it and things had led up to it
nicely, and once he'd finally got a chance to put the mule in
the barn it had been real all right, but had it been this good?
Was anything worth a hole like this: roaches the size of
cigar butts on the floor; one little, barred, and net-wired
window; and a companion who needed a bath?

Rufe looked at the little drunk, not able to remember
when they had brought him in. He'd gotten into the bad
habit lately of sleeping sound as a rock.

The drunk saw him looking his way and leered back.

''Reckon you're in some deep shit here, boy. Mayor's
wife ain't the ticket for a colored. Not here. Everyone else
in town was fucking her, but not with a black dick, no sir.
That's gonna get you sent up.''

''Secrets are real well kept around here, aren't they?''
Rufe groused.

''Nope, they ain't, and that's a fact,'' the drunk grinned.

At the end of the hallway, Rufe heard the door open
and the drunk whispered, ''Shit, here comes Braddock.
Don't look like I been talking to you, will ya?''

Braddock came over to the bars and grinned.

Rufe thought the sheriff looked like an oversized Butterball turkey that had learned to wear clothes.

"Mornin', boy," Braddock snickered.

"I guess that pleasant greeting must be for me," Rufe growled, wishing he could reach through the bars and strangle the bastard to death.

"The mayor don't like his wife being soiled by no burrhead," Braddock rasped. "He's having her put out to pasture, just 'cause of you. And you . . . well, you're going to be breaking big rocks into little ones real soon, and the mayor aims to make sure there's some guards up at the state pen paid off to bust your balls real regular-like."

"I'm not there yet, Sheriff."

"No, and that's a fact, and I'm right proud to have you here as my guest, boy. You and me, we're going to have ourselves a little fun back here before your case comes to trial, ain't we?" Then he turned to the drunk, not waiting for a response from the big, angry, glaring black man.

"All right, Leroy, get your ass out of there."

Braddock took out his revolver and held it against his leg. He unlocked the cage with the other hand, let Leroy out and closed the cell door, putting the gun away again and smiling at Rufe.

"Leroy must be real dangerous when he's sober," Rufe noted.

Braddock patted his holstered sidearm.

"That was just in case you tried a little end run. And you know, I think I'd like that. Yessiree. I'd give you a warning shot right upside your head, boy. See you later."

"I'll count the minutes," Rufe growled, watching Braddock and the drunk disappear down the hallway outside the cell. He sat back on his uncomfortable bunk and grumbled sourly to himself and the cell floor, "Way to go, Rufe. A nigger's nightmare and you jumped into it feet first . . ."

About two-thirty in the afternoon a car pulled up in front of Braddock's office.

A tall man in a tall hat wearing shiny lizard-skin boots got out of the driver's side, while the other door yielded a muscular man outfitted in a workshit, jeans, and chuka boots, and a Pentax camera slung around his neck, riding on his chest. They went inside the office.

Braddock sat behind his desk, a deputy across from him, playing checkers.

"What can I do for you?" Braddock demanded tersely, moving inhospitable eyes over the new arrivals.

"Sheriff Braddock?" the man with the tall hat asked.

"You're talkin' to him."

"Name's Harold Richards," Hawkeye Hawkins said. "This here is Jim Mosby." He motioned to Cody. "We're over from Carrington County. I'm a deputy over there. Jim here's a friend. He's the one going to make sure this is all official-like."

"Make sure what's official-like?" Braddock glowered.

"Well now, Sheriff, I reckon that's going to depend on whether or not you're interested," Hawkins winked. "It's not, shall we say, law business, but it is, uh, official in a way, if you want to call money official."

Braddock stood up and came around his desk, sort of smiling.

"Well shoot, I've always thought of money as official; right official."

"Well," Hawkins went on, "it is kind of private."

"Oh, don't mind Willie Bob," Braddock assured them with a nod at the deputy. "Willie Bob ain't gonna say shit if'n he ain't supposed to, right, Willie Bob?"

Willie Bob nodded, and Hawkins and Cody nodded as if that suited them.

"Well then, Sheriff," Hawkins continued, "first off, I got to tell you I'm right proud to meet up with you. Heard a lot about you, yessir."

"You have?"

"You bet I have. Your gambling feats, Sheriff. Word is you're one of the best. Bet on anything, all kinds of odds. You're practically a legend."

Braddock puffed up.

"Well, now, I figure a man ain't a man unless he's willing to take a chance now and then."

Hawkins nodded. "Fact is, you're kind of the inspiration for this whole deal, you and your betting. Like I say, word is you'll bet on anything. So, some of the boys, and the sheriff . . . You know Sheriff Tywater, don't you?''

"Know who he is.''

"Sheriff Tywater got this all started. Uh, you do have a prisoner in your jail at the moment, don't you, Sheriff?''

"Hell, yes. Got me a nigger in back.''

"Well,'' Hawkins chuckled pleasantly, "they're usually prisoners, aren't they?''

"I always say ain't nobody fills out and looks right in a striped suit and ball and chain better than a coon,'' Braddock snickered. "Don't I always say that, Willie Bob?''

Willie Bob nodded. "That's what you always say, Sheriff.''

"Well then, Sheriff,'' Hawkins went on. "I'm not going to beat around the bush any longer. I'm going to come straight to the point. We're having ourselves a dick measuring contest.''

"A *what*?'' Braddock and Willie Bob replied together.

"You heard me right. The old leather swing, the peter, the hammer, the dong. We're gambling on who's got the biggest one.''

"Well now,'' Braddock said, slowly. "I am a betting man, but I ain't holding my dick out there to be measured—''

"Not yours, Sheriff. The prisoner's. We're measuring prisoners' dicks. See, Sheriff Tywater got himself a boy in our lockup over to Carrington County. Happened to get a look at that boy in the shower the other day, and whooee, talk about hung! The sheriff never seen anything like it and, well, being as he's a gambling man hisself, I reckon he figured he'd make some easy money. He sent me over to make a wager of two hundred bucks that there ain't a prisoner in your jail hung the way his is. You game, Sheriff?''

Braddock looked as if he'd been stunned with a slaughterhouse hammer.

"Two hundred skins for the biggest dong?''

"Yep,'' Hawkins nodded. "Like I said, it's inspired by you. Word is you'll bet on anything, and Sheriff Tywater was talking about that—''

"But I don't know Tywater."

"Ah, but he knows you, Sheriff, or your reputation, I should say. Said it would do you proud; was your kind of game. Whatcha think?"

"Do it, Sheriff," Willie Bob urged. "That boy in back's bound to have himself a well rope. They's known for that, and he's one big sonofabitch."

Braddock made up his mind and started smiling.

"Willie Bob, go get the coon. And keep your gun out, otherwise he just might tie you in a knot."

"Yes sir, Sheriff," Willie Bob nodded, and he scampered to the back.

A moment later, Rufe Murphy came through the door, hands on his head.

A yard behind him, his gun pointing at Rufe's back, came Willie Bob.

Rufe saw Cody and Hawkins and almost smiled. Almost.

"Well, well," Hawkins grinned, "if the contest was for ugly, this black motherfucker would win hands down."

"Who these honkies?" Rufe growled, not missing a beat.

"No matter to you, boy," Braddock snarled. "You gonna win me some money. Drop your pants."

Murphy blinked.

"Say what?"

He looked at Cody.

Cody nodded very faintly, so faintly had Rufe not been looking for a sign, he wouldn't have noticed it.

Rufe sighed. He unbuckled his trousers.

"You white breads sure are a fun-loving bunch."

"Shorts, too," Braddock ordered. "We're going to measure your dick."

"The hell you are, shit-for-brains."

"It's either that," Braddock said, "or Willie Bob here is going to shoot it off."

Rufe frowned at Hawkins and Cody.

They smiled back.

Rufe sighed again and lowered his shorts.

"Good godalmighty," Braddock said, looking at Rufe's

tool. "To think something like that's wasted on a spade. Guess that's what Ellie seen in you, huh, boy?"

"It didn't hurt her feelings none," Rufe conceded with a smile, and he placed his hands on top of his head again.

"Well, fellas," Braddock invited, stepping back, "Measure away."

"Uh-uh." Hawkins shook his head. "You've got to do your own measuring. Them's the rules. We just validate."

Cody pulled a cloth measuring-tape from his jeans pocket and tossed it to Braddock. "There you are, Sheriff. I'll get the picture." And he began adjusting the knobs and dials on the Pentax.

"Picture?"

"Of his thang," Hawkins said. "Lot of money changing hands here, Sheriff, we can't just have our say so that your prisoner's hung like a bull moose. We've got to have proof. Need a picture of the tape on the meat, so to speak."

"Willie Bob—" Braddock started.

"Nope," Hawkins said. "Got to be you, Sheriff. Them's Sheriff Tywater's conditions on this little deal or it's no go."

"I don't see what it matters who measures the damn thing," Braddock whined, regarding Rufe's principle male tendon as if it were a snake that might leap up and bite him.

"But them's the rules," Willie Bob added hastily.

"You shut up," Braddock snapped at his obviously relieved deputy.

"That's right," Hawkins said. "Them's the rules. I didn't make 'em. I'm just helping enforce this little bet, to make sure it's done right. I'm getting twenty bucks and a half day off to see it's done the way it's supposed to be."

"I'm getting cold," Murphy grumbled. "It gets small when it gets cold."

Braddock sighed, then shook the measuring tape out.

"Oh, all right, but I sure don't like it. I might have to touch it."

"That is a problem," Hawkins admitted.

Braddock circled Rufe like a shark, frowning at the instrument of the contest. Finally, he settled on his knees, slightly to the side of Rufe, and measured.

"Godalmighty," he marveled, "it . . . it ain't human."

"Ought to see me when I'm happy," Rufe grinned.

Cody snapped a series of pictures with the Pentax, moving from left to right to get them.

"You, uh, getting it?" Braddock asked.

"Oh yeah," Cody said. "Guess that about does it, Sheriff."

Braddock handed Cody back the tape measure.

"When'll I know if I've won?"

"We'll get back to you," Hawkins promised. "And soon."

"Hey," Rufe called, "what about me?"

Cody smiled at him.

"Well, prisoner, if I were you, I'd start by pulling my pants up."

Two hours later, Cody and Hawkins returned, Caine accompanying them this time. Cody had a large manila envelope under his arm. When they came into the sheriff's office, Braddock turned and looked over his shoulder at them. He was nailing a framed photograph on the wall. It was a photo of him holding an extremely large catfish on a chain. Braddock was smiling, the catfish wasn't.

Deputy Willie Bob was nowhere in sight.

"Well now," said Braddock. "Back already. Who's your friend?"

"Doesn't matter," Cody said. He took the envelope from under his arm, opened it and tossed some enlarged photographs on the sheriff's desk. "That photo service in town here, it does prints just as fast as they say. Faster when you pay them a little extra."

Braddock looked confused. He picked up one of the photos.

It showed him down on his knees beside Rufe. Rufe had his hands on his head and was smiling in a satisfied way. From the angle the photograph had been taken, you couldn't see the measuring tape. In fact, it looked as if Braddock were . . .

"My God!" Braddock exclaimed. "You boys can't use these! You can't see the tape!"

"No shit," Hawkeye smiled.

Braddock colored as realization seeped into him. He snatched the pictures up, tore them to pieces furiously.

"You missed a piece," Hawkeye offered, handing Braddock a large corner of one snapshot that had drifted to the edge of the desk.

Braddock tore that up too.

"You dumb asshole," said Hawkeye, still smiling. "You think those are the only copies we've got?"

Braddock eyed the three of them evenly.

"There wasn't no contest, was there? You just wanted to get them pictures, to make it look like—"

He couldn't finish.

Hawkins finished for him.

"Like you're tooting Rufe's horn, Sheriff. Yeah, that is what it looks like, don't it?"

"You . . . you bastards know that nigger, don't you?"

"Bingo," said Cody. "And I'd forget putting your hand on that gun, Sheriff. We might be forced to hurt you. We don't want to do that."

"These pictures are going to hurt you bad enough," Caine put in, "if you don't listen to reason."

"I got no money," Braddock told them. "I ain't got nothing you'd want."

"You've got one thing we want," Cody corrected. "You've got Rufe Murphy. I want you to let him go."

"But I can't do that! Man's in here on grand theft auto."

"He didn't steal a thing and you know it," Caine countered. "We know about the mayor's wife, mate, and we know that's why Rufe's in this pigsty you call a jail."

"But I can't just let him go!"

"Let me outline this for you," Cody said. "We've given copies of these pictures to some people here in town. And we've told them if anything happens to us, or Rufe, they send copies to certain individuals. People see these, and . . . you figure it, Sheriff."

"Dick-honking sheriffs are frowned upon highly," Hawkins offered, his smile right in place.

"You goddamn sonofabitches," Braddock snarled without moving from behind his desk.

"Three of the biggest," Caine agreed.

"Now," Cody said, "here's what you do, Sheriff. You go back there and bring Rufe out. Then you'll just have to do something about that grand theft auto stuff. Drop it. Say it was a mistake."

"The mayor—" Braddock started.

"The mayor wouldn't want those pictures flashed around either," Cody said. "Could prove to be extremely embarrassing for your town, don't you think?"

"Yeah, Sheriff," Hawkins said, "If you're going to play the skin flute, you're going to have to learn not to have pictures taken of you doing it. Not smart at all."

Braddock's mouth opened and closed a few times but nothing came out, as if the words were too thick and had lodged in his throat.

"You know," Hawkins continued easily, "we could send you one of these framed and you could put it up there next to your fish picture. Be kind of nice, I think, you showing how you caught a couple of big ones."

"I ought to blow your heads off," Braddock hissed.

"You do," Cody said, "and those pictures get sent."

"Besides, my good man," Caine interjected, "it would be to your considerable disadvantage to try. We'd be forced to cripple you."

"At the very least," Hawkeye added.

"Enough." All the humor had gone out of Cody's voice. "You go back there and get Rufe. I'd like it best if you'd put that revolver on the desk before you do. If you don't want to do that I'll take it away from you."

Braddock eyed the three of them, not seeing a gun among them, but there was something about the way they stood, the confidence they radiated. Slowly, he placed his service revolver on the desk.

"Good man," Cody nodded. "Now bring Rufe out."

Braddock opened a desk drawer, slowly, and got out a ring of keys. He went to the back, returning with Rufe Murphy.

The huge black man looked very happy.

"Howdy, boys." He moved quickly away from Braddock to stand by his friends from ten years ago, then said, "Sheriff, baby, looks like you've just had your ass stung, but don't feel too bad. It was done by the best."

Braddock's cheeks were hopping about as if infested with jumping beans, but he didn't say anything.

"And remember," Cody said. "Clean slate for Rufe here. And you try and stop us, push this matter in any way, your wife gets a copy, the mayor gets a copy, just about everybody gets a copy. Got it?"

Braddock nodded, glowering.

"Let's hear it," Cody snapped.

"Got it," the sheriff said, biting off the words.

"Bye now," Rufe said.

They turned to go out the door, Cody watching Braddock, as first Caine, then Hawkeye, left the building. Rufe was almost out, then stopped and turned to Cody as if he had been fighting a battle inside himself and just lost.

"Sorry, Sarge," he told Cody, "but I gots to."

And he crossed over quickly, before Braddock could scuttle out of the way, and delivered a backhand slap that was hard enough to lift the sheriff off his feet and pitch him back over his desk, to where he balled up in an unmoving, loudly snoring heap in the corner.

"Damn, that felt good," Rufe sighed.

He and Cody got out of there.

They drove by the park in the town square on their way out of town, and Cody parked idling at the curb at Hawkeye's request.

Hawkeye took a package off the car seat, got out, and went up to the bench where Old Joe—as usual—was seated.

The oldtimer looked up.

"Fifty bucks again?" he asked hopefully.

"Something better," Hawkeye chuckled, opening the package. He took out a framed, glassed picture of Sheriff Braddock and Rufe, Rufe's head having been strategically scissored out of the picture. "Keep this for insurance, pard. Never know when you might need it."

Old Joe looked over the photograph and laughed so hard he nearly fell off the bench.

"Goddamn, boy, you got him, didn't you? You got him good."

"Yep," Hawkins said. "You take care, Old Joe."

"I will," the oldtimer promised between laughs.

Hawkins shook hands with the old man and went back to the car, smiling all the way.

Cody slipped the car into gear and drove them out of town and no one tried to stop them.

After several miles Cody said, "Rufe, I've got a proposition for you . . ."

CHAPTER
EIGHT

Captain Tom Ward completed the shutdown procedure.

The 727's massive jet-engine power whistled, hummed and vibrated away to nothing, leaving Flight 766 from Athens to Tell Aviv sitting all by its lonesome on the tarmac fronting the north side of the Beirut airport terminal.

The 727's flight deck crackled with tension and body odor, and the plane's air conditioning did nothing for the sweat Ward felt beading his forehead and upper lip. He restrained himself from making even the slightest move to wipe away the perspiration.

He did not want to make the woman holding the pistol to the nape of his neck anymore nervous than she already appeared to be.

Larry Jenks, the copilot, flashed Ward another secretive sideways glance, awaiting some sort of indication of what to do, but Ward ignored him, as he had from the beginning of this ordeal, a long sixty minutes ago when Flight 766 had been cruising routinely, halfway to its destination, high above the troubled lands of the Middle East. The endless expanse of the blue Mediterranean flowed by far beneath as if there were no such thing as terrorists and hijackings, something that was always on the mind of pilots and crew in this part of the world these days. But for all the hijackings that had occurred in the past few years, the total was but a minute fraction of the daily air traffic in and near the trouble spots, and a job was a job. Flying was a profession Ward loved, and all you could do was hope and pray that your luck would hold.

Ward knew their luck had run out.

The flight navigator, Yamir, lay stretched out dead on the floor of the flight deck, where he had fallen when he reacted in the first moments of the takeover.

It had been an A-B-C, by-the-numbers operation all the way: the first thing Ward had known of anything being wrong was the frantic knocking on the cockpit door and a woman shrieking something frantic, unintelligible.

Ward had nodded for Yamir to open the door, thinking perhaps one of the passengers was panicking from some sort of air-flight phobia and had come forward. This happened from time to time.

The door to the flight deck had slammed inward then, knocking Yamir off his feet, and then Ward had known instantly what was happening when he saw the dusky, Arabic features and the guns the man and the woman both held.

Yamir had started to get up, to protest.

The man had kneed him brutally in the face and the kick had jammed his nasal cartilage up into his brain.

Then the woman had aimed her weapon at Ward's head, where it had remained except for the brief time during the landing.

Ward had followed the man's orders and landed the jet here on the rough, uncared-for runway of Beirut International.

Every pilot's nightmare.

Passenger's nightmare, too.

He had not gotten much of a look at the woman, but one glance at the man had been enough to make him do as he was told and fly the plane and not cause trouble, which is also why he had not encouraged his copilot to take action, either. He had not only his own but the lives of all his passengers dependent on how he reacted.

The man—the woman terrorist had referred to him as Abdel—had about him the look of a born killer. Ward had flown in Vietnam and had seen some men like this before; men who had lost their souls to what they had been through and lost even their reason for fighting on, and had begun to enjoy the killing.

Abdel strutted back into the cockpit, now that they were landed.

Ward did not twist around to look out into the passenger section, but he knew other terrorists would have that part of the plane secured. He didn't know how they could have gotten these weapons aboard the flight, but it didn't really matter now, anyway. Athens security was a joke. His gut region burned to *do something*, but the woman had not removed the gun snout from his neck.

Abdel stepped over the sprawled form of Yamir, leaned forward past the pilots and picked up the cockpit radio.

"Attention, tower. This is Flight 766, do you read me?"

"We read you," the radio crackled back. "Go ahead."

Ward looked out and down at the group of people standing in the early morning light in front of the terminal. He could see cameras and some uniforms, but no one from there came forward.

"This plane is now in the control of the Palestinian Liberation Guerrilla Force," intoned Abdel without inflection.

"We demand the release of seven-hundred revolutionary heroes now held by Israeli forces in the prison camp outside Tel Aviv within the next forty-eight hours. What is to happen is intended to prove we mean what we say. If our demands are not met, we will commence executing the passengers aboard this plane one per hour. *Allah wa-akbar!* God is great!" Abdel replaced the headphones and stepped back, turning to the woman. "Watch them closely," he instructed, then he glanced at Ward. "I would advise you and your crew not to attempt anything, Captain. We needed you to land this plane. We don't need you now. Understood?"

"I understand that," Ward grunted. "What I don't understand is why you people always bring God into it when you're getting ready to massacre innocent civilians."

The terrorist hissed and delivered a short, swift chop with his Uzi to Ward's forehead, making the world seem to spin around with a burst of pain inside Ward's head.

Ward righted himself to keep from falling, shaking his head to clear it, turning in time to see Abdel leave the cockpit.

The woman stepped away from Ward now so she could keep both him and copilot Jenks covered with her pistol and riveting, dark eyes.

Ward looked back at the woman and thought about trying to say something, but he caught his tongue.

If Abdel had looked like a man who would enjoy killing, this one had about her the look of the haunted, the damned, like she had a mad-on for the whole damn world; as though she had just lost her best friend and was only waiting for the right opportunity to let the anger and hate inside of her boil over so she could start pulling the pistol's trigger.

Something about her scared Ward even more than Abdel had, and the only thought Ward had at that moment was, God help us all. . . .

Farouk Hassan had positioned himself and Hallah in the rear of the jet's passenger section, while Abdel and Tahia had found seating toward the front.

The prearranged passing through of customs with their weapons had been managed without a hitch, thanks to connections made at the airport by the PLGF's local cell.

Farouk's only real concerns had been the depletion of his unit, the fact that they were not carrying the full armament and ammunition required for an operation such as this, and the fact that Tahia seemed to be suffering from such a state of nerves that he had feared she might draw suspicion to them before the hijack even began. But that had not happened.

He had signaled the others that the operation was to commence when he had stepped up to the magazine rack at the front of the passenger section.

That was when Tahia had gone into her act up front and

within minutes the crew and all one-hundred-and-fifty passengers had come under their control.

He knew how Tahia felt. He felt the same way. It had been only hours since he had seen Ali bloodied and dying. A cold rage filled him to deliver some kind of retribution, even if only upon this collection of tourists and businessmen and miscellaneous travelers, but he knew he must control his grief until the time was right and he must trust his brother's lover to show the same strength, as she had up to now.

At this moment, Hallah stood at the rear of the plane after having collected the passports of all aboard and separating the Israli and American passports from the others.

The passengers remained seated, frightened, immobile, under the weapons aimed at them.

Abdel emerged from the flight deck and nodded.

"We are ready. I have radioed the message. It is time to select the first one."

Sharon Adamson had been in the galley with one of the other stewardesses, chatting about nothing, in the moments before they were to begin walking down the aisles, collecting emptied drinking cups and the like, when the woman's screams from up front had brought them running—into the barrels of the automatic weapons held by Arabs, one at the front of the plane, one at midsection.

She stood now near the front entrance, where she and the three other flight attendants had been told to stand. She watched the drama unfold before her with the numbing shock of realization at how quickly one's life could be turned upside down.

The Athens–Tel Aviv flight was not a long one, but glancing out across the passengers, she felt the same sense of responsiblity she always took to heart, only magnified.

Her eye caught the elderly American couple that had been so nice coming aboard—the Marcuses, their names had been; charming folks who had been bubbling with enthusiasm for their travels, their "second honeymoon," as Mr. Marcus had chuckled affectionately.

There was Mrs. Vereen, an overweight woman in

middle-age whose shortness of breath and flushed complex-ion made Sharon think the woman probably had a heart condition.

And the children, at least a dozen of them.

She was afraid, she readily admitted to herself, but not so afraid that she could look away from the anxiety etched across the face of every passenger aboard.

The terrorist she had heard referred to as Abdel emerged from the cabin and spoke to the other man, who was obviously the leader, who nodded and turned to Sharon while Abdel and the man at midsection kept the hostages covered.

"Miss," the man said, with a nod to the stack of passports that had been gathered and placed in an empty seat nearby, "I want you to reach into this pile of American passports and hand me one."

She lost her voice for a moment. Cold fingers seemed to wrap themselves around the base of her spine. She knew the methods of these madmen and she knew what was about to happen, and yet she was stunned that she was being asked to be a part of it.

This can't be happening! her mind screamed.

"W-why?" she asked before she could stop the word from coming out. "You . . . you're not going to hurt any of these people, are you? They haven't done anything to you!"

He glared at her straight on for a moment and she saw things she did not understand in his eyes.

"You will do as I say. Pick one of the passports. Hand it to me. That is an order."

The passengers overheard this exchange, and nervous murmurings began rippling through the rows of seats.

She suddenly felt very strange, as if somehow detached from what was happening around her, as if this was all happening to someone else, not to Sharon Adamson of Ft. Lauderdale, Florida, with a planeload of tourists on a hijacked jet in Beirut, Lebanon.

She said, very quietly and in a voice she did not quite recognize as her own, "I will not help you. Do with me what you will."

The man named Abdel started to turn in her direction, raising his weapon.

"The bitch. Farouk, let me—"

Farouk lifted a hand.

"No." He stalked over close to her and she could smell him. She *smelled* his hate.

"It is too late to help anyone," he told her.

Then he made a fist and hit stewardess Adamson on the jaw.

Sharon's eyes rolled back in her head and everything went black for her.

CHAPTER
NINE

Ten minutes after Cody received word that they had a
mission, the four of them kicked out of the new style
military "Jeep" in front of their operations center on the
sprawling Andrews Air Force Base.

All four were grimy, splotched with camou black on
hands and face. They wore camou fatigues well dirtied after
a grueling four-hour exercise in the woodsy, marshy section
at which they had been training for the past two weeks.

"About time they hand us something," Hawkeye groused
with a belch.

"It has been getting real tedious," Murphy agreed.
"Almost got me to longing for my choppers and that
mayor's wife."

"Imagine this will shoot teatime all to Hell," Caine
snorted.

Cody knew what they meant. He'd been getting restless, too.

Cody's Army, as Lund had dubbed it half kiddingly,
was ready, and for the past two weeks it had been a case of
all dressed up with nowhere to go.

The training helped relieve the tedium but it had proved

unnecessary. Caine, Hawkins, and Murphy had kept themselves hard and in shape, every bit as battle-ready as they were back in Nam.

Most important, to Cody's way of thinking, was that these good friends—Hawkeye Hawkins, Rufe Murphy, and Richard Caine—had lost none of their enthusiasm for a good scrap if the cause was just.

He led the way into a squat cinder-block building that showed only one story above the ground but dropped three levels below.

"Lund said it was a big one. Let's see what they have."

Two minutes later, they walked into the third basement level of their quarters, an elaborate electronic war room with one twenty-foot-long wall covered with a huge video map that was computer-programmed and adjusted. Now an out-of-sight hand changed the screen to Europe, then to the Mideast, and at last zoomed in on Beirut, Lebanon.

There were a dozen soft, swivel, rocker chairs in the twenty-foot-square room. Each chair fronted a long table at which microphones perched expectantly beside steaming cups of coffee and platters high with sandwiches. Rufe grabbed four and began chowing down.

Besides Cody's Army, four more men sat in the chairs. One was Pete Lund, next to him sat an Army general, then a Marine colonel, and a civilian who had State Department stamped on his forehead where frown wrinkles were growing deeper by the second.

Lund led it off.

"Gentlemen, welcome to Beirut. This is not a replay, this is a whole new shoe, another incident, almost a carbon copy of the TWA hijack a few months back. But this one is not going to last as long or end the same way.

"The takeover of the Air Mediterranean Flight 766 from Athens to Tel Aviv was by the Palestinian Liberation Guerrilla Force. We know little of this group, which we are assured is a radical splinter from the PLO. Members of this PLGF have been involved in only minor bombings and some kidnapings before, nothing this ambitious.

"The PLGF are demanding the release of seven hundred Lebanese revolutionary prisoners still held in an Israeli camp outside of Tel Aviv. These were captured in the Israeli invasion of Lebanon more than two years ago.

"The PLGF has given Israel and us a forty-eight-hour deadline, then they will begin executing one passenger an hour if their demands are not being met. Now please watch this satellite transmission from Beirut television. The hijackers notified the Beirut tower well in advance so that television crews were on hand at the airport when the hijacked plane landed.

"We taped this transmission less than an hour ago from a satellite transmission, showed it to the President, and he told us to come right over here and get into operation. Roll the videotape please."

The screen went black for a moment, then an eight-foot-square lit in the center of the wall and they saw what had to be the Beirut airport.

An excited voice came on speaking Arabic, which was quickly translated into English, sometimes overlapping.

"Here we are at the Beirut, Lebanon airport where the Air Mediterranean flight 766 has just landed. A band of courageous Palestinians on board have liberated the airliner and are holding the crew and passengers in custody."

As the voice continued the camera moved closer to a 727 commercial passenger aircraft, where two persons appeared at its passenger door. A boarding ramp was hastily rolled up to the airliner.

A gunman wearing a long black hood that completely covered his head appeared at the door and waved the two ground crewmen away. When they were clear, the gunman pulled forward a gray-haired woman who seemed to be in her sixties and motioned for her to go down the steps.

She hung back. The gunman slapped her twice with his open hand, jolting her head from side to side.

The translation picked up again.

"Now a passenger is being brought out. The radio man at the tower said the woman would be Mrs. Esther Marcus of New York City—oh, she fell!"

On the screen the elderly woman could be seen to trip

and then fall against the railing. The Arab gunman with his Uzi submachine gun jerked her up and pushed her forward.

A moment later an elderly man appeared at the door of the plane and was forced down the steps. He was about the same age as the woman.

"Now Mr. David Marcus is coming down the steps. Mr. Marcus has a heart condition and high blood-pressure, but he was selected for the honor and so he must participate," the translator droned on.

The two hooded terrorists now had the man and woman on the tarmac under the nose of the plane and forced both to kneel. The woman fell down but was hoisted to her knees while her skirt slid up her thighs.

The narrator translator continued. "I'm not sure what they are doing now. The Marcus couple are looking at each other, yes, they both are weeping."

The camera zoomed in on a tight shot of David Marcus. Tears seeped down his cheeks. He held one arm protectively around his wife. One of the hooded gunmen forced the old man's arm away from her. The hijacker lifted the submachine gun and held it at the back of David Marcus's head.

The woman screamed and pushed the gun away, throwing her arms around her husband. The second hooded figure slammed his Uzi against her head, stunning her, and pulled her away from David Marcus.

The translator came on again. "The gunman shouted, 'I do this for the liberation of my seven hundred fellow countrymen being held illegally by Israel.' Oh, my God!"

The camera zoomed in close again on the weapon's muzzle pressed against the back of David Marcus's head. Then the Uzi fired.

The man slammed forward, blood and skull fragments sprayed in the air. David Marcus jolted to the tarmac face-first; his body twitched two or three times, then lay still. He was dead before his face skidded onto the black surface. A pool of crimson-red blood formed on the tarmac below his head. The woman beside him screamed and swung her fists at the hooded murderer, then in total frustration and agony dropped on top of her dead husband.

The two masked figures dragged Mrs. Marcus off her husband's corpse and forced her to kneel next to him.

"My God! They killed him! Shot him in cold blood. I'm sorry, it's so tragic. The translation, yes, I forgot. The killer shouted that he was doing this for Lebanon. He shouted that the criminal Israelis must set his starving seven hundred countrymen free. Then he murdered David Marcus. Now . . . oh, my God! Now they are forcing Mrs. Marcus to kneel. Surely they are not going to . . . they wouldn't dare to . . . not again!"

The zoom lens showed only Mrs. Marcus's face now on the giant screen. In back of her there was some motion. Then the camera pulled back a little to show the Uzi's muzzle against the back of her head.

The weapon fired once and Esther Marcus's eyes widened, her mouth flew open before her whole body smashed out of the frame to the blacktop runway.

"My God! They did it again. They murdered Mrs. Marcus and the gunman said the same thing as before!"

The giant screen showed a wider shot of the scene now that included the plane's nose, the two bodies, and the ramp. One of the hooded terrorists went to Mr. Marcus and fired a three-round burst into his head, then moved to the woman and did the same. He lifted his weapon in the air, and then both the terrorists hurried back up the steps. They returned from inside the plane a minute later and threw the body of a man to the runway. Then they left and closed the plane's door.

Over this scene the translator continued with a shaky voice. "A short time later, by radio, the terrorists made these demands: One. The United States and Israel must make plans at once to release seven hundred Lebanese prisoners Israel still detains. These men must be returned to Lebanon within forty-eight hours of the current time.

"Two, there will be no attempt made to free the hostages from the aircraft or all will die.

"Three, there will be no retaliation against any PLO organization or personnel, or all the hostages will die.

"Four, if satisfactory negotiations are not completed for the release of the seven hundred within forty-eight hours, one of the hostages will be killed every hour on the hour.

"Negotiations are to be made through the good offices of Majed Kaddoumi in Beirut. Set our prisoners free!"

The lights came up softly as the image faded on the screen. When the TV feed was gone the lights were up fully.

Cody felt the familiar rage building in his gut. The anger against all those who took advantage of the weak and defenseless. The brazen brutality of these killings sickened him.

"Bloody bastards!" Caine whispered.

"Fucking sonsofbitches!" Hawkeye blurted.

"I owe them muthus! I owe them hard!" Rufe raged.

The four-star Army general stood and looked at Cody. "Gentlemen, this will not be another TWA flight 847 hijacking. The United States government cannot permit that to happen. We must deal with this quickly, with total dedication, and we must fight as deadly and as dirty as the terrorists do. No negotiations and no prisoners is our firm resolve in this matter."

He looked at the four men. "I am assured by the President, and by Mr. Lund, that you four are the men to do the job. I hope they are right. You have the full resources of the United States government and military establishment at your disposal. I wish you luck, and more to the point, good hunting."

Pete Lund stood as the general eased into his chair. "So far we have little to go on. You will be briefed in code on your flight. You leave in a B-52 taking a training flight to Tel Aviv in exactly one hour and twenty-two minutes.

"We are not certain how many hijackers there are. At least two, the hooded ones we saw on the ground in the film. There must be more, perhaps as many as six to eight more on board. The deadline time clock began at 18:36 Beirut time, which was 11:36 today here. Beirut is seven hours ahead of us. We were notified of the hijacking at 12:02. We have a less than forty-six hours before the next innocent hostage is scheduled to die.

"The third person to die on the aircraft was the flight

engineer, Yamir Abudah, an Egyptian national. He was killed, evidently, in the takeover of the plane.''

A phone blinked beside Lund. The civilian next to Lund picked it up, listened, then whispered to the CIA man.

''We have just been informed that the hijackers have utilized contacts at the airport and rolled onto the field with a heavily armored column. They have commandeered airport buses and taken away the one-hundred and twenty passengers and the crew of seven from the aircraft.

''They left the airport, which is under control of the Amal Militia, without a shot being fired. Then under heavily armed escort have transported the hostages somewhere into West Beirut. We no longer have the advantage of knowing where they are, or of the chance for a friendly rescue attempt with the aid of the Christian Forces Militia who control East Beirut.''

''So now we have to find the hostages before we can do anything,'' Cody growled.

''Exactly, and you'll be dealing within a hostile nation. These men and women of West Beirut are in a constant state of war, heavily armed and eager to die for the glory of Allah. Our man from the Near East desk at State can help us understand the situation in Beirut.''

The civilian stood. He looked even more worried now than before.

''Gentlemen, this will be difficult. Beirut is a madhouse. There is little stability there and no consistency except that of terror and constant warfare. There is no central government that has any power. Amin Gemayel is the president, with almost no authority or day-to-day operating muscle. He is leader of the Phalange Party. All of the major political and militia groups oppose him.

''Yes, yes, I know. From time to time they have accords, cease-fires and treaties among the three major forces fighting in Lebanon, but just as quickly these are shattered.

''Several of these groups opposing the East Beirut forces include:

''The Shiite Amal Militia, one of the stronger and

better-armed outfits in Beirut. The Sixth Brigade is one of their largest units.

"Hezbollah, or the Party of God, is a large, heavily armed group. This is a rival Shiite faction, not controlled by the Amal. Often they shoot at the Amal people, and sometimes at each other.

"The Sunni Moslem Mourbitoun are a group backed by Libya and Yasser Arafat's PLO.

"The Islamic Jihad, or the Islamic Holy War, is a fourth band fighting for a homeland. This is a shadow group of Shiites loyal only to themselves. They are Moslem super-fundamentalists closely tied to Iran's Ayatollah Khomeini, and display all of his radical, extreme tendencies.

"The Druse Moslems are a group who vow to fight President Gemayel to the death.

"The only force that is friendly to the Western world is the Christian Lebanese Forces, who control most of East Beirut. They are led by Elie Hobeika. All of the previously described groups are Moslem and they all fight the Christian Militiamen. It makes for exciting times on the streets.

"This Lebanon situation is unlike anything most Westerners have ever seen. It is not a civil war, it is like six civil wars going on at once. Generally the only security you will have as Westerners will be in the east half of Beirut. It's easy to tell the east. There is a line of blood called the Green Line that separates East Beirut from the west.

"Almost constant fighting takes place along and across the Green Line. There might be a fourteen-year-old boy firing a fully automatic rifle across the line at random. There could be a blooded killer of eighteen firing a rocket-propelled grenade at a moving car or truck. The fighters then return home and play with their toys, try to feed their families, and argue. For the moment their war is over.

"In Beirut, trust no one; your best friend is your loaded SMG, and the U.S. Government has never heard of you if you are captured or come under some foreign nation's official jurisdiction.

"You may have any weapons you want. You may order more or different arms on your flight. It all will be ready for you at your final landing point, the U.S. Embassy in East

Beirut. You each will have plenty of cash, in U.S. dollars, Israeli shekels, and Lebanese pounds. Your team leader is authorized to draw up to five-hundred-thousand dollars if needed for equipment that may be needed later. Are there any questions?''

"What is our exact mission?" Cody asked.

Lund leaned forward.

"You are to proceed to Beirut as directed, locate the missing hostages of Flight 766, then penetrate the area and rescue the hostages, removing them with the cooperation of Israeli Air Force choppers. You pick up liaison and radios for Israeli contact in Beirut. The Israelis will operate from Haifa, only seventy-five miles from Beirut."

"The rescue of the hostages, then, is our major concern?"

"Absolutely. We are not opposed to as much retribution as required to discourage the terrorists; however, their annihilation is not our prime objective."

"Understood."

The Marine bird colonel lifted his hand at Cody. "The President has asked me to tell you that you have his strongest possible support on this mission. If you need anything and can't get it through channels, call me direct. My number is in your briefing papers."

Lund stood. "Thank you, Cody; men. This is what we hope is the start of a new attack on terrorism by the United States."

"Good luck, and good hunting."

A half hour later, Pete Lund sat in the Oval Office with the President and his top advisor on military operations. The advisor was Brigadier General Will Johnson, in mufti.

"I still don't like it, Mr. President," growled Johnson. "Sure, this Cody has a good record, he gets things done, has had military combat duty, and worked with the CIA. But it still doesn't seem right."

The President turned to Lund. "Comment?"

"Absolutely, Mr. President. Will, you haven't been on the ground. You haven't fired a shot in thirty years. You are not thinking logically when you say a battalion-sized landing party in Beirut would do the job simpler, and better. You could never gear up a battalion to move in forty-eight hours, let alone put them on-site.

"You could not determine the reception of the dogfaces or Marines on the objective. Cody will go in, do the job, if it can be done at all, and get our people and the other passengers out of there with minimum losses. And we do not stand to get our noses bloodied in any fashion."

"People already know about his move," Will protested. "I had a call from a reporter asking about our task force to Lebanon!"

"He was out fishing, Will," the President said. "No, there would be nothing covert about sending in even a thousand men. That would create a worldwide flap we might never live down."

"But *four* men, Mr. President?"

"Depends on the men, Will," Lund said quickly. "I'll put Cody and his four up against a platoon of regular troops any day."

"Gentlemen, this is moving us nowhere. When is their plane set to take off, Lund?"

"It left ten minutes ago, sir. I checked just before we arrived here."

"Enough. We have made a committment. I thought then it was the right move, and I still do. We support them all the way. If something goes wrong, it's only four Americans not connected with the government in any way. Now, on to other, more pressing matters."

Lund listened, but his thoughts were with Cody's Army team in that B-52 heading for Cairo, Egypt. He prayed real hard that this would not somehow prove to be another double-cross—the way Cody had been set up in Nicaragua.

CHAPTER
TEN

Officially, the four civilians on the Air Force B-52 bomber were hitchhikers. Unofficially, the flight had been arranged to take Cody's Army from Edwards Air Force Base to an Egyptian airfield just outside of Cairo.

Time was the essential consideration. At first they had toyed with the idea of using jet fighters with two seats, but when they took a second look at Rufe Murphy and his 260 pounds of muscle, they changed their minds.

The B-52 could make the 5,200-mile jump to Cairo in a little under eight hours, depending on the headwinds. The four passengers flaked out on the floor of the big bomber and slept, later sat in jump seats and talked. It was the longest flight any of them could remember.

They were going as civilians, wore mufti, and had suitcases, and there was not a single weapon among them, not even a knife. They would be picking up their working "tools" at the American Embassy in Beirut, from the Marine detachment on guard-duty there.

It was 05:32 when they landed at dawn at the Cairo airbase, where they were met by the U.S. Ambassador to Egypt. Cody had not realized what a high priority this mission had until then. They had lost seven hours in transit. They were driven directly to the Cairo civil airport, where they had been booked on a 07:00 Alitalia Airlines flight. The Italian commercial jet would take them to Beirut in under two hours, nonstop.

Cody stared out the window at the desolate landscape and knew he would soon be fighting on land that was much the same: hot, dry, and with little natural vegetation. He disliked the idea that they could not bring in familiar weapons. But it would cause too many problems. They could go with new tools from the Marines.

He preferred his own weapons, but it would simply take an hour to become familiar with the SMGs and other tools they had ordered. He hoped the Marines had come up with all the right weapons. Some of his crew were particular about the tools they used.

As they turned on their final approach to the runway at Beirut, Cody could see three different downtown buildings smoldering. There was probably no water pressure to put out the fires even if there happened to be any firemen still on duty.

What once had been the jewel of the Mideast, one of the most beautiful cities in the world, lay a gutted, defiled ruin. He knew it would look even worse once on the ground. This was simply the continuation of a 400-year-old war. How could a people survive with only occasional stretches of peace, freedom, and prosperity?

He looked around as much as possible as they taxied toward the terminal, but he could not see the captured airliner. It probably had been towed to a far corner of the field. They moved quickly down the ramp and into the terminal. At the incoming gate three Americans waited— their reception committee. Their suitcases were claimed from the baggage check, and they moved through customs with no trouble.

Cody knew dozens of men from the CIA, but he recognized none of the three They could be from the skeleton diplomatic staff at Beirut.

The airport terminal showed scars, pockmarks, in some

of the concrete and plaster exterior walls. One room had suffered bomb damage, and one section of wall lockers was still twisted and warped where the explosives had been set off. Blast marks showed on the ceiling and smoke stains marred the walls.

The three embassy men had said little in the terminal. Once in the embassy cars, moderate-size European-made rigs, they relaxed a little. Each embassy man carried a snub-snouted Ingram submachine gun under his coat on a strap around his neck. They were so small as to be practically invisible.

It was 09:12 hours.

Cody's team traveled in two cars. The embassy type with Cody nodded tiredly once the car door was shut.

"So far, so good. We were afraid something might have leaked and you would have a hotter reception. This place has been wired for action ever since the hijack."

"What do you have?"

The man in the backseat with Cody held out his hand.

"My name is Gerry Oxe, cultural attaché. Damn little, I'm afraid. Not much that will help. Your cover is as a TV news team, right? We've got some equipment for you, and an expert to show you how to use it enough so you can get by."

"What about our working tools?"

"We have everything you asked for. The Marine Corps armorer is at your disposal, and you can test and fire-in any of the weapons you want to. We have an underground range. Your contact will be Jack Gorman."

Gorman.

And the past hurled in to punch Cody in the gut. Lund had neglected to mention Gorman back at Andrews . . .

The diplomat let a smile creep over his face.

"I see you know and love Mr. Gorman, the fair-haired boy of the Mideastern section of the Company."

"I won't work with Gorman," said Cody. "Radio Langley that I want a new contact."

"No time. He's your man, like it or fly home."

Five minutes later, Cody and his men milled around a

table inside the embassy that held coffee, beer, and snacks. Cody looked up as Gorman walked into the room.

Gorman saw Cody, and a sneer twisted his face as he started to say something, while at the same moment Cody fought down an impulse to finish what he'd started eighteen months ago in Nicaragua. But just then the ambassador himself scurried up.

His name was Stewart Tabler; an excellent money-raiser for the party and a wasted diplomat in an impossible situation, he appeared oblivious to the brittle atmosphere between these men.

"We've got troubles," he blurted without preamble.

"My number-two man will brief you and your crew, Cody, on the political situation here.

"In Lebanon, *everything* is politics. Don't expect to move with any freedom in the western half of the city or in the countryside; it's all hostile territory.

"Even the east section is not always safe for Americans."

"We're Australian."

"Yes, that's right. So, let's get at it."

The political briefing took fifteen minutes and covered much the same material they got in Washington. Then all four went to the weapons room.

The Marine sargeant in charge was in his forties, an E-12 with stripes all over his sleeve. He had red hair and a big grin. He stood with his fists planted on his hips in front of a folding table that held the weapons each man had requested. In back of them were two dozen other assorted handguns, automatic weapons and SMGs.

"Understand you boys know how to use these tools," Paterson growled. "Damn well better. You fuck up these weapons and you'll answer to me." He grinned then and waved at the table. "Take your pick. I can get almost anything else you want, domestic or foreign. Problem is, though, I'm fresh out of Sharps, Spencers and Gatling guns."

"I think we'll get along," Cody acknowledged.

The men went to the weapons. Each had a silenced Uzi 9-mm submachine gun. This model had a blowback system and an overhung bolt that reduced the overall length of the unit.

Cody picked up two of the 32-round magazines and a clip that fastened them together so that when one of the clipped-together magazines was dry, it could be pulled out, flipped over, and the second magazine, still filled, was slammed home for thirty-two more quick rounds.

Cody liked the Uzi. It spat out 900 parabellum rounds a minute, about three seconds of sustained firing per magazine. The Uzi was a close-in weapon with a maximum effective range of 200 yards. Cody figured most of their work would be eyeball-to-moustache anyway.

He took a trusty Colt Commander .45 as a sidearm, and then began picking out a collection of knives and specialty weapons for his kit, including a garotte wire with wooden handles on each end and a half dozen other silent killers.

"We standardize on Uzi's," Cody instructed. "Pick out another SMG if you want one, but keep it a 9mm parabellum so our ammo will match."

Cody added an M-203 grenade launcher attached to an M-16 rifle. The rifle and launcher could both be fired at the same time. The launcher gave him a 380-yard throw with the small 40mm grenades.

Cody test-fired his Uzi in the adjacent firing range. With the spray effect of an SMG there was little need to fine-tune the sighting. The Colt Commander was different. At twenty yards, he wanted to know where the cluster of hits would be on the target. Cody blasted off six rounds and had the target brought up. The weapon fired slightly high and to the left. He would remember that.

Twenty minutes later all four men had picked their weapons. Caine went for a Beretta, Hawkeye grabbed his ordered .44 Automag.

Caine held the big weapon and almost dropped it. The 6.5-inch barrel made the overall length 11.5 inches.

"You really going to carry that anchor?" Caine bellowed. "Thing weighs a ton."

"And it will stop a charging bull elephant," Hawkeye gloated. "Fires a 240-grain slug with a muzzle velocity of

1,650 feet per second. The round is produced by mating a .44 revolver bullet with a cut-down 7.62 NATO rifle cartridge. Closest by-damn thing to a rifle you can get in a handgun.''

Caine went with Cody to another table, where they selected the latest plastic explosive, the Army's C-5, and the necessary detonators and timers. Cody let Caine finish that part of his job and thanked the sergeant.

They moved their weapons and ammo to a room that would serve as their home base.

Next came a briefing by a TV newsman. He was a reporter for CBS and looked them over for a moment.

''Sorry, men, you just can't fake it as on-camera reporters, and you don't want to carry around a twenty-pound sound camera. Let's make you advance men for the reporting team. You're looking for locations, hot spots, trying to set up interviews. That you can get by with. You'll need an Arabic-speaking translator unless you can jabber the lingo.''

That briefing was over and Cody sat down across a table with Gorman, who had stayed well removed from Cody's group the whole time.

''Kill any nuns and children lately, Jack?''

''You're not a professional, Cody, you're just a killing machine with no brains. You want this assignment or do I fire your ass right here?''

''You can't, but I can clout you to death. Now tell me what else you know about the hijacking and then I never want to see you again . . . alive.''

Gorman paused a minute

''All right. Truce for now. We know damn little. This is a new splinter from the PLO. We have no location for them, no headquarters. All we know is that Majed Kaddoumi is the current front man, the negotiator who is supposed to know where they are.

''Farouk Hassan is their leader, and he works with an ice-cold killer called Abdel Khaled. Our best contact is a real TV reporter named Kelly McConnell. She's trying to find Kaddoumi with the hopes she can locate the hostages.''

"Any idea where they took the passengers?"

"Not a prayer. They could be anywhere in the west sector, or they could be in a village or halfway to Tripoli or Damascus."

"We need a starting point. You must have something."

"The McConnell woman is your best lead. She stays at the International Hotel. You might try her there by phone. Outside of that, you know as much about it as we do. Incidentally, our countdown clock has now been running for almost eighteen hours. We have a little over thirty hours before the next hostage is scheduled to die. It's now 11:36 hours. Now stay out of my way."

Cody found his men back at the room.

"Our problem is intel. We don't have any. I'm taking Caine with me to try to find our contact. We've got two cars to use, with drivers who know the lingo. Just cool it here for a while."

Minutes later they were in the car driving to the place where Kelly McConnell had told the switchboard she would be if anyone tried to contact her. As the old Fiat pulled away from the American Embassy, a vintage Chevy slid away from the far side of the grounds and followed the Fiat, holding well back in a professional tail-job.

Kelly McConnell sat in her Volkswagen bug parked near a one-story building that had been blasted into rubble by a bomb or an artillery shell and waited. She was good at waiting. She poured a cup of coffee from a steel vacuum bottle and handed it to Cal Vanloo, her cameraman.

"You sure this is the spot, Kell?"

"As sure as I am about anything in this crazy town." She sipped the steaming coffee, light blue eyes squinting against the perpetual sunshine. She was a tall, slender woman, just over five-nine, with a figure she tried to tone down and a mind sharp enough to have earned her the top spot in her graduating class at the Columbia Graduate School of Journalism just three years ago.

She wore her free-flowing blonde hair as a badge in this brunette world to advertise that she was an American. It had helped her nail down more than one good news story.

"Is that our man?" asked Vanloo, pointing through the windshield at a figure walking across the street.

"No." Kelly was positive. "Kaddoumi is a small, stout man, clean-shaven, with wire-rimmed glasses. He almost never comes on the street in the daylight. The contact man we need is a fatso, about five-nine and two-hundred and fifty pounds."

"Trouble," Cal whispered.

She saw them coming around the corner, a ragtag group of teenagers with automatic rifles, one carrying an RPG, a rocket-propelled grenade on its rifle-like launcher. Small raiding parties like this roamed both sides of the Green Line, often taking what they wanted from whomever had fewer arms and less of a stomach for fighting.

There were eight of them, all in their teens. They moved up cautiously, then when they saw who was in the car and the TV camera, they became bolder.

Kelly rolled down the window and spoke to them in her passable Arabic. The apparent leader of the group, a pimple-splotched youth of no more than sixteen, laughed and replied in English.

"You crazy come out here. This is our street. You got to pay to sit here. Instead you pay to take my picture. Put us all on the American TV, yes?"

"I'm waiting to see an important man. You probably now him. Majed Kaddoumi."

The name cause a stir among those who did not know English. The young leader of the pack took a step backward.

"You lie. Nobody, no American, ever talk to Majed." The youth glared at her, turned to listen to someone in his group and laughed. "My expert on women says he wants to see you with your clothes off, see if you have blonde hair other places."

"Your expert on women is a little boy who has never had a woman and wouldn't know what to do with one," Kelly shot back at him in Arabic. It caused hoots and howls of laughter among the group. The only one not enjoying the joke surged up to the car and slammed his rifle butt into the windshield, cracking it.

"Get out, American whore!" the enraged youth spat.

He turned the rifle and fired a round into the side of the rear door.

Kelly never moved. "What's the matter, big general? Can't you even control your troops?" Again she spoke in Arabic.

The leader shrugged.

The youth with the rifle glanced at the leader, then swung the rifle so it pointed at Kelly. "Get out, you stinking American whore! Get out and strip off your clothes . . . or you die right where you sit!"

CHAPTER

ELEVEN

"**H**old it right there, small boys," John Cody barked in his top-sergeant's voice. "One move and you join Allah."

He stood fifteen feet away with his Uzi leveled at the group. They had taken the silencers off them for this first run, so they could hide the weapons under loose-fitting shirts.

Caine braced to one side for a crossfire angle with his Uzi lined up perfectly.

The leader saw the situation and shouted a quick order to his team, freezing them.

"You with the rifle pointing at the woman, put it on the ground, carefully," Cody commanded.

The street bandit looked at his leader. Sweat broke out on his forehead, and his whole body shook. He picked up the silent command from his leader and slowly bent to put the weapon on the ground.

The others whispered and growled, but a sharp command from the teen boss quieted them.

"You a big hero or something?" the bandit leader asked him.

"Mostly something," Cody growled. He walked up to the group and slapped the youth who had fired his rifle. The blow slammed the teen sideways, but he caught his balance before he fell.

"You understand enough English, small boy," Cody said to the one he had just slapped. "You like to see people naked, try it yourself. Strip down, right now."

"No way," the youth said.

Cody hit him with a short right fist that slammed him backward so hard he lost his balance and found himself sitting in the dust of the street. Before the kid could move, Cody darted forward and slid a four-inch honed straightedge razor against the downed Lebanese's throat.

"Strip down right now, punk, or I slice your clothes off you! I won't mind cutting you up a little in the process."

The boy, who now looked his fourteen years, nodded and unbuttoned his shirt. A few seconds later he kicked out of his pants and slouched there in his shorts and shoes.

"All the way, gutter rat! Next time you think twice about ordering a woman to take off *her* clothes."

Hatred showed on the boy's face. He turned around, away from Kelly, and pulled down his shorts. He kicked them off his feet, then looked at Cody over his shoulder. Suddenly, he began crying, and Cody waved the whole band away.

"Get lost, punks. Come back when you grow up, in about ten years!" Richard Caine shouted at them as they ran.

Cody motioned to the woman. "Get in that rig and move it fast! Those hotheads will be shooting this way as soon as they get behind cover. Move it!" Kelly jumped in the car, where her cameraman had stayed, and spun the wheels in a U-turn as she tore back down the street.

Cody and Caine sprinted for the mouth of the alley, surged behind solid walls, and waited. Two shots blammed through the quiet street from the direction in which the teenage bandits had vanished.

Cody shrugged, got back in the car they had arrived in minutes before, and raced down the street after Kelly. She had stopped two blocks ahead to wait for them.

She stood beside her car and laughed with a trace of nervous tension when Cody stepped up beside her.

"Who the hell are you and where did you come from when I needed you?" she asked, a brassy but sweet California-girl grin on her pretty face.

"I'm Cody, that's Caine. We need to talk to you somewhere that's relatively safe and where they serve beer."

Kelly held out her hand and gripped his with a firm handshake. "I'm Kelly—"

—"McConnell. Famous TV correspondent," Cody finished for her. "I know. We came hunting you. Where can we talk?"

Ten minutes later, all three settled down over beers in a small cafe.

12:25 hours.

"I can't tell you how glad I was to see you back there, Cody. I've been here over a year now prowling the streets, and I've never been threatened with guns like that before—certainly not by one of those teenage gangs."

"I'm glad we were there," Cody said. "Any luck finding Majed Kaddoumi?"

Her soft blue eyes darted up to watch him with concern, then a touch of alarm. She grinned. "Okay, that must be it. You know Jack Gorman and he told you I was Kaddoumi-hunting. Which means you're either State, which I doubt, or CIA. Right, CIA. You're on the hijack."

"You always do your logic out loud?" Caine asked with a grin.

"When I'm with friends. I owe you guys."

"Any luck on Kaddoumi?" Cody persisted.

"A short fat man was supposed to leave that house I was watching and go to Kaddoumi. We probably missed him. And with that gunfire in the street outside his house, he won't show his face for days."

"You must have more than one lead."

"Why should I tell you?" she asked. "You could be an advance team for another network."

"How many network news hawks do you know travel with a pair of Uzi submachine guns?"

"Good point. Look, I got this job the hard way. I am

not just a bimbo over here pretending to be a newsperson. I get more than my share of stories with hard-nosed, digging-it-out work. I thanked you for showing up back there just in time. My virginity was not at stake, but a gang-bang is not something that turns this lady on. And so, Mr. Cody and friends, when I say I owe you, that's all there is to it.''

''And we both have a job to do,'' said Cody. ''I'm on a tight schedule, Kelly. I'm sorry. Where's your other contact?''

''Across the Green Line.''

''Shiite territory.''

''Exactly. I go over there as little as possible, but it looks like I'm out of options. I have a friend who is a double and has great contacts on the other side. I can take one man with me. I'll take you, Cody, and leave my cameraman here. Are you game?''

Five minutes later they drove down Avenue Dugeneal Fouad Chehab, turned right onto Rue Bechara El Khoury.

The Green Line was established years ago to divide Beirut into Christian and Moslem sectors, but for many years now it had been a bloody line, militia on one side firing at anything that moved on the other side.

Now it was a symbol, and a barrier, and a spot where few wanted to be, let alone cross over.

Kelly turned right onto a side street. They were in the Bachoura section of East Beirut; only two blocks over was Rue De Damas, the Green Line. Just across the line was the old St. Joseph's University in the Yessouieh section of Moslem West Beirut. She parked a short way down the street behind a red Fiat. A man with a submachine gun slung on a cord around his neck leaned on the back of the Fiat, smoking.

''If he was not smoking, we would not have stopped,'' Kelly said. ''It's our all-clear signal.'' She got out of the car.

Cody made sure the Uzi was out of sight under the loose sport shirt he wore as Kelly walked past the man and turned into the alley, then he strode along beside her.

Halfway down the alley a door stood open. Kelly stepped in and motioned for him to follow her. Inside the dingy building the light was faint, and what light there was came from a small skylight two floors up.

The building could have been there for a thousand years. It was made of stone and much plaster and many coats of paint. It smelled of hundreds of years of living, and cooking, grease and unwashed bodies, and now the strong musk of recent lovemaking.

Kelly turned, noting the scent.

"People here must live for the moment," she said quietly. "They never know how long they will survive." She continued through the room, past two people sleeping on mats on the floor and into another room that had a square table made of heavy, black wood. A man sat there smoking a water pipe. He did not look up as they sat down in two chairs facing him.

The man was ancient, at least eighty years old. When the old man's eyes opened, Cody could see the white growths that covered all of the cornea and half the other.

"Small flower," the man wheezed through a protesting throat. "I am pleased to see you again."

"I must make a special trip to see Majed, ancient one," she said in Arabic. "It is vital I move as quickly as possible."

"Youth, always so impatient. How old are you, girl, child?"

"Twenty-five."

"Oh, to be even fifty again!" The old man blinked his nearly sightless eyes. He clapped his hands once and a small boy of nine or ten ran in. "Take them to see your uncle," the old one wheezed in English.

"Yes," the boy said. He leaned in and hugged the old man, who blinked back a tear, then closed his eyes. The boy smiled at them and hugged Kelly, then held out his hand to Cody

"Dahr, this is Cody, he will be going with us," Kelly said.

The small boy nodded, turned and walked away. Kelly followed him and Cody was close behind her. They continued through the building to another alley, down it to a building that had been hit by an artillery shell, and finally through a basement door under the rubble.

Once in the basement, Cody saw that the area had been cleaned up and that several families lived there. Dahr walked through without speaking to anyone. No one looked at them as they stepped into a closed room, and Dahr pulled aside a blanket that covered a door. He took a flashlight from a niche in the wall, and shone it forward. A dirt tunnel extended as far as they could see.

Now Dahr took Kelly's hand and led her into the cavern. Cody had to stoop in places to get through, but it was dry and the air was good. After they had walked an estimated fifty yards, Cody could see light, and soon they were in a room in which a blanket had been pulled back to let the sun shine through a window and almost directly into the tunnel.

"We're now on the Amal and Shiite side of the Green Line," Kelly said. "Here we are in true enemy territory." As she said it she took a large kerchief from her purse and put it around her hair. She then put over that a black shawl with a veil that Dahr handed to her.

"I must look like a proper Moslem woman on this side or I would attract attention," she said. "Your Western clothes are acceptable here for a man, and you are dark enough. A blonder man would have trouble."

Dahr led them out of the room, through several passageways and then into an alley. They walked through three blocks of the alley, crossing main streets quickly, then came to a door where Dahr knocked. A dark face showed through a two-inch crack.

Dahr said something in Arabic, and the door opened.

"Inside, quickly," a deep voice said speaking English. They moved past the door and found they were in a modern, well-decorated living room. The man who had told them to come in held out his hand. He was slight, short, dark brown with black hair and a patch over one eye.

"You may call me Abu. I know Kelly. This gentleman is . . ."

"Cody, John Cody." They shook hands.

"Kelly, fragrant flower, I know why you are here. It is

a tragic affair. Most of us wished that it had never happened. It is bad for all of us. Arafat with the PLO is furious. He knows his movement will be hurt by the similarities in name. The Amal are unhappy. All of the Shiites believe it was a mistake. Even the Hezbollah think it will hinder, not help, our causes."

"Then help us end it," Cody said softly. "Tell us how we can contact Majed Kaddoumi."

Abu looked at Cody quickly, smiled, then glanced back at Kelly. "A woman so beautiful should not concern herself with politics. I have told you that before, Kelly. You are welcome to join me here anytime. Your working days will be over. You will have a life of leisure . . ."

"Abu, get back to the subject," Cody insisted. "I have a deadline, it is running out quickly. Where can I find Majed?"

"Mr. Cody, you are insistent." Abu paused, walked to an alcove and brought back a hand grenade. The pin was firmly attached. It looked like an old American-made bomb. "We all must be patient, Mr. Cody. This whole section is ready to explode. I don't want to be responsible for pulling the pin."

"Abu, I have twenty-eight hours to meet my deadline."

Abu turned to Kelly. "You, too, have deadlines, daily ones, as I remember. Do you also wish to see Majed?"

"I must, Abu. It is my work, and it is partly for my country. Remember how you told me one had to be loyal to a nation or one was cast adrift?"

"I remember." Abu stared at a picture on the wall. It was a good print of a French impressionist. "Very well. I'll show you. Dahr has returned to his home on the other side. This way."

They left by the same door they entered and were half a block down the street when submachine gun fire chattered from a window across from them and shattered glass over their heads. They dashed for a doorway and rushed inside for protection.

More weapons began firing, and then a bomb blasted death and destruction down the street.

"It came sooner than I expected," Abu said. "Out this

way!'' They ran through the building toward the alley, and had just lunged from the structure when riflefire flared in the alley. The firing was away from them. They ran from doorway to doorway, moving away from the fighting.

A jeep rolled into the end of the alley ahead of them. It had a belt-fed machine gun mounted on the center post, and a gunner began raking the alley with lead.

They each dove behind a large metal trash bin and lay panting in the dirt of the alley.

"It has to be the Hezbollah!" Abu shouted over the sound of the firing. "They would sell their mothers into slavery to gain the upper hand over the Shiite Amal. They do not have good leadership."

"Where is Majed, in case they get lucky?" Cody demanded.

"You're right, I should tell you. But first, let's get out of here. That door, right over there on the far side. If we can get to it we'll be well out of the firefight by the time we get through the building."

"Not a chance crossing the alley with that machine gun up there," Cody said.

Before he finished the sentence, firing increased from the far end of the alley, and he saw a dozen fully uniformed men rush into the space and flatten in doorways and behind cover. For a moment, lead from both sides slammed through the confines of the ages-old alley.

He leaped three feet from the protective bin to the doorway on the near side of the alley and pounded on the panel. It was locked. Before he had time to shoot the lock off, the gunfire increased again. He had to get Kelly out of there! She would do him no good wounded.

He made one surging run to the trash bin and saw Abu standing up behind it, sending signals to the troops working their way slowly up the alley. They must be friendly. Perhaps they could knock out the Jeep and end the threat.

Before he could work out a plan of action, the decision was taken away from him. He heard the engine whine and then roar as the Jeep with the mounted machine gun began a mad dash down the narrow alleyway, the .30 automatic weapon firing twenty-round bursts, sweeping away everything in its path.

There was no place to hide.

CHAPTER
TWELVE

Cody motioned for the other two to stay behind the protective metal trash dumpster. He pulled a smooth hand-grenade from his pocket and took a quick look around the side of the trash bin to judge how far away the Jeep and its blazing machine gun was.

Still thirty yards. He waited. He jerked the ring and drew out the safety pin from the small hand-bomb and held the arming handle firmly in place.

The machine gunner had switched to five-round bursts. His barrel was probably overheating. The bullets slammed past them, jolted into the metal dumpster, careened off the stone and bricks of the buildings, as the Jeep came forward, more slowly now. The driver and gunner examined each doorway.

Twenty yards.

Still too far. He had to be sure.

"We must do something!" Abu screamed.

"We will in another twenty or thirty seconds," Cody barked. "Keep your head down."

Kelly McConnell stared at him with a combination of

admiration and bewilderment. She probably had never been in the middle of a real combat fire fight before.

Cody risked a peek around the trash bin.

The Jeep was ten yards away and stopped. *Now!*

He lifted up, pitching the grenade with a stiff-elbowed overhand toss to get it over the dumpster.

He dropped as soon as he let go of the grenade and edged to the outer end of the dumpster, the Uzi safety off and ready for action. He had a 32-round magazine in the chopper and another in his pocket.

Four-point-two seconds after the arming handle sprung off the bomb, it detonated. The grenade had landed in the rear seat of the Jeep and bounced upward a foot before the time fuse ran out and the grenade exploded with a cracking, echoing roar.

Cody sprang from around the dumpster and sent a burst of eight parabellums into the Jeep. The gunner on the chatter gun had been nearly torn in half by the explosion and lay draped over the side of the rig.

The driver had taken a dozen shrapnel wounds but none were fatal. He furiously tried to shift the Jeep into reverse. It was the first time he had driven the stolen vehicle, and no one had told him about reverse.

Cody chopped him into garbage with a six-round burst into his chest.

There was an eerie silence after the sound of the Uzi's firing faded away. Then came screams from behind the Jeep, and foot soldiers swarmed forward, firing as they came. That triggered the opposition at the far end of the alley, and the fury of the automatic weapons battle climbed to the deafening zone.

Cody dove behind the dumpster.

"You all right?" he shouted to Kelly.

She nodded, afraid to show how frightened she was.

"Where to?" Cody shouted again, this time at Abu.

Abu was calm. He pointed to the nearby door.

Cody lifted the Uzi and blasted four rounds at the lock, saw the door sag as it came unlatched.

"I'll go first and cover you two," he instructed. "Then send Kelly, and you come last."

He surged the three feet across the unprotected area between the dumpster and the wall and landed in the relatively safer doorway alcove. He looked left. The men who had been firing there had retreated halfway to the street. Automatic weapons still blasted from the other way.

The attackers were almost to the dumpster.

"Now!" he bellowed.

Kelly looked at him for reassurance, then stood and hurried across the opening.

A Hezbollah partisan pushed next to the side of the dumpster and fired twice at his only target, Kelly McConnell.

Cody shifted the Uzi upward and with four rounds turned the attacker's face into bloody, lifeless pulp. He looked back at Kelly, who staggered the last step toward him, then fell in his arms. He saw blood on her chest. He pulled her fully into the protection.

Abu spurted across the danger zone, kicked open the door and helped Cody with the girl.

Inside the dimly lit room, Cody slammed the door shut and pushed a chair under the handle. He put Kelly down in a big chair, in a living room of sorts. He had not heard Kelly make a sound since she was hit.

He pushed the shawl aside and saw blood on her blouse. He touched a carotid artery in her throat. Twice more he tried. There was no pulse. He pinched her nose, but she was not breathing.

Kelly was dead.

He stared at the pretty face. He had seen a lot of people die, right, but this was a shock. He had never expected it. She had been so vigorous, assertive, bright and lovely just moments ago . . .

He kicked the couch, slammed his fist into the cushion, growled a string of curses.

"She's . . . gone?" Abu asked in a stunned voice.

"Yes." Cody picked up Kelly gently, cradled her in his arms and fisted the Uzi in his right hand. "Now get us out of here, and on the way tell me exactly how to find Majed Kaddoumi, or you're going to be next."

"Yes . . . through here."

They moved through the unoccupied building, down a

long hallway that led away from the fighting, out a door into the street, across it to an alley, and down that for two blocks. Then Abu stopped in a deep doorway.

"Majed is in his palace, his fortress, to the south, nearly out of the city, in an area called Furn El Chebbak, off the Rue De Damas near the Beirut River. The exact address is 1194 Rue Hassanein. You'll need help to find it."

"I have plenty of help. Don't get any ideas about telling Majed that I'm coming. If he knows, I'll come back here and slit your throat, Abu, even if you *were* a friend of Kelly's. Now, how do we get back to Kelly's car? We parked it on the street north of that tunnel under the Green Line, in the alley."

"It will take time, but I can bring the car here. Do you have the keys?"

Cody took out the keys and held them. He could feel Kelly beginning to turn cold in his arms. He put her down on the steps, arranged the black shawl over her blonde hair and adjusted the veil.

"I think I'd better go with you. You could get lost in all of these streets and alleys. Wouldn't want there to be any foul-ups. And I'm running out of time."

An automatic rifle chattered two streets over, answered by a small-caliber pistol of some kind, and then a grenade went off before things quieted again.

"Don't you people ever give up and try to live together?" Cody asked.

"As you would say, American, it is a matter of principal. These are fanatics. All of them believe they will live forever if they die fighting for Allah."

"Spare me the details." Cody picked up Kelly, cradling her in his arms. "Let's get to that car the quickest possible way, without getting killed."

It took twenty minutes. They had to go around one combat zone in which three men with automatic rifles were engaged in a death struggle with two other armed men in a ruined building.

They came to a street that had been devastated, nearly every building on both sides blasted, bombed, or shot up. They saw no one in the street, heard no one.

"That is the Green Line, my new friend," Abu said. "No one in his right mind tries to cross it during daylight. There is one quick passage through a storm drain if I can remember where it is."

They backtracked half a block, and a shadow stepped from a doorway and spoke to Abu. For a moment there was an argument, then the other man nodded.

"This way. An old friend will help us. He believes that the dead should be treated properly. He will help not you, but he will help the dead woman back across the line. You may come if you wish."

They entered a building to the left, went down steep steps to a basement and along a partially finished hallway for twenty yards, then turned sharply to the left to face a tunnel that was only three feet high.

"An old escape route for a rich man," Abu said.

The man who led them there brought a large cardboard box. He indicated that Cody should put Kelly in the box.

"We crawl and drag the box," Abu said. "It is the only way to get across here without waiting until dark."

It took them a half hour to crawl through the thirty yards of the narrow tunnel. There was not room enough to pull the box efficiently.

Once on the far side, Cody brushed off his clothes and picked up Kelly. Her body was starting to stiffen and cool.

When they came to the street, the red Fiat was gone, but Kelly's bug was in place, undamaged. Cody laid Kelly tenderly in the backseat, then looked up at Abu.

"The information about Majed better be right, my new friend, or I'll be coming back for you."

"It is right. But the great man is not always there, remember. Let us hope you get lucky."

"Luck, yeah. Watch your backside, new friend."

Cody started the bug, shifted into first, then drove back to the U.S. Embassy entrance. He showed his ID and went through a telephone check before he was allowed to drive through the maze of road blocks and gates and concrete barricades to the embassy building. They were taking no more chances with a dynamite loaded truck and a kamikazee driver.

He told the Marine guard about Kelly, then gently picked up her remains and carried them up the front steps.

A senior aide showed him where to take her, a room to one side, with a couch. The aide said he would handle the rest. Cody hurried away from there, submerging emotions that cut deeply into him.

He looked at his watch.

14:28 hours.

And he didn't have a solid lead yet. Those forty-eight hours, and hopes for survival for 130 hostages, were melting away too damn fast.

CHAPTER
THIRTEEN

Sharon Adamson sat beside the window and looked out at the lovely green of the trees. They were cedars, the cedars of Lebanon. An Arab with an automatic rifle slung over his shoulder passed the window every two minutes. He looked and waved but she ignored him.

She had no idea where they were. She had recovered from the blow to the jaw she received on the plane. It was the first time she had ever been unconscious. For a while she was in a fuzzy haze, but when the terrorists insisted that they all leave the plane to board the buses, she had hustled back to her job of taking care of her passengers.

She had made sure that the older people were given time to move along the aisle and that they were not harmed. She had felt a strong responsibility for the passengers. That was simply her job; she had to take care of them.

There had been little problem on the bus. She had talked with everyone on the big airport bus, and kept them calm. She was surprised when they left Beirut and moved into the countryside, and then she realized they were heading south along the coast highway. Abruptly they took another road that doubled back north, then turned inland toward the low-lying hills behind the city.

The road was not as good as the first one. Now and then a Jeep filled with armed men would speed ahead, then stop and watch them pass, and then follow them again. There had been no orders to blindfold the passengers.

Sharon tried to keep track of their position, but she spent more time comforting some of the elder passengers. She did see a sign that said they were twelve kilometers from Choueifete. Shortly after that, they turned due east and climbed into the low-lying hills.

They passed several settlements, and she saw a sign that said they were approaching Quadi Chahrour. But they never arrived at the town. They turned off at the top of a long grade and drove through barren hills to a high gate that now had riflemen perched on top of it.

Sharon figured that this place had once been an estate of a tremendously rich man, but now was used by the terrorists who had taken over the plane. The long drive ended when they went through a second, higher, wall, which had gun emplacements on the top. She was certain she saw some mounted machine guns.

She had been surprised at the amount of plants and flowers that were on the grounds. It was a virtual forest in places with many cedar trees, hardwoods, and plots of flowers. To one side she saw a swimming pool, but it had not been taken care of and now was fouled and empty.

Sharon left the window and went quickly down the big room to talk to a woman passenger who had a heart condition. It was about noon, the day after the capture.

Mrs. Vereen was worse. Sharon took her pulse and knew it was too fast. Her blood pressure was probably far, far too high as well. Sharon knew the woman had to have medical attention. She went to the door and pleaded with the guard to let her talk to Farouk Hassan. The guard merely grinned.

Down the hallway in the large, palace-like structure that had three wings, Captain Tom Ward pounded on the door until the guard came. This one could speak some English. Ward was far past being afraid by now. He was furious at the way the passengers were being treated. He felt that the surviving 123 ticket buyers and the crew of seven were still his responsibility.

The guard leveled a strange-looking automatic rifle at Ward as he pushed the door open.

"So, talk," the guard said in English.

"I want to see Farouk Hassan, the man in charge. I demand to see him. We have a lot of things to discuss. You go tell him what I said."

"I tell, but do no good," the guard said and slammed the door.

Ward was on the second floor in a room with sixteen other men. There were eight cots there. The younger men slept on the floor the night before. The windows were barred, had been made that way years ago to keep people out. Now they worked very well to keep the hostages inside the rooms.

Five minutes later the guard opened the door.

"Ward, come."

Ward grinned. "Men, we must be getting some action. We can at least have decent living conditions while we're being held here. I'll be right back."

A minute later his hands were tied behind his back and he was marched down a hall, up steps to the third floor, and into a luxuriously decorated room in which Farouk Hassan had just finished a seven-course meal.

Ward had decided on the civil approach. His hands tied with twine behind his back dented his resolve, but he continued.

"Mr. Hassan, I am Captain Ward, the pilot of the aircraft."

"I know who you are. What do you want?" Farouk said in a British-accented English.

"I want only humane treatment for my passengers and crew. We have not been fed since we left the plane almost twenty-four hours ago. There are not enough beds and no bedding. We must have these necessities, or we will be no good as hostages for you."

Abdel Khaled came up behind Ward and slammed his fist into the pilot's left kidney. Ward screeched in surprise, slowly dropped to his knees and fell to the floor, his knees drawn up to relieve the pain.

"You were saying?" Farouk asked softly.

Ward struggled to get to his knees; then, with good balance, he stood. "Dead hostages will not help you. Sick and dying hostages will only enflame the civilized world against you. The press will paint you as savages—"

Abdel slammed his fist into Ward's kidney again, just over his belt and slightly to the rear. Ward went down, retched violently, then threw up on the floor. Abdel kicked him in the stomach and the shoulder.

"Filthy pig!" Abdel screamed. He kicked Ward twice more, in the stomach, before Farouk waved him off.

"Captain Ward, it seems there is some problem with your complaint. We'll consider it and see what we can do. Clean up this mess before you leave. Abdel, cut him free."

Abdel's knife slashed the cord binding his wrists and put a three-inch-long slice up his forearm. Abdel laughed at him as he tried to stop the bleeding.

"Now you have more of a mess to mop up, Mr. Ward. Be quick about it!" Farouk snarled.

Abdel threw him a towel and Ward slowly wiped up his vomit, mostly bile and water. When he had it done he tried to stand. At last, he had to crawl to a chair and boost himself up with his arms.

"Get out of here," Farouk said with disgust. "You're what I hate most about Western people and their countries; your arrogance, your phony superiority. You're trash. Get out of here!"

The armed guard caught Ward by one arm and led him out of the room. He stumbled and dragged one foot, and his final look at Farouk was one of hatred.

When the door closed, Abdel smiled. "It looks like we have found our next sacrifice candidate to the United States government."

Farouk nodded slowly. "Yes, you may be right. He could be a troublemaker. We don't want any of the passengers causing complications at this point."

"That's why we will feed them only once a day, and provide them with no blankets. If they are worried about staying alive and getting some sleep, they won't have the strength to plot against us in any way."

Farouk saluted Abdel with a mug of black coffee. "It's settled, then, about our next victim. Now all we need to decide is when we must give the United States and Israel another reminder that we are serious about our plans to kill the prisoners."

Abdel grinned, and for a moment Farouk saw there again the expression of a man who loved to kill, who had slipped over the line from loyalist to fanatic, from a soldier willing to kill for the cause, to a madman who killed now for the thrill of saying yea or nay to the life or death of another human being.

The expression passed and Farouk breathed a little easier. No one person was more important than their cause, not the loyal guards in the hallways and around the estate, not himself, and certainly not Abdel. He hoped he would not have to make a tough decision about Abdel before this was over.

Back in the big room, Ward lay on one of the cots for half an hour, recovering from the kidney punches. At last he sat up and called over his co-pilot, Peter Jenks, a big man at six-foot-four who had played tight end on the football team in college but was not sharp enough to make the pros. He had joined the Air Force instead and become a transport pilot.

"How you doing, Tom?"

"Making it. How are our people?"

"Hurting, some of them. Lots are unhappy and one or two are near to going over the edge. I haven't seen the rest of them since we got here, but we talk."

"The next room?"

"Right. There's a kind of pass-through up near the center of the room. Sharon is on the other side. She's really taking good care of those people with her."

"Good, help me get up there; we need to see what kind of plans we can work out, what strategy. Reasoning with these animals doesn't work. I found that out the hard way."

At the center of the room's long inner wall was a serving counter with a sink and cabinets under it. On the wall itself were panels that could be pushed open. When they were opened on both sides they created a foot-high pass-through to the next room. Jenks opened it and knocked softly on the opposite panel. A moment later it opened. Sharon looked through.

"Captain! Thank God you're all right. I heard they had taken you away." Sharon's look of concern emphasized the dramatic change that had taken place in her during the past twenty-four hours.

"I'm still alive, Sharon. I'm relying on you to take care of our people in there. You have that woman with the bad heart, don't you?" Sharon nodded, her face pinching now with worry about the drawn, painful expression on the captain's face.

"Take care of her. If she gets worse, if she needs medical attention, call your guard and make a fuss. These Arabs treat their women badly, but they are sentimental about them at the same time. Play on their sympathies."

"Captain, I think you need a doctor, too."

"No, just a sneaky kidney punch. We've got to talk about how to get out of here."

"They have a series of roving guards with submachine guns, Tom," Jenks reported. "Place is crawling with guards. Then at the wall, which is maybe thirty yards out there, there are more guards on top. At the one end I can see is a mounted machine gun."

"Great, the place is a fort."

"I heard a State Department man talk to some pilots about a month ago," Jenks said. "He told us the government would never let there be another drawn-out hostage situation. He said Uncle Sam would move in and end it."

"Sounds a bit ominous, doesn't it." Sharon said. She scowled. "Well, I'm going to take care of my people the best I can. And I won't be afraid to complain if I need to. The first thing I'm going to demand is more cots. We have only six in here and eighteen women. It's degrading and inhuman."

"Be careful how you talk to these men, Sharon," Jenks warned. "They are not diplomatic."

"We've got to get out of here," Ward growled. "I

have a bad feeling. I think they are going to kill more of us to send a message to our government. I have a black, terrible feeling.''

''No, Captain, they made their point at the airport,'' Sharon argued. ''They know those two brutal deaths shocked the whole world; it's enough. Any more would be overplaying their hand. These men seem smarter than that. What we have to do is hang on and work an escape if we can.''

''We probably shouldn't let them see us talking through here,'' Ward said. ''Close up most of the panel, just leave part of it open.''

''That won't really help you any this time, Captain,'' Abdel suddenly snarled as he looked through from the women's side. He slammed the panel shut and screamed, ''What you doing, dumb woman!''

The others had backed away, but Sharon stood there in front of him, her arms folded under her breasts. She still wore the white-blouse and blue-skirt airline uniform. She had given her blue jacket to one of the women the previous night.

''Are you in charge here?'' she demanded in a strong, no-nonsense voice. ''If you are, I want to tell you that we need more places to sleep. We have eight elderly women and they simply can't sleep on the floor. We need cots, and sheets, and blankets . . .''

Abdel grabbed Sharon's arm and pulled it upward until she had to rise on her tiptoes.

''Shut up!'' Abdel hissed. ''Western women are all whores. Look at you! Your big tits are pushing out against your shirt. You don't even cover your face. And your legs, you show off half your legs to tease a man. It's a wonder you don't get raped every hour!''

He let go of her arm and reached toward her breasts. She slapped his hand away. Before she could admire her quick work, Abdel had one hand grasping her breast and the other with a sharp knife blade pushing against her throat.

''You strike me again, American whore, and I'll strip you right here and spread your legs and make you beg for death.''

''Take your hands off me!'' Sharon shouted, her voice

steel and fury. "Take your hands off me or I'll find you wherever you are and castrate you with a dull knife."

Abdel stepped back as if he had been shot, stared at her in disbelief, and then put the knife back in its belt sheath.

"Yes, American whore," he said quietly, ominously. "I will enjoy tearing your clothes off and showing you how a woman should be treated. You will learn to love it."

He stepped back and slammed the wall panel shut.

"There will be no more talking through the wall, no more plotting to escape. And there will be no more cots or blankets. This is not a resort. You are my prisoners, and I will deal with you any way I wish to!"

Abdel turned and marched out of the room.

Sharon ran to the door and heard the lock click in place, then a heavy bar slide into brackets.

She turned to the women in her care. They were her only concern. She checked on Mrs. Vereen again. She was stable, but Sharon was sure the woman needed medical care.

She turned toward the other women who watched her. "Is one of you a nurse or doctor? Mrs. Vereen needs care." She watched the women shake their heads and went back to Mrs. Vereen.

"Now, don't you worry, Mrs. Vereen. We're going to be out of here sometime tomorrow, and we'll have a doctor take good care of you. Just try to relax, and hold on."

Sharon held her hand and the woman looked up and smiled. It was something, she thought. At least she could be doing something for her passengers.

It was 14:12 hours, the day after the hijacking.

CHAPTER
FOURTEEN

Gorman stared across his desk at the slightly built Lebanese man. He was not yet twenty, but already he had killed a U.S. diplomat and tried to bomb an embassy car. Gorman did not believe in turning trash like this over to the East Beirut militia.

If the killer knew the right people in the Christian Forces militia, he could go free, despite his being a Shiite. Sometimes the Christian Forces operated in a strange fashion. Better to settle matters right there on United States soil and have it over with.

"Camel shit, you little bastard!" Gorman bellowed. "Who else worked with you when you killed Phillips?"

There was no reply. Gorman nodded and one of his men drove his fist into the Shiite's unprotected belly. He grunted and sagged forward. Another man behind him grabbed his bound wrists and jerked him erect.

"We have all day, asshole!" Gorman snarled at him. "The games we play get rougher and rougher. You ain't seen nothing yet."

It had been established that the Arab spoke English, at

least enough to understand the questions. He only glared at them and tried to spit on Gorman.

"Filthy pig!" Gorman screamed and slammed his own fist into the man's jaw. Gorman pulled back his aching hand. He had forgotten how it hurt a hand to smash it against a hard jawbone.

"Who were you working with? Was it the Amal, or the Hezbollah, or the Jihad? Maybe you're a Sunni. Tell me, damn it, and you might have a chance to live."

"To die for Allah is everlasting glory!" the prisoner screamed.

"Allah? You murder and bomb and rape and steal for Allah? Sounds like some real kind of a camel-shit god."

The Lebanese man surged forward, his right foot lashed out, grazing Gorman's scrotum enough to bring a sharp, piercing pain.

"Bastard!" Gorman rushed the man, his hands around his throat, choking him. The prisoner's struggles only increased Gorman's fury. His hands tightened around the yielding flesh until he saw the Arab's eyes bulge.

"No, damn it!" he said, relaxing and stepping back. "That would be too fucking easy for him, too quick. Take him down to the storage room, where we can have a little bit of privacy."

The prisoner gasped and coughed, wheezed to get his breath back, and was still wheezing and gurgling when the three agents hurried him out of the second floor office and down the back steps to the storage room that Gorman had used before. He followed them a few minutes later, after detouring to the kitchen to get one small item. He carried the tool in a paper sack as he went to the basement and found that the guards had already stripped the prisoner naked.

"He don't look so fucking tough to me," Gorman said. "Like in Nicaragua. Those damn gigaboos didn't know when they had a good thing going. We had to move in and teach them a damn painful lesson. Got to be the same way with this asshole, I guess. Where's the stick?"

One of his men handed Gorman an electric cattle prod that had the power turned up to the maximum amps.

"Know what this is, killer?" Gorman asked the Arab, who was sucking in breath with an effort. The prisoner nodded.

"So why don't we make it easy. What's your name?"

"Ronald Reagan," the Arab spat.

"Asshole." Gorman sighed. He touched the metal end of the prod to the prisoner's thigh, causing him to leap away, his whole body trembling.

"Tie him," Gorman said. Quickly, the guards bound the Arab's hands to an overhead beam and then fastened his ankles to twenty-pound cement pier blocks on the floor. He was spread-eagled standing up.

"Now, camel dung, what's your name?" Gorman asked.

The prisoner made no reply.

Gorman held the cattle prod against the man's scrotum and pushed the button. Four, five, six seconds he pressed the jolting rod against the young Shiite soldier's testicles. The prisoner screamed and then clamped his mouth shut as his body shook and jolted with the electric shock.

When Gorman pulled the prod away, the prisoner sagged forward, held up only by his wrists tied to the ceiling beam.

"Passed out, Chief," one of the agents said.

"Too quick. Maybe he's faking." Gorman touched his cheek with the prod, but there was no reaction to the sharp jolt of electrical current.

"Wake him up. I've got another idea that you guys are going to get a boot out of." He took the eight-inch, heavy meat cleaver from the paper sack. "I figure we can play fingers and toes with our young killer. Hard to keep quiet when you're losing your fingers one joint at a time."

A knock sounded on the door. Gorman motioned with his hand for one of the men to see who it was.

"It's Nelson, sir."

"Yeah, let him in."

Nelson took one look at the prisoner, lifted his brows, then spoke softly to Gorman.

"I followed Cody and his bunch like you told me to, but they parked down by the Green Line, and the next thing I knew they vanished down an alley. By the time I got there, nobody knew anything. I hung around for an hour and they didn't come back. Maybe he and the girl got themselves blown up over on the west side.''

"Not likely. Nelson, you really fucked up. How in hell do you expect me to . . . forget it. Get out of here. Maybe I'll have more luck with this piece of stinking meat than I did with you.''

Nelson took one more look at the unconscious man and hurried out of the room.

Several miles to the southeast of the American Embassy, below the hippodrome and the beautiful pine forests around the Palace Omar Beyhum, lies the section of Beirut known as Badaro. This part of Beirut borders on Rue De Damas, the general dividing line between East and West Beirut, commonly called the Green Line.

All her life Oma Yafi had lived across the Green Line on the West Side of Beirut. She and her husband ran a small shop for copper goods across from the law courts building and beyond Avenue Sami Solh. Their shop had provided enough income to feed their young family and pay most of their bills.

She looked up quickly now as the bell rang over the door, and she saw her husband rush into the store. She was nursing her four-month-old baby at her large breast, still flushed and heavy with milk.

"Hurry, hurry!" her husband, Nabih, screamed at her. "We must get the panels up over the windows. There is trouble outside. I just saw a dozen armed men down the block and they are not from this area. They could be another faction, one who hate the Amal!''

Nabih struggled with a four-by-four-foot square of half-inch-thick plywood toward the front door of the little store. Just as he opened the door there came a blinding flash, then a roar such as Oma had never heard before, and everything in the shop came crashing down around her and her baby. She fell to the floor, holding her daughter to her breast, and rolled under a heavy table.

Hundreds of copper pots and pails and decorations

cascaded from the walls and ceiling, where they had been carefully hung to show off their best features.

The sound had been terrible. Oma was sure she could not hear a thing. Her ears rang like cymbals being clashed. The air was thick with the dust of centuries, but the table kept the heavy copper and brass pots from her and her baby. Huge chunks of the plastered walls and ceilings fell as well. Some of the plaster was four inches thick where it had been recoated decade after decade.

Oma lay under the table until the last of the pots had fallen. Slowly she realized that she could hear rifle and machine gun fire outside. Her hearing was coming back.

For a moment all was quiet, then another explosion shook the building and more plaster fell. This blast must have been outside, perhaps next door. She waited again.

Men yelled.

Machine guns and automatic rifles stuttered out their deadly messages.

A grenade exploded.

Then a sullen, strange silence filled the street and the ruined store where Oma and her daughter lay. Slowly she pushed back from the protection of the table. She kicked a vase worth forty pounds out of her way and crawled from under the table.

Tears sprang to her eyes as she stared at the destruction of the shop. No one could have done a more complete job if he had planned where to plant the explosives. The small room's dividing wall had been blasted into rubble, the front windows were blown outward, three-foot-square chunks of heavy plaster littered the floor. Copper pots and pans and vases had been smashed and scarred and strewn about like garbage in the street.

For the first time she thought of her husband. Nabih was just ready to go out the door! Where was he? She kicked through the pots toward the front door. At first she saw nothing, then from a large chunk of plaster she saw a hand extended. There was blood on the palm.

"Noooooooooo!" She rushed to the spot, fell to her knees and with a strength she had never possessed before, lifted the plaster block upward and tilted it until it crashed backward.

On the floor lay Nabih. His chest was a mass of blood. His neck had been riddled with shrapnel. Only his face escaped, and on it was a worried expression that had been frozen in place, and now would remain there forever.

Oma let the tears come. She fell on her dead and wailed and cried for long minutes. Then she lifted up, made sure her daughter was comfortable in the front carrying-sling around her neck and shoulder, and walked through the splintered wood, crashed glass and plaster to the open front where the door had been.

Once through the rubble, she headed aimlessly down the street. She could hear weapons firing ahead. She paid no attention to them. A machine gun chattered half a block down.

Bullets zipped through the air near her, but Oma Yafi did not hear them. She kept walking.

Halfway down the block, a Shiite soldier saw her and called to her. At last he ran out, grabbed her, saw the baby and led her to the safety of a doorway.

"You can get killed out there," he scolded. She looked up at him, not understanding. Oma wore no veil, her blouse still sagged open where she had been nursing her baby and her left breast was in plain sight, large and bouncing with each step. The soldier stared at her undraped breast for a minute, then urged her deeper into the doorway. His hand reached for the woman's naked nipple, but a rifle barrel cracked his wrist.

"No!" came the sharp order. The soldier's sergeant loomed over him. "This one we save for the commander. He likes them young like this and he can even taste her milk!"

The sergeant caught Oma's hand and helped her up. "Come with us, little mother. We have a safe place for you until we kill these pigs who attack us. Then I will take you to see the great Majed Kaddoumi himself."

For the first time since she had seen her husband's body on the floor of the shop, Oma Yafi took notice of where she was. She slowly shook her head.

"No, loyal soldier of the Shiites, I can't go with you. By all that is sacred to Allah, I must go bury my husband. The sons of a camel blew up our store. They killed my husband! You have to let me go bury him properly."

The sergeant reached down and fondled her breast. It was the first that she realized she was not covered. She slapped away his hand and pushed her blouse together, quieting her baby's faint cries.

"I am a good woman, loyal to the Shiites and to Allah. I must go and bury my husband."

The sergeant, nodded. "Yes, that would be proper. Come down the alley a-ways until the fighting is over. Then we will take you to your husband when it's safe to walk the street again."

He took her three houses down, led her into a building that had a sentry on the alley door. Then he put her in a small room that had a bed, a chair, and a washbasin. When Oma looked around, the sergeant was gone. She tried the door and found that it was locked.

She sat down on the bed and tried to cry, but no tears would come. She was at the mercy of this band of militia, from whichever faction they were. Trapped in the middle of a war that she knew nothing about, she wished only that it would end.

She lay on the bed and began feeding her daughter.

CHAPTER
FIFTEEN

Ambassador Stewart Tabler peered over Cody's shoulder and looked at the map and the circle Cody had drawn on it around the Furn El Chebbak section of Beirut just across the Green Line and west of the Pine Forest Park.

"Damn it, Cody, you're supposed to be trying to find and rescue those hostages. That does not mean you are to commit suicide on a trip like this. Do you know anything at all about conditions on the other side of the Green Line?"

"Mr. Ambassador, no disrespect, but a couple of hours ago I carried Kelly McConnell's body through a tunnel under the goddamned Green Line. Damn right I know about the Green Line. But to find out where the hostages are, I need to talk to Majed Kaddoumi. You going to invite him here for tea or midday prayers or something so I can talk to him?"

"Easy, Cody, take it easy," the Ambassador said. "If you do go in there, you'll need to wait until dark, at least, then get a damn good guide."

"Ambassador, we don't have the time. It's 15:20 already. It won't be dark for five hours at least. We have to move now. Do you have any Lebanese you can trust on your staff who could get us through the Green Line in the daylight?"

"No, I won't allow that. If they got caught they would be killed."

"Great, fix me up with a Gray Line tour of the Green Line then." The other three members of his team sat around the table. They were in fatigues, with their weapons and equipment in place and ready to move and to fight. Richard Caine kept checking his favorite handgun, a Beretta 92 DA. He kept slipping the loaded ammo clip in and out until the Ambassador stared at him.

Hawkeye kept looking at the map and grumbling. He wanted to get moving. Rufe Murphy sat on the chair, waiting patiently. Now and then his eyes closed and his breathing evened out in just under a snore.

"Kelly got me through, maybe some of the other news people have more contacts than you do, Ambassador. It's worth a try. What hotel do most of them use?"

"The Royal Garden, but I don't like the idea."

"Show me a better way, and I'll grab it."

Someone came to the door and the Ambassador waved him inside. The man, a Lebanese, whispered to the Ambassador, who shrugged. The messenger left.

"Cody, there's someone at the gate to see you. The guards won't let him in but he says he must talk to you. He's about ten years old and his name is Dahr."

Cody laughed and a smile cracked his too serious a face. "Yeah, we might just have found our meal ticket. Dahr helped us get over the Green Line this morning. I bet he could do it again, even in broad daylight. Tell the guards to let Dahr in and bring him up here."

Five minutes later Cody finished a serious talk with Dahr. The boy had told Cody that Kelly was the first American ever to be honest and fair with him, and that he helped her whenever he could. He was angry that she had died, and now he wanted to help Kelly's friend.

Cody told Dahr the street address, and he knew at once where it was. He touched the map in the Najmeh section, where they had crossed the Green Line that morning.

"Safe to cross there again, if I with you. About . . . oh, three kilometers to the address you need go to in the Furn El Chebbak section."

The ambassador shook his head. "Maybe you can get the men across the Green Line, Dahr. But how can you lead them through the heart of West Beirut for three miles?"

"Just can," Dahr said. "How can you be big-shot ambassador?"

Rufe bellowed with laughter and they all joined in, even the ambassador.

"You're hired," Cody growled. "Fifty dollars a day. That's about two hundred Lebanese pounds. Now let's get out of here. We're wasting time."

Dahr looked at the four men and shook his head. "Too damn clean," he said. "Dirty clothes. Two shirttails out. Each different hat. Look too much like real army."

In their supply room downstairs, the men picked up their combat ammo, grenades, all the special tools they each had ordered and got ready to move out. Caine wore a small Israeli combat pack filled with C-5 plastic explosive and his detonators, all of the timed variety.

Dahr looked at the four men again and shook his head. "Most militia don't have uniforms," he said.

Cody waved at Caine and Hawkeye. "Get out of the camous and back in pants and shirts. Nothing too new. Let's push it!"

They rode toward the Green Line in an older fiat. Cody drove. Before they arrived at the parking spot, Dahr told them they would be using a tunnel and that once across the Green Line he was their guide. They must do exactly what he told them.

"If we get into a firefight, then I take over," Cody warned him.

"We might. Several factions in this area. None of them like the other. Oh, I not ten, I am twelve years old. I did not get all of my vitamins."

Getting into the buildings and then the house and to the tunnel was no problem. At the far end, Dahr talked with them before they left the building in West Beirut.

"Keep weapons pointing down, slung," he said, touching an Uzi. "No marching; militia don't march. They run, scramble, and get lost. No English, point, motion. Keep quiet as possible. We stay in alleys most of time."

They were a curious-looking contingent as they came out the doorway into an alley in West Beirut. The boy went first, swinging a stick he found. The four men grouped loosely, about five yards apart, heads down, caps covering obvious American features. Rufe wore a floppy white hat to help hide his big black face.

The first four blocks went without incident, then on the next one they saw a barbed-wire barrier on the main street and expected security of some sort in the alley nearby. An Amal Shiite stepped into the alley as Dahr came midway in the slit between the one-story buildings.

Dahr tossed a rock and tried to hit it with the stick he still carried. The militiaman guard jabbered in Arabic with Dahr, then held up his hand as Cody came within a dozen feet of him. The Shiite had just begun to swing up his automatic rifle, when Cody beat him to the punch and sent three silenced 9mm parabellums into his chest. The rounds slammed him backward and killed him before he skidded off the wall and crumpled in the dirt.

Murphy, bringing up the rear, effortlessly picked up the dead soldier and dropped him in a nearly full trash bin. They double-timed out of that alley behind Dahr and resumed their southerly route, crossing over a wide street called Mar Maroun, and two more blocks south past Rue Huvelin.

Dahr ducked into a safe place beside a stone building and pointed ahead.

"From here it get little tougher. We run out of alleys. We be on small streets, but there more people. Be casual, don't look like from out of town."

"Yeah, and if we get into a firefight, let's do it with the silenced choppers," suggested Hawkeye. "We have four of them. Let's not alert anyone we're on the way until we have to."

They moved at a good pace, but not with any kind of military precision. Usually Dahr was ahead with his stick.

Often small boys trailed or led militia groups wishing they could be a member. Most could not wait until they were fourteen so they could have a real weapon and join the militia.

Down two more blocks they passed a park that had not been watered or cared for and had turned brown. They found an alley again that led south and to the east. The Green Line slanted that way and so they had to move with it.

They came to an area with many more shops, wider streets, and hundreds of people. It was some kind of an open-air market. They went two blocks around it, and continued south.

Ten minutes later, Dahr bellied down at the end of an alley and motioned Cody forward. His men vanished behind doorways, and he hurried up to lie beside the young Arab boy.

"This is the place," Dahr said. "Thought I knew address. It is fortress. On outside many buildings, no windows. Then inside is real fort. Also courtyard. Once saw chopper fly from this courtyard. Big place, many Amal soldiers."

"First we watch the fort, Dahr. See what forces they show."

Five minutes later an old convertible came around the corner ahead. It moved slowly. There were three militiamen in the big backseat. Two had the long rocket-propelled grenade, RPG, launchers. The third a submachine gun. The driver moved slowly, cautiously along the narrow street, and down to the corner, where he turned to the left to circle the block.

"So, they have a mounted patrol. What else?" Almost as Cody said it a pair of militiamen without uniforms but with camou fatigue shirts, came around the far corner, where they had first seen the convertible. The men were young and did not check the alley mouth, and so did not see Cody and Dahr lying there.

Five minutes later a second pair of roving guards, with no camou fatigues at all, strolled by, chattering and then laughing at some joke.

Cody did not have to lay it all out and determine a plan of attack. He knew instinctively. He sent Caine and Murphy up the street to the first doorway that was deep enough to hide them. They were to take out the first foot patrol to show up.

Cody figured the mounted patrol in the old Ford convertible would come past next, and it was first on the list. He brought up Hawkeye and they split up the targets.

"I'll take the driver and the man with the rifle," Cody said. "You get the other two. At this twenty-yard range it will be like picking your teeth."

The convertible appeared next and made the same trip as before. The men were not talking among themselves this time. One actually stared into the alley, but the contrasting brilliant sunlight and deep shadows made it impossible to see far.

When the Ford was exactly opposite them, Cody gave the signal and they both fired. Cody's round slammed into the Shiite driver's head, jolting him sideways, spraying the ages-old rock with blood, bone fragments, and brain cells. The dying man kept his grip on the steering wheel, and when his body was flung to the left, he turned the wheel that way as he fell.

The convertible turned sharply to the left and smashed into the stone building, skidding for a dozen feet before the engine stalled.

The sudden movement of the Ford jolted the two remaining live passengers. Hawkeye's first round had killed his target, but the second shot of both men missed when the car swerved. The two live Shiites dove over the side of the convertible and got between the vehicle and the stone wall.

Cody and Hawkeye unleashed a sheet of hot lead from the two silenced Uzi's, emptied 32-round magazines, and replaced them. In the quiet spell, one of the Shiites lifted up and blasted twelve rounds into the alley.

Cody looked at the convertible, figured out where the gasoline tank was, and put six carefully aimed rounds into the area he had selected.

Before he could fire again a small blue flame licked out from under the rear bumper, then the convertible exploded,

flipping end over end twice down the street, spewing burning gasoline along the way. The two Shiites were charred
beyond description in the few seconds they had after the
blast.

With all the noise and firing, Cody knew he had to
move fast. Cody jumped to his feet, charged across the
street to the first doorway. It had a new heavy door on it and,
he figured, a good lock.

By the time he got there Rufe and Caine joined them.
Cody tried the door; locked. He fired six times at the
doorknob, and just around it. When he tried the door the
next time it came open.

Cody kicked the door forward and charged on through,
his Uzi down and ready for anything that lay on the other
side.

Caine, Murphy, and Hawkeye followed him in.

"16:30 hours," Caine noted.

"Let's hope this dude Kaddoumi has the poop we want
on where those hostages are held," Rufe grumbled.

"And let's hope we can stay alive to do something
about it," Hawkeye tacked on.

Amen to that, thought Cody

They pushed ahead, deeper into Hell.

CHAPTER
SIXTEEN

As Cody came through the door into the outer ring of buildings that formed the defense around Majed Kaddoumi's West Beirut headquarters, he found only an empty room in front of him. It was an entranceway, with a long hall extending to the sides and a short one to a door straight ahead.

Dahr had been left in the alley. He agreed to stay there as long as he could, and he would try to find them when they came out of the fortress. They would get back to this spot if possible. If he had not found them in an hour, he should go back to the east side.

Rufe took the door ahead, kicked it open, lumbered into the room and swept it with his Uzi chattering softly in its silenced mode. There was no return fire. He came to the door and motioned and the three men darted into the room. It had been a dayroom for off-duty troops. Three dead Shiites sprawled on the floor. Each had an AK-47 Russian-made rifle with the 30-round curved magazine loaded with the 7.62mm NATO cartridges.

Cody ran to the small window that looked on a court-yard. The building next door extended deeply into the open space, so from here Cody could see little. What he did see did not make him happy. A cadre of twenty men was being screamed at by an officer twenty feet in front of the window.

Cody had heard that many of these "soldiers" received two hours of political diatribe which made up their complete training. Then they were given a rifle and expected to be expert fighting men.

"Put a charge near the window," Cody snapped at Caine. "Thirty-second timer. We stay together. They've got too much firepower for solo."

By the time Cody was through talking, Caine had pulled a quarter-pound of C-5 from his backpack, sliced it in half and inserted a timer. He pressed the plastic explosive at the side of the window and set the detonator/timer for thirty minutes. He pushed the start button.

Cody led the way into the hall and almost stumbled into an Arab man backing out of another room. When the door closed and the man looked up, he started to scream, but Hawkeye put two silent rounds into his mouth, removing a chunk of his skull four-inches-square and most of his brains with it. Cody caught the body and lowered it soundlessly to the wooden floor.

The four men ran lightly down the hallway to where Cody figured the longer building was located. He found a hallway that led away to the left. Somewhere a woman screamed. Cody shook his head and pointed down the hall.

They made it safely to the end room. Rufe kicked in the door and charged into the room. There was no one there. They were now on the second floor, since the land had fallen away downhill.

Caine closed the door as far as it would go, while Cody looked out the window. Now he could see the open area. It was at least forty yards wide, with no trees, a few shrubs, and no grass. A misshapen child's swing set had been tipped over on one side. A squad of six men made a pitiful attempt at close-order drill near the center of the cleared space.

On the far side of the courtyard the appearance of the inner buildings changed. They had bars on the windows. There were guards outside some of the doors leading to the interior. Then, at the far side, but detached from the square of buildings on the rim, Cody saw a structure that had to be Majed's headquarters. It had windows, so it couldn't be that tough.

He had to work his way around to that spot, then find a way to breach the more heavily defended GHQ, and he had less than half an hour before the first blast went off.

Cody looked over the area again, more slowly this time. At the far side he saw something under a canvas camouflage.

"Rufe, take a look at this. Is that a bird over there under that camou?"

Rufe checked it out and nodded. "Yeah, Yugoslavian make, a copy of something. Looks a lot like a YZ-24. I can fly it if we can get to it."

"Just checking. Caine, set another present for them, here," Cody instructed. "Give it twenty-eight minutes and let's move."

Caine planted the bomb so it would blow out the wall of the room into the courtyard and cause a lot of excitement—and, he hoped, confusion.

They came out of the second room on the run, charging down the hall to the outer rim, then to the left again to get closer to the building that almost certainly was Majed's headquarters.

Twenty feet after getting back to the rim corridor, they ran head-on into three militiamen. Hawkeye was on the point. He sprayed them with half a dozen silent rounds before they could get a shot off, and Cody finished one of them, who had only been wounded. They charged on past, sure now that the dead men would be noticed behind them at any time and an alarm sounded.

Before that happened they came to the last turn. Somewhere ahead would be an exit they could use to get to the headquarters.

Fifty feet down the hallway, a sandbagged position erupted with hot lead. Cody's men dove into doorways and splintered one door on their way inside.

"Casualties?" Cody shouted. All were intact except Rufe, who took a hot slug through half an inch of his upper left arm. It would bother him about as much as a mosquito bite.

Hawkeye was closest to the enemy position, still about forty-five feet down the hallway. He pulled a grenade pin and heaved the bomb, hoping on lots of roll. The grenade went off with a shattering roar, echoing and with the sound building as it raced down the hallway.

A hole in the floor showed where the hand bomb had been short. Firing came again from the sandbagged position and now from Shiite men at the other end of the hall.

"Give them a Caine special," Cody snarled.

Caine had it almost ready. He used the half a cube of C-5 explosive and formed the plastic around a hand grenade, but left room for the arming spoon to fly off. Then he pulled the pin, and exposed himself for two seconds as he threw the bomb with all his power down the hill.

He ducked back inside the door and clamped his hands over his ears. After the 4.2 second delay, the grenade and C-5 went off in one tumultuous sympathetic explosion.

Cody looked out his door and saw the sandbags leveled, the position behind it only splatters of human flesh and blood on the walls, and one wall on the inside of the courtyard, blown into the room it had been forming.

"Let's go do it!" Cody yelled. The four men came out of the rooms firing. Two gave covering fire to the rear, the other two used assault fire to the front as they charged down the hallway to take the territory their bomb had just won for them.

They leaped over parts of bodies, blasted sandbags, and twisted remains of a tripod-mounted machine gun, and continued down the hall.

Two militiamen in civilian clothes jumped into the hall firing automatic rifles, but the spraying Uzi's jolted them out of their socks and drove them into the floor and straight into Allah's waiting arms.

For a moment there was no firing in front or behind them so Cody kicked in a door, motioning them inside the room. It had been an office at one time. A desk remained, but mattresses had been scattered on the floor for some of the troops to sleep on.

Cody looked out the window cautiously, saw the head-quarters not more than thirty yards away. From there it looked more imposing than it had before. It was two stories, made of stone and plaster, and had heavy bars on all the windows and guards on the two doors he could see.

Just then, across the courtyard, the first of the C-5 timed bombs erupted.

Majed Kaddoumi sat at his desk, looking over plans he had to solidify his grasp on the southern half of West Beirut. If he could win ironclad control here, it would boost him for a bigger job—trying to bring the more moderate factions of the militia together. They must unify. They could not expect to win against the Christian Lebanese Forces of East Beirut unless they were unified and strong.

The first explosion came as only a faint shock to him.

A man rushed in to report the bomb inside the complex. It had never happened before.

"You can handle it," said Kaddoumi. "Send in Abbas, he always wants the toughest jobs."

He leaned back in his swivel executive rocking chair after the man hurried away. He was not worried about these minor skirmishes, not even here at his headquarters. There had been dissidents from time to time. He had crushed them all. Just as he would eliminate this probe.

His main concern now was that cursed hothead, Farouk. Kaddoumi had done his best to sabotage the PLGF, placing Najib Yaqub among them, instructing Yaqub to inform on what he learned to the Athens police. But that bit of subtlety had failed, and now here sat supposedly the most powerful warlord in Lebanon at a time when the least attention would do the most good in achieving his goal of putting the country's warring factions behind him. Those radicals, Farouk and Khaled, had picked this moment to slaughter helpless American tourists on worldwide TV, and Kaddoumi had no choice but to feign approval while in truth he would have preferred watching Hassan and Khaled and their crew die screaming by slow inches.

He heard a second explosion, which shattered the wall across the complex.

Strange that anyone could have penetrated.

He picked up the telephone and discovered that it was working. Sometimes it did and sometimes it did not. He dialed Farouk Hassan and the call went through.

"Farouk, how is the mission?"

"Well, old friend Majed. We wait for the jackals to meet our demands."

"I did what I could for you at the airport and later with the reporters," Kaddoumi worked to make his voice cordial, "but one can never tell when dealing with these Western cold fish. They say one thing and do another. They are not reliable."

"My undying gratitude, old friend."

"I want more than your gratitude, Farouk. I want your men, your organization, to join mine. We are rapidly growing to be the largest of the Shiite militia. Soon we will control all of Beirut."

"When the time comes, Majed, I will side with you. For now we each have our priorities. Now I must take care of my charges, one in particular, and I must watch Abdel."

They said good-bye and hung up.

The guard at Majed's door saw that the conversation was over and opened the door. A soldier pushed a young, most attractive woman into the room. She did not wear a veil, so she was not a respectable Muslim woman.

Majed looked at her again and saw the infant held at her waist. She was pouting, and angry.

"What is this?" Majed asked.

"A small flower we found in the rubble, most worthy general. She has agreed that it is not possible to do otherwise, and is now ready to do your bidding."

"Let her speak for herself." Majed stared at her.

"I am not afraid of you, of any of you," the woman said with a firm, assured voice. "My husband spent many years in the West. He treated me as an equal."

"What is your name?" Majed asked.

"I am Oma Yafi, widow of the copper merchant Nabih Yafi. My daughter's name is Jasimine."

"Oma, I too have lived in the West, where the women wear no veils and they expose their bodies wantonly. But I have known Western women who were intelligent, brilliant, fascinating. Later I will see if you can meet those standards. Right now I have a small problem on my hands, and a war to win.''

He motioned to the guards. ''Take her to a safe place, and let nothing happen to her or the child, or you will personally answer to me.''

The guards showed much more respect for the woman now than they had before.

Another explosion shattered the stillness. This one came closer.

Majed scowled.

''And get out there and put an end to this, at once!'' he shouted.

Cody and his team had bored another twenty yards toward the main headquarters.

They had holed up in a small room with a window that opened inward and had no bars on it. The window was less than thirty yards from the rear entrance to the Majed GHQ.

Again, Cody's long experience in battle and strategy took over, and he pointed to Hawkeye Hawkins, the shorter of the three men.

''Hawk, you and I are going to get into that fortress over there. We're going to walk in, not blast our way in. What we need are some raunchy-smelling clothes and a pair of AK-47 rifles and a pair of those fatigue caps they wear, the ones that look like they've been sat on for a week.''

''Got one right here,'' Caine said, looking down at the dead militiaman on the floor. ''You want his shirt and hat and long gun, right?''

Cody grunted and Caine began stripping the shirt off the man.

Rufe went to the door. ''Didn't we leave another body or two across the hall?'' Hawkeye nodded at him. ''Then 'pears like I should take a small walk and bring back the right wardrobe. Anybody give me some cover?''

Hawkeye moved to the door, edged it open a crack and looked out. He waved Rufe forward and the big man went across the hallway and into the room opposite in 1.4

seconds flat, a new Beirut record. Hawkeye eased the door closed when two militiamen ran down the hall, shouting something behind them.

Two minutes later Rufe shot back into the safe room with a shirt, soft hat, and an AK-47 with three extra magazines.

"Now, we need a small diversion, Richard," Cody said. "I'd say about half a cube of C-5 out the window and thrown down away from the GHQ over there. Make it go off on impact. That will give Hawkeye and me a chance to get out this window and work our way toward the GHQ main doors. I hope my six words of Arabic are enough."

CHAPTER
SEVENTEEN

Caine added some C-5 plastique spice to the hand grenade he threw thirty yards north out the window and into the inner courtyard of Kaddoumi's fortress. The small bomb rolled near the side of a building in the protective ring and blasted with a vengeance, bringing screams and shouts from all quarters.

As soon as the sound came, Cody and Hawkeye rolled out the window, looked at the blast site and then ran toward the headquarters. They wore the Amal camou militia shirts and hats, and each carried a Russian-made AK-47 rifle.

Cody walked at a fast pace the last ten yards to the side door of the headquarters building. Two guards there stared at him.

"Trouble," he growled at them in Arabic. "Kaddoumi himself called us to come."

"Pass?" the guard asked.

"No time, camel dung! Let us past!"

The guard shrugged, stepped aside, and Cody and Hawkeye slouched through the door and into a hallway. Men in parts of uniforms scurried down the hall, into rooms. Several held rifles.

"Kaddoumi's offices?" Cody asked the first man he could stop. The Shiite frowned, jabbered something Cody missed. The man pointed down the hall and said 'number seven.' They hurried that way, found room seven and barged in, safeties off the Russian automatic rifles.

Just coming out was a militiaman and an Arab woman without a veil, carrying a small baby. The guard leered at the woman, stroked her breasts with one hand, then patted her bottom and moved her into the hall.

The look of anguish and desperation on the woman's face almost made Cody turn from his main objective. But he realized he had a higher calling for the moment. He saw a man sitting at a desk staring at him.

"General Kaddoumi called us," Cody said in poor Arabic. The desk man snorted, said something softly, then louder he said: "He's busy. Some trouble."

"Yes, that's why he called us!"

The desk man stared at Cody a moment, then lifted his brows and pointed to the second door. Hawkeye had snapped a night lock on the door leading into the office; now he paused beside the clerk and with one swift stroke sliced the soft neck from ear to ear. The desk man fell forward without a sound and bled to death all over his reports.

Cody eased up to the door. It was a soft probe turned hard and anything could happen now. He thrust open the door, found one man behind the desk and two others bending over papers.

"Majed Kaddoumi?" he asked with his best Arabic accent.

"Yes, yes!" snapped the smaller man behind the desk, who had graying hair and wore a full general's uniform.

Cody shot one of the aids with his forty-five-caliber auto, and Hawkeye pumped two of the 7.62mm NATO rounds through the other man's face.

Kaddoumi held both hands tightly to the big desk on which they had been touching a map. He looked up slowly now, first at Hawkeye, then at Cody.

"So, the Americans come at last. I have been waiting for you." He spoke in British-tainted English.

"Tell us quickly where Farouk is holding the aircraft hostages and you'll live," Cody snarled.

"They are in the country, well protected. All will die if you try to rescue them. The whole place is mined with explosives. I had my men set up the place."

"You have thirty seconds to tell us the exact location and how we get there," Cody threatened quietly.

"You are inviting disaster, the deaths of all those innocent passengers. I am on your side. Didn't I speak with the hijackers at the airport? I was trying to get the hostages released. I'm the good guy here, as you would say. I spent time in the United States, yes? I have a green card to work there. Why have you killed my aides?"

"Time's up," Cody intoned in an icy voice.

Sweat beaded the Shiite's forehead. He slumped in his chair.

"Keep your hands on the desk or you're dead meat!" Hawkeye roared at him.

Kaddoumi obeyed.

"It would be suicide for you, and death to all of the hostages," he protested. "These Palestine Liberation Guerrilla Force members are a splinter group. Small, unreliable, and unstable. They could kill everyone and vanish into the countryside."

"We know who they are, and their leaders," Cody countered. "Time's up, so we do it the hard way. Hawkeye."

Hawkeye had moved beside the smaller man. His scalpel-sharp blade drew a three-inch-long bloody line across Kaddoumi's forehead.

A sharp scream by Kaddoumi came not so much from pain as from the surprise and fear.

"Now we talk about the hostages," said Cody. "Are they outside of Beirut?"

"Yes . . . to the west."

"Near what town?"

"Nearest to Quadi Chahrour, but not quite to it. Twenty miles from here, out toward Baabda, not as far as Aley."

"Draw a map the best way to get there. And tell us about the place. Men, defenses, arms, buildings, best way to get in—everything."

An occasional burst of gunfire came from the outside. Cody hoped that Rufe and Caine were keeping a low profile.

"The estate is large, five hundred acres. It is in the hills, mostly barren, but around the buildings, lots of cedars and other trees. It has a good well and they water everything. There is a security wall, eight feet high with barbed wire on top. Inside that is another wall of six feet, and machine guns have been positioned there.

"My guess is that they have about forty men, total. That is their whole force. They are a small group with big ideas."

He finished the map, showing approximate direction, distances, and other small towns.

"The hills are not high, maybe six-hundred feet at the most. The roads are two-lane, narrow, and a long drive leads into the estate. There are road blocks all along the drive, so do not try to motor in. I'm not sure if the estate is mined or not. Farouk is a little crazy. He would rather kill all the hostages than not get what he asks for. His brother was killed yesterday. He is crazy . . . and bitter. A dangerous combination."

Someone banged on the door to Kaddoumi's office.

"Answer!" Cody hissed.

Kaddoumi spoke in Arabic. Cody didn't catch all of it, but enough to know the leader told whomever it was to get out there and defend the headquarters. He was safe.

Whoever it was evidently didn't believe his leader. A big man kicked in the door and burst into the room. Hawkeye took him from the side with a six-round burst through his back and his head. He skidded to a dead stop almost at his leader's desk.

The sound of the automatic rifle fire in the closed space was like an alarm. Hawkeye rushed into the outer office and closed the door to the hall. It had been forced open, so it would no longer lock.

*   *   *

"Praise Allah!" Kaddoumi snarled in English. He stood, and as he did his hand came out from behind his side where he had been holding a small automatic. He got off one round, nicking Hawkeye's shoulder before Cody's forty-five caliber blasted twice, sending death through the Shiite leader's forehead, dumping his lifeless corpse behind the desk.

Cody had already folded the map Kaddoumi had drawn and put it in his pocket.

"Let's get the other two and move toward that chopper."

As they came to the outer office, a guard holding an Arab woman by the arm hurried in. Her face was flushed and furious. She spat at the man, who only laughed. When he saw the big .44 Magnum Hawkeye pointed at him, he began to shake, and spoke rapidly in Arabic.

"Adios, hairbag," the Texan muttered.

The forty-four-caliber hand cannon roared, slamming a 240-grain bullet at 1,455 foot-pounds of muzzle energy into the Shiite's left eye. It powered upward and then slanted to the side, blasting half the left side of the man's skull against the wall.

"Bring her!" Cody snapped, and they moved into the hallway. Two militiamen stood there listening to the echoing sound. Hawkeye held the woman by one hand, and fired the AK-47 with the other, chopping both Shiites into Allah's garden before they could get their weapons up.

The two men and the Arab woman with her baby ran down the hall. She clung to Hawkeye's hand in desperation, sure that these men would help her.

Cody kicked in a door to a room that he knew should look out on the inner courtyard. The room was empty, only a desk and a filing cabinet. He motioned the other two inside, closed the door, and ran to the window. The courtyard swarmed with a hundred Amal troops, all looking for someone to shoot.

As he watched, a nearby window in the outer ring of buildings exploded with what could only be one of Cain's small helpers. Then, down the line, two more of the bombs went off, not ten seconds apart. Half of the militiamen in the courtyard pounded into doors that led to that area.

Just as they vanished, two more blasts came from the far side of the court as two more rooms collapsed in a rumble and roar as the C-5 detonated. These blasts drew most of the enemy troops near that side into the outer-rim buildings to find the bombers.

Cody and friends were on the first floor of the headquarters.

"Out the window," Cody ordered. "We make a break for the chopper down there; and hope that our men see us and support, then follow. They must be watching."

Hawkeye picked up the Arab woman and motioned out the window, then eased her out so she could step to the ground. A militiaman sprang away from the building.

Cody blasted him dead with two rounds from the AK-47, then he and Hawkeye were both out the window, walking across the courtyard as if they owned it, the woman in tow as if a prisoner.

They got halfway across the open space before anyone challenged them. Then a squad of six men in full fatigue uniform and bright red berets jabbered at them to halt, but rifle fire from a window stripped that fighting force of four of its six men in an instant, and Cody cut down the other two.

Hawkeye and his group were running for the chopper. Rufe Murphy bailed out of a window and angled toward them, his silenced Uzi cutting a swath through six more Shiites who had straggled up to the sound of fighting. They never even knew where the fatal firing had come from.

Two more C-5 bomb blasts rattled the compound. Window glass sprayed the court; stones and bricks flew as two more sections of the old buildings collapsed where Cain's small wonders did their work. Caine rolled out of a window on the side where the chopper sat, and sprayed silent killers at the two guards around the bird. He carried two Uzi's.

Cody gave the big black man a hand signal and they all angled toward the fly bird.

The woman stumbled and fell. Hawkeye looked at her quickly. She had a gash in her leg from a bullet. He scooped her up, changed his AK-47 for his trusty decapitating .44 Magnum and rushed forward.

Cody sprayed with his AK until he ran out of rounds. He grabbed two loaded magazines from a downed Shiite, dodged behind an old Mercedes parked in the middle of the court, jammed in the new magazine and covered Hawkeye, who had brought his double burden to a sliding stop behind the vehicle.

The woman protested in Arabic that she could walk. Cody told Hawkeye what the Arab woman said as he scanned the defenses between them and the chopper.

Rufe, with his two Uzi's, had dropped into a defensive foxhole somewhere ahead of them, blasting silent death at the Shiites wherever they appeared.

Caine was nearly at the helicopter, held up by a knot of a dozen Shiite Amal near a Jeep.

Cody evaluated the situation. Time was the factor. He had sixty-four rounds for the AK-47. They were fifty yards away from the bird. As he watched he saw Rufe jump out of his hole and charge forward, an Uzi in each hand blasting as he charged toward the bird. He would need three or four minutes to get the engine started and warmed enough to risk a takeoff. All Cody and the others had to do was get to the bird without getting blown full of holes.

CHAPTER
EIGHTEEN

Tahia Ahmed watched Sharon Adamson with twinges of envy and respect. The young stewardess was not as old as Tahia, yet she had stood up to Abdel in the plane, and again here in the mountain fortress.

Her strength fascinated Tahia. In the Arab world women were still second-class citizens (and would always be to devout Moslems), pushed around and in many nations treated like little more than animals. Even Lebanese men believed they "owned" their wives. Sharon would put up with no such foolishness, and perhaps Tahia should not, either. Tahia had achieved much more than most Arab women ever would. She was on the team, the takeover team that had captured a multimillion-dollar jet passenger aircraft with 129 hostages!

But the men still told her what to do. She had been in on none of the planning, only the execution. She looked at her watch. There were only a few minutes left until it would be twenty-four hours since the deadline had been issued. Halfway to the final, deadly cutoff that Farouk had given the Americans.

She knew there would be another execution. She had

hardened her heart and mind to it, as she had to poor Ali's fate back in Athens. Allah's will be done.

She knew the next victim would be the captain of the aircraft. He had proved to be a troublemaker, just as this Sharon had. Because of his importance he had been selected as the next victim. Perhaps the Adamson woman would be the first to die after the forty-eight-hour deadline.

She went about her job now. All of the passengers and crew were to be assembled in a small courtyard toward the rear of the main house. There they would be under machine-gun guard as the captain's execution was to be videotaped. The tape would be rushed into Beirut and broadcast to a satellite relay station as soon as possible as a second warning to the slow-moving Americans and Israelis.

The infidels would learn! There was no way the Americans could prevent the captain's death, no way to rescue the passengers. The slow-to-retaliate Americans would cave in again and do what was asked to prevent the death of any more of their citizens.

She unbolted the door to the women's hostage room and stepped inside.

"You all will get up and follow me," she snapped in her good English—one of the reasons she had won the job on the takeover. "None of you will be harmed. We are going to the courtyard for a lecture on the eventual victory of the Muslim world over all infidels. Hurry now. Line up by the door."

When the twenty women were in line, she told the door guard to bring up the rear and keep them close together. They walked without trouble to the court, and she sat them on a low wall that ringed a terrace.

"Why are we really here?" Sharon Adamson asked.

"For the reason I gave you," Tahia responded. "You would do better not to be so militant in your actions. Those who cause trouble will be punished."

"I am responsible for my passengers until they safely reach their destination. That's my job; I must be concerned."

"Then do it quietly; keep it to yourself. Do not irritate Abdel, or it could be tragic."

Guards then came with more lines of the hostages until all 128 were sitting or standing in the courtyard.

Abdel strode in followed by three militiamen who carried a pole. With a shudder, Tahia noticed that the pole had a crossbar. It was a cross, a Christian cross, the kind that was used for executions in ancient times . . . crucifixions! Not even Abdel would stoop to such a fiendish trick. It must be a device to frighten the next victim.

The cross was lowered into a pre-dug hole in front of the hostages, it was straightened, and dirt was filled in the hole and pounded down until the cross was freestanding.

The hostages had buzzed with surprise and alarm when they first saw the cross.

Then two men came in with a self-contained TV minicamera. It could record color TV tape with the sound. The unit ran from battery packs strapped around the cameraman's waist like a SCUBA diver's belt. The cameraman took some readings, judged some shots, and then waited.

The cameraman and his assistant began to shoot as soon as Farouk Hassan walked into the courtyard and stared at the hostages.

"I am truly surprised and sorry that we are gathered here. I had fully expected cooperation with the United States and Israeli governments by this time. They must be reminded that we are not to be toyed with, lied to, or put off. Any blame lies with the two governments, not with the Palestine Liberation Guerrilla Forces.

"You must remember that whatever happens, any blame, and any blood, is on the hands of those negotiators who have not talked in good faith with us. They are the terrorists, not us."

Tahia saw now that as he spoke the TV camera had been recording his words.

"So, I say to all Americans, to all Israelis around the world, that you must put pressure on your governments to do what is right. The detainees in Israel are there illegally. We chose to fight that illegality with some of the same. We fight fire with fire, blood with blood.

"What you are about to see is not pretty, but it is necessary. We also think it is highly symbolic."

Sharon sat on the wall, unable to believe what she knew must be happening. They had been brought out to this space in late afternoon to be witnesses to a murder! There was no other explanation. She was not sure if the cross was only a symbol or if it might. . . . She refused to think further along that line. No.

She watched the Arab girl who had been on the team of terrorists. She seemed to be about Sharon's own age, perhaps a year or two older. There was a tenderness about the woman that came through even when she was waving a submachine gun, or when it hung over her shoulder on the sling as it did now.

She was Arab dark, black eyes, black hair, an olive skin to shed some of the brilliant sunshine. Sharon wondered how they would have reacted to each other in a more pleasant setting.

Sharon gasped. She could not help it. Some of the women began to sob. Captain Ward was led down a path with a rope round his neck, his hands bound behind him.

"No! No, you can't!" she shouted.

Tahia swung the muzzle of the SMG until it was only inches from Sharon's chest. Then she slapped her across the face with a quick, forceful blow. Sharon jolted to the left, caught herself, and stared hard at Tahia.

"They're going to murder him!" Sharon whispered.

Tahia locked her eyes with Sharon's. "Probably." Tahia whispered back, her face stern. "If they do, then you could be next. Do you want that? Control yourself if you wish to help your passengers."

Sharon sucked back a sob and wiped her eyes. "How can you be so hard, so terrible?" She kept her voice low so only Tahia could hear. "That's a human being out there they are going to torture! How can you be part of this?"

"Quiet!" Tahia said.

Abdel Khaled had led the procession with the cross and held the rope around Ward's neck. When he was satisfied that the cross was firm he had Ward stand on a two-foot-high box at the base of the cross. His hands were untied and his arms stretched out. They were at the same height as the cross-beam of the cross.

Sharon looked at the TV camera on the man's shoulder. It was aimed at the cross now, and she realized all of this was being recorded so it could be broadcast to America!

Abdel had one of his men tie a stout rope around the pilot's waist, binding him to the cross. Then Abdel had a man hold Ward's right hand open, its back against the sturdy cross-beam.

The witnesses gasped, some shouted, others cried as they saw Abdel take out a hammer and a large spike and position the big nail over Captain Ward's hand. The hammer slammed against the thirty-penny spoke. Ward screamed as it drove through his palm and into the cross-beam.

One woman among the hostages fainted. Many were now weeping. The procedure was repeated on Captain Ward's left hand, then the box was pulled from under his feet. He sagged until his feet nearly touched the ground when the rope around his waist was taken off.

Ward hung by his nailed hands, agony etching his face.

"This can't be happening!" he screamed in pain. "Not in a civilized world!"

Abdel slapped him four times, rocking his head back and forth. There was no easy way to nail his feet to the upright, so they were tied.

Abdel took out a six-inch knife and approached Captain Ward. He sliced his shirt off, then poised the blade next to the Captain's right side.

"For the Glory of Allah! For the Palestinians! For the freedom of our brothers in an Israeli concentration camp!" As he shouted the last he drove the blade deep into Ward's side and slashed downward until the blade grated his hipbone.

The eight-inch wound gushed with blood. Ward had not made a sound. He seemed unconscious for a moment, then his mouth opened and he screamed his death song, a long shriek of agony and disbelief.

Abdel stepped back and looked directly at the camera.

"This American dies because his country's leaders will not bargain with us. We have heard nothing! America, you have only twenty-four hours left, then one American dies every hour on the hour! We are serious. If you do not talk with us, America will be wallowing in the blood of its innocent citizens because of the stupidity of its President!"

He went back to Ward. The pilot lifted his head once more, tried to speak, but blood seeped from his mouth and a great gush of air escaped from his lungs as he died.

Sharon held her face in her hands and sobbed.

In the Oval Office of the President of the United States, the Chief Executive listened to the diatribe and fought back tears as he saw the American being tortured, then crucified. When the segment that had been taped from the satellite finished, the President gave a long sigh and wiped his eyes, then looked at Pete Lund.

"Did we do the right thing, Pete?"

"Absolutely, Mr. President. No negotiations, no blackmail, no concessions, and if possible no terrorist prisoners. This is the only method that will eventually defeat the terrorists. If they know they must be martyrs when they plan something like this, it will discourage many, and eventually prevent them from continuing."

"Oh, I agree about no prisoners, but we're going at it all wrong," General Will Johnson brayed. "Like I said before, you meet deadly force with superior deadly force. We call in an air strike on West Beirut with twenty Navy Tomcats and let those F-14s wipe out two hundred Shiites. The Israelis do it. We should too."

"You want to sink as low as the terrorists, Will!" Lund rasped. "A raid like that would kill two-thirds of the women and children."

The President looked at each man. "I stand by my first decision, gentlemen. The best way to go is covert. We wait and watch for Cody and his team. He still has twenty-four hours. He has communication gear, you said, Pete?"

"Yes sir. He has a transmitter that can reach the satellite and will be relayed to us here, and to our people in Haifa. That's only seventy-five miles from Beirut. We can get choppers or jet fighters over Beirut there in minutes. That can be our own or Israeli."

"Let's hope he calls. Now all we can do is wait. This is the hardest part."

"No, Mr. President, the hardest part is for those surviving hostages who are wondering if they will be the next to be tortured and killed."

CHAPTER
NINETEEN

Cody and Hawkeye, thinking alike, both pulled grenades from pockets and discarded the safety pin at about the same time. Cody raised himself from behind the old Mercedes and threw the hand bomb as far as he could toward the red-beret-topped Shiites who were peppering them with rifle rounds.

The *karump* of the exploding grenade kept the red hats down long enough for Hawkeye to come up right behind the sedan and get a good throw. Cody's bomb .fell ten yards short, but with a good roll, Hawkeye's Shiite killer spattered six of the red caps all over the landscape.

Cody and his firing partner began picking off the out-in-the-open troops as some of them tried to move forward, then gave up and raced toward the protection of slit trenches that had been dug around the perimeter of the open space.

Just when Cody thought the attackers were beaten back, a Jeep roared, gears clashed, and a jolting green rig sped from a shed affair, and a machine gun mounted amidship began yammering. Cody took his AK and turned his sights on the Jeep. He got one shot through the windscreen but the rig kept coming forward.

The rounds from the heavy MG laced through the old Mercedes, and Cody and Hawkeye shifted their position to the end. Hawk concentrated on the red berets and Cody slammed round after round at the jolting Jeep. He kept his Russian rifle on single shot to conserve his long-gun ammo.

Caine saw the problem. He had gained the chopper, put down a guard and another militiaman who had been hiding there. Then he turned his silenced Uzi on the red berets and bedeviled them with 9mm parabellum rounds.

When the last of the beret-topped defenders rushed for the perimeter trenches, Caine turned and watched the Jeep. He had six grenades left. He souped up one with half of a quarter-pound blob of C-5 plastic explosive and ran forward to the first cover he could find. The protection turned out to be a dead Shiite militiaman.

The Jeep turned and struck a new angle. The driver seemed determined to get to the chopper, probably to protect it. The closer the Jeep came, the quieter Caine lay. He wanted to look like another dead body. For a moment he thought the rig would run over him, but it missed him by six feet.

Caine had pulled the pin; now he let the Jeep jolt past him, then he lifted up and flipped the C-5-laced grenade into the front seat and saw it roll to the floor.

For a moment, nothing happened. Then a scream shattered the afternoon as both men in the Jeep's front seat and the gunner on the MG tried desperately to exit the vehicle.

They did, but only with the help of an ear-jangling blast as the grenade triggered the C-5 into a roaring, thundering explosion that decorated half of the courtyard with stray bits of Shiite militiamen and Jeep metal. A secondary explosion detonated the fumes left in the gasoline tank, and then a quiet settled over the parade grounds.

Rufe had silenced his immediate problem, a pair of Shiites who knew how to shoot. He caught one as he came out of a trench, and the other before he made it into the next one. Both went down in sprays of hot, silenced Uzi lead.

Then Rufe legged it for the chopper. For just a moment he dreamed of being a defensive end with the Dallas Cowboys.

He had just blocked a pass, knocked it up in the air and then caught it, and he was wide open sixty-five yards to the enemy end zone! Before he made it to the end zone, he saw Caine, who had fallen back to a defensive position at a trench nearer to the chopper. Rufe dove into the chopper, checked out the controls a moment, then started it. The four-place ship had room for five. He let the big rotor spin slowly as the engine caught and purred contentedly.

He ducked down behind the heavy metal protection and let the chopper warm up for two minutes. Then he gunned the engine as a signal to his team that he was ready to fly. Caine got back to the bird first. He used a captured AK-47 and laid down covering fire as Cody, the woman, her child, and Hawkeye made a series of classic retreats toward the spot at which they had wanted to be all the time.

Cody pushed the woman on board and pointed to the far-back area. She squeezed in and crouched there with her baby. Caine jumped in next, then Cody and Hawkeye provided the final covering fire out the off-pilot side as they lifted slowly off the deck. A rifle round punctured the thin plastic bubble on the front, but Rufe punched her in the throttle and they jolted nearly straight up and slanted quickly over the buildings and out of range.

"What kind of armament does it have?" Cody shouted over the roar of the big rotors.

"Six rockets in pods, and a fixed fifty-caliber machine gun," Rufe shouted back.

"Let's give them a taste."

Rufe swung the bird around, hanging just behind the rim of two-story buildings. Then he lifted up, zeroed in on the small headquarters fortress and blasted off two rockets.

The small missiles flew true, jolting through the facade before exploding inside. Half of the building collapsed. Cody grinned and Rufe trained the fixed machine gun on the Shiites scampering around the parade ground.

Rufe blasted until he figured he was half out of ammo and stopped.

"Bus driver wants to know what your stop is," Rufe shouted.

Cody looked at the woman. He asked her where she wanted off, East or West Beirut. She told him she had some family in the western part of the city. Rufe picked a parklike area near Corniche Pierre Gemayel, a wide street, and let her off. She stood on the grass for a moment, looking at the men.

"Thank you," she said, her only English.

Cody told her in Arabic they were glad to help. He watched her for a moment. He knew nothing of her background, of her life up to now, but she seemed to represent all of the tragedy that slams down on civilians in any war.

The very people the generals say they are fighting the war to benefit are the first ones to be victimized. He reached in his pocket and took out a wad of Lebanon ten-pound notes, and gave them all to her. She looked at him in surprise, then he told her in Arabic to go and find a place to live in peace. She let tears spill from her eyes as she stepped back.

As the big chopper lifted away from her, Oma Yafi wondered if she would ever see the kind men again. She decided they had to be Americans. They had treated her so gently, with such compassion, had rescued her and saved the life of her daughter.

For just a moment she thought of her dead husband lying in the shop. She should go back and give him a Muslim burial. She could not. If she went back she somehow would be caught up in the war again. She would walk west. She would find a small village that needed a copper worker. She had learned to make pots and other items that were always in demand.

She hurried with her baby to the edge of the park, plunged into the railroad yards. She knew where she was. She would cross the tracks and come out near the bridge that led across the Beirut River, and go to the Sinn El Fil area. From there she could slowly work her way out of Beirut itself into the western hills.

There were many small villages there. She was remembering Mkalless, where some of her relatives lived. Yes, she would go there. It was not until she had crossed the tracks and she was in the warehouse area that she thought of the wad of money the American had given her. She found a hiding place under an old wrecked truck and took out the roll.

Slowly she counted the bills. There were forty ten-pound notes. Four hundred pounds! It was more money than she had ever seen before in her life! She hid it in several pockets in her clothes, and walked out to the bridge. She would stop at the first store she came to so she could buy a proper veil. It was unseemly to be without a correct veil. Then she would find a cafe and have something to eat. She was hungry and the little one would want to eat soon again.

For a moment, Oma Yafi blinked back tears. It had been such a terrible day in her life, but the strong American had made it possible for her to go on living. She would make it now, yes; she could go on and raise her daughter.

Cody sat in the seat next to Rufe, pawing through maps until he found the one he wanted.

"Yeah, the hills west of Beirut. Any idea where we are, big guy."

"Not far from where we started," Rufe shouted. "I've got a traffic circle down here, there's the park where we let the woman off, and we're still on the east side of the river."

"Roger, let's head due west. Be a hell of a lot easier to find this place before it gets dark. What time you got?"

"About a half hour to sunset, twenty minutes after that to sit-down time, somewhere."

"Agreed. Let's move south, try to find a secondary road going due south out of Beirut. Down around the airport somewhere a smaller road, probably dirt or gravel, turns off and goes east into the mountains. Should be a piece of cake."

Rufe laughed, then winced when he shook his arm. "Hell of a lot depends who baked the cake, and who is on the navigation plotting board."

"Give it a try, we'll find it," Cody said. He took his knife, slit Rufe's left sleeve where he had caught the bullet and dumped on some antibiotics and wrapped it up while they flew.

"We're looking for a village called Quadi Chahrour, but we don't get all the way there."

"Sounds too easy," Rufe grunted, and dropped down so they could read the street signs.

Somebody took a shot at them.

"Folks must have seen you fly before, Rufe," Cody said.

" 'Pears as how. What you think of that road over there? It's no four-laner, and I can see the edge of the airport to our right and down a-ways."

"Give it a try. Everybody check your ammo and supplies. We'll be up against forty to fifty men out here somewhere. And we can't stop by at the hardware store for some more boxes of rounds."

CHAPTER
TWENTY

Just before sunset they spotted the small village they were looking for and backtracked toward Beirut two miles to where they saw the lane leading off along the top of a ridge toward a swatch of green a mile distant. They went to four-thousand feet and flew over the estate below.

Cody used binoculars and confirmed that had to be the place. It had two walls, the outer one with barbed wire on top, and he was sure he spotted machine guns on the inner wall. They flew out of sight, then snaked down a valley, circled around and flew to within a mile of the mountain hardsite to a small clearing, where Rufe set the bird down as lightly as a bumblebee invading a tulip.

By the time they were loaded for combat and were on the trail, darkness closed around them. They followed the graveled road that led into the estate. There were no cars or trucks on it as they walked along cautiously twenty yards to one side.

Cody was in the lead. He held up his hand and in the soft moonlight the men saw the signal and stopped. He gave them a down command and moved ahead quietly through the harsh land, being careful not to kick a rock or snap a dry stick.

He found what he had expected, a roadblock. It was a log about a foot in diameter, but it would take two men to move it if a car or truck were to come. There was no way to drive around the log.

Two men sat in the dark shack next to the edge of the road. Cody went back to his team, detoured them fifty yards to the side, and then back to the road.

Twice more they found two-man guard posts with logs across the road. There did not appear to be any depth protection on either side of the blocks.

Two hundred yards from the last roadblock they came to a small house, which must have been a gatekeeper's residence at one time.

Lights blossomed inside, and the men could hear radios or TVs playing. They circled this spot as well and moved forward. Cody had told them they would keep it a soft probe as long as they could. He had no thoughts of going hard so close to daylight.

There was no chance he could get the Israeli choppers in before daylight anyway. Rufe had stayed with the chopper, and would charge into action as soon as Cody called him. They each had small pocket-sized radios that were powerful enough to reach the European Communications Satellite.

The signal was then multiplied in power and rebroadcast so Rufe, and Washington D.C., as well as the U.S. people waiting with the Israeli Air Force liaison in Haifa could get it.

Cody had checked twice with the small radio, and he had picked up Rufe with no trouble. Now he had to see what kind of a setup he had to fight against, do a complete recon, and then work out a plan. At least half of the work should be done before daylight. That way it would make it easier when the sun brightened this half of the globe.

The physical setup could have been better. The estate had been positioned on the rim of the ridge and flowed down the eastern slope. The wall probably circled much more than the buildings of the estate that they could see.

He established a base of operations where a small ravine left the ridge and dove under the first wall. With a little work they could enlarge the opening that the runoff water had eroded and worm inside the compound. He sent Hawkeye one way and Caine the other to scout the outer wall, report any fixed weapons, any sentries, any more lookouts. He slid under the ten-foot-tall first wall and checked inside, looking for roving guards, dogs, and machine guns.

A half hour later he came back to the base. He told them he had found two machine guns, manned, both on the inside twelve-foot stone wall. Six guard towers were built above and inside the wall, but no guard dogs and no roving foot patrols between the walls.

The other two men had found nothing of importance. The wall kept going for miles, they decided. There were no gunners, no guards, only the barbed wire. It was probably to help keep the prisoners inside, they decided.

Cody said they would hit the two machine guns first. A thin nylon rope with a fold-out grapple hook gave Cody the first look at the top of the second wall. It was twelve feet high, made of native stone and mortar, and looked to be three feet wide at the base. He would go up it fifty feet down from the machine-gun position, which was manned but not lighted.

He threw the grapple and winced at the sound it made as it went over the wall. He waited thirty seconds, heard no response, and so pulled gently on the line. Too far! Before he could stop it the grapple grated over the top of the wall and fell at his feet.

A guard in the tower called softly, but got no reply. He gave up.

Cody tossed the grapple again, this time a dozen feet farther down the wall from where he had been. The hooks caught something and he put all his weight on the line. It held. He put the silenced Uzi on a strap over his back, pulled on his tough leather gloves, and began walking up the face of the slightly in-sloping wall.

When Cody was halfway up, Caine materialized out of the shadows near the base of the wall and held the flailing loose end of the line. Cody got near the top and peered over. The top of the wall was nearly two feet wide, smooth. He bellied down on it, let the line go slack. He felt it tighten as the next man began climbing.

Cody paused, letting all of his senses work for him. He could hear the man breathing in the machine-gun guard tower fifty feet ahead. He stood up on his rubber-soled boots, checked his balance, then walked forward with the silenced Uzi held in front of him and ready for action.

The guard was facing the other way, and by the deep, even rhythm of his breathing, Cody knew he was sleeping. He slid the four-inch straight razor from his fatigue pocket and flicked it open. When he was three feet away, the sentry snored in his sleep and woke himself up. The guard changed positions, swore softly in Arabic, and went back to sleep.

Cody had not breathed during the small ritual. Now he took a long, slow breath, then stepped forward, clamped his left hand over the Lebanese terrorist's mouth and nose, and slit his throat with the razor. After a twenty-second struggle, the dead man shifted forward a foot, then rested on the small platform on which the machine gun sat.

By the time Caine had scaled the wall, Cody had checked out the field of fire, the amount of ammo, and the target opportunities. It would work. With the Brit's help they tilted the dead man over the back side of the wall. They had stripped his shirt and hat off, and put them to one side.

When Hawkeye arrived a minute later, they knew this was a key firing point.

"Hawk, when it's nearly daylight, you hightail it back here and man this weapon. The minute we go hard, I want you to hose down everything in uniform that moves. Get transport first, then the troops. Put on this hat and shirt when you come back. We'll take the other MG out and then get busy planting our timed little friends. Next trip we're going to use radio-detonated charges."

"Why didn't you say you wanted them? I have backup for up to twelve frequencies. I always come with two controls."

"Good, we'll use them. Let's move. Hawkeye, you go get the next machine gunner. He should be about fifty feet down this wall. Use your knife and leave him in place so it looks like he's sleeping. Drop out all the ammo, and pull the firing pin on the MG in case they send up a new gunner. We'll go down the ladder here and meet you at the bottom of the ladder around the wall.''

Hawkeye walked casually down the top of the wall like a steelworker. Nothing bothered him. He saw the MG position, and almost at once a small laugh came from it. The voice was soft and accusing. Hawk had not the slightest idea what the words meant.

He simply growled at the man and continued forward with the silenced Uzi ready. He was within ten feet of the sentry before the man sensed something was not right. Hawkins shot him twice in the chest and he was dead before he could utter a word or cry out in surprise.

Hawkeye pulled the MG apart as much as he needed in order to take out the bolt and the firing pin, then put it back together. He dropped the ammo over the outside of the wall and bent the dead guard over his weapon so it looked as if he were sleeping. He found the ladder and worked down it silently.

Cody and Caine were waiting for him at the bottom of the ladder. They moved more cautiously now. There had to be interior guards here, foot patrols. They lay quietly at the edge of the green brushy area for ten minutes.

No one came past.

They moved forward toward the first building with lights. It seemed to be a dayroom and dormitory for the troops.

It was built off the ground where the land fell away on the downhill side. Caine snaked under it, planted two charges of quarter-pounders, both set with frequency 1. He locked in the tabs on his control panel and they moved toward the next building, which seemed to be some sort of office. Through a grimy window they saw a man sitting at an old manual typewriter, using the hunt and peck system to write a report.

Six men in the room seemed about ready to go on guard duty. They formed up inside, and a small man with a crisp fatigue uniform inspected them, then gave a curt command, and they did a left face and marched out the door.

The Englishman vanished under the side of the building. Cody and Hawkins fell into step behind the last man on the guard roster. Cody reached around from behind him and slit the guard's throat. He died before he knew he was hurt. Hawkeye hooked his left arm around the next man's throat, stopped him, and drove his knife into the guard's heart.

The next man in line turned and saw a problem in the moonlight. Two Uzi's came up whispering nearly silent death. When the last four guards stopped moving, Hawkeye and Cody dragged them into the bushes and hid them—at least they would stay hidden until daylight. Caine caught up with Cody and Hawkeye as they headed for the main mansion.

Cody guessed it was forty rooms. There were three wings, all double-storied. The captives had to be inside, but Cody's Army could do little about them until morning. They pulled back, found another building used as a motor pool. Only one man was on duty.

Caine looped a strand of piano wire around his neck and pulled the wooden handles on both ends. The thin wire sliced through the Shiite's windpipe and both carotid arteries, and he was dead in twenty seconds. Caine stuffed him in the trunk of an old Fiat. Then he dumped a fifty-gallon drum of gasoline over so the fluid spilled out and puddled on the concrete floor.

"Nice touch, but hold off on the igniter," Cody whispered. "Let's see what else we can find."

The Brit left a half-stick of C-5 there—the gasoline would do the rest—and set the frequency number on his detonation code.

Outside they all paused to listen. A radio sounded softly somewhere, a piano player tried hard inside the mansion, but somewhere else Cody heard a purring hum.

"Generator," Cody said. "Let's find it."

They moved toward the sound but sound can be tough to trace. After two false leads they found the generator building. It had been soundproofed, but the throbbing diesel engine could not entirely be muffled.

Cody slipped inside the building, checked the engine with a pencil flash and promptly drained all the fuel out onto the floor. The diesel sputtered, coughed, and stopped. The lights dimmed in the buildings and on the two poles, then came back bright.

Outside, Caine grunted, "Damn battery backup."

"Just the same, somebody will come to check the engine," Hawkeye whispered.

As he spoke, two fatigue-clad soldiers swung down the path from the building that served as the troops office. One of them opened the door to the generator building and switched on his flashlight.

"What the hell?" he said in Arabic. The other man joined him inside. As they stood looking at the diesel-oil spill on the floor, twin silenced shots from two Uzi's blasted the men out of this life.

Caine and Hawkeye dragged them out of the building and down twenty yards, where they rolled the bodies into a gully. They had saved the men's AK-47s.

It was 20:00 hours.

None of the dead guards had been found. Evidently the guards who were supposed to be replaced were all sleeping on duty. No one else had come to look at the generator.

Lights in the buildings were still as bright as ever, but some had been turned off.

"Let's try one of the wings," Cody said. "Maybe we can get some of the hostages to a safe place before the shooting starts."

There wasn't time. A siren went off.

Cody pointed at Hawkeye. "Get on that MG and watch out for the civilians. Don't open fire until we go hard. We may have three or four hours yet, or it could be until daylight. Richard, you and I find a nice comfortable OP up here behind the main wing and watch whatever happens. I think they must have found some of the guards, or maybe the honcho is worried about running down his batteries if the generator won't start again."

Caine and Cody watched from a good hiding place thirty yards beyond the end of the east wing of the mansion. A man with a Doberman pinscher on a leash left the center section of the big house. He carried no weapon, but had two men with SMGs on each side of him as he walked toward the generator shed. One of the guards carried a stream light, a battery-powered light that could shine for a mile. It lit up the area like noontime.

"Bet the honcho gets mad," Caine said. "Wish I could blow the generator shed when they all are in here."

"No, we wait. We don't go hard until we want to, we take all the advantages we can get. They don't know anyone is here yet. I'd bet this outfit has a discipline problem among the troops."

CHAPTER
TWENTY-ONE

In the center wing of the mansion, Mrs. Vereen, the hostage with the bad heart, clutched at the woman's hand beside her.

"I feel terrible," Mrs. Vereen said. "Seems this is the way it was just before I had my heart attack."

"Try to stay calm, Mrs. Vereen," the woman who sat beside her said. She had taken Mrs. Vereen's pulse and worked with her hands around her arm for a moment to try to get some reading on her blood pressure.

"Mrs. Vereen, I'm a nurse, and I'll do everything I can for you. We're talking with the leaders now, trying to get you out to a hospital."

"You're an angel, thank you. So many nice people here, like that stewardess, Sharon. You thank her for me for everything she's done for all of us, especially if I don't make it."

"I promise. But you hush that kind of talk. You're going to be fine. Now you try to get some rest."

In another large room where some of the men waited, Co-pilot Jenks sat slumped on one of the folding cots they had provided for half the hostages. He was *not* a leader. He was *not going to stick his neck out!* It was only a job, for Christ's sake! He had no ordination to take care of these folks. His responsibility ended when the aircraft touched down safely. Period.

Damn right! Then why did he feel like shit? He had watched Tom Ward be crucified, and something deep down in his gut changed, something snapped and crashed and withered and he knew that he would never be the same again. Hell, nobody even looked at him cross-eyed. He had taken off his uniform jacket and his wings. He doubted if the terrorists even knew he had been co-pilot.

Damn it! He should have stood up and protested! He should have taken over where Tom left off, bitching about no food and no cots and blankets. He should be the one looking out for the passengers!

Jenks huddled lower on the cot, pulled a blanket up around him and tried to relax. He kept shivering. Again and again and again he saw the nails driven right through Tom's hands! He could feel the steel piercing flesh! He could feel the ring of the hammer on the steel spike! He could hear again the rending scream by Tom!

When the knife had plunged into Tom's side, Jenks had fallen to one side, thinking for a moment that he himself had been knifed. The real pain of it shot through the co-pilot, and even as he watched his commander dying, the sensation billowed through him, touched him, changed him into a coward.

He had admitted to the word. He was a coward. He could only tremble, and slide lower on the cot, pulling the blanket up over his head so no one could see him shaking. Tom Ward was a hero; Jenks was a coward.

In another room in the center wing, Sharon stood in front of a desk and quietly told Farouk what they needed.

"Our first problem is Mrs. Vereen. She's been a heart patient, and it looks like she's about ready to have another heart attack. Her pulse rate is too high, and I'm sure her blood pressure has skyrocketed. She needs to see a doctor—tonight if possible.

"There's a small town nearby; could I take her there to

see a doctor? She should stay, but I promise that I will come back with your guard and not make any trouble.''

Farouk Hassan watched the woman in front of him. She was pretty rather than beautiful. She did not have big *tsaydes,* like many American women, and she did not dress to attract attention. She would be good in bed, he could tell. He pushed his thoughts off sex and concentrated on what she was saying. When she finished he shook his head.

"No, she can't go to a doctor. There is no doctor in the village who could help her. She would have to be driven back to Beirut, and I can't spare the two men and the vehicle. She must take her chances along with the rest of you.''

"Mr. Hassan, with her it is not a 'chance.' If she has another heart attack here, she will die. The odds are good that she will suffer another attack unless she has medication to prevent it. Any doctor could give that drug to her.''

"I'm sorry, Miss Adamson. It is impossible.''

"You are condemning her to death.''

"Whatever is the will of Allah.''

For a moment Sharon wanted to scream at him. He was hiding behind his religion. Whatever he did was for the glory of Allah. Whatever happened must be the will of Allah or the god would never let it happen. Rubbish!

She trembled for a moment, working to control her anger. At last she folded her arms in front of her in a basic body language of defiance and stared hard at the man.

"You must have a wife, a family. Are they well? What would you do if they were threatened? Attack, kill, destroy? These people on this plane are my family. They are my responsibility. Perhaps I should follow your example. When my family is in danger I will protect each one. I will attack, kill, and destroy. How can you object if I follow your own rules?''

"You made up the rules, Miss Adamson. Even so, they are rules for the hostage keepers, not for you. Any more complaints?''

"Yes, we need more cots, more blankets, and a humane supply of good food. We are not animals in a cage. We must be fed.''

Farouk shook his head in dismay. "Miss Adamson, why do you continue to do this? You saw that we chose Captain Ward for the next execution victim when he kept protesting. Doesn't that make any difference to you?"

"None whatsoever. If we're out of coffee on board I yell at the captain and the head attendant. If we're short on beds and food here I yell at the head man, you. Whatever happens to me, happens. I'm a little bit of a fatalist. But you can bet that I'm going to fight and claw and scrap to the last fraction of a second if it comes down to saving the lives of my passengers. What I won't do is crawl, especially not to a coldblooded murderer like you."

Farouk sighed. He motioned for an armed guard to bring in his second in command, Abdel Khaled.

Abdel came in and glanced up and down at Sharon. He smiled.

"Has she decided to be nice to us yet, Farouk?"

"Unfortunately, no. She wants more blankets, but she has not once offered to take off her blouse and her skirt to help get covers or more food for her charges."

"If I thought it would have worked, that would have been my first ploy," Sharon said. "The problem is, you don't have enough supplies here for your own men, let alone another hundred and thirty of us. Logistics is the word in English; it means supplying the troops and supporting units. You are a lousy soldier."

"How would you know that, soft woman?"

"I know. I grew up on army posts all around the world. I can shoot a .38 or a 1911-issue .45 automatic better than you can. So don't underestimate me. I'm fighting for my passengers and their right to life. Compare that to your gonad logic and see where you get."

Abdel looked at Farouk. "Gonad logic?"

"Balls; gonads. She means sex." Farouk looked out the window a moment, then waved at the guards. "Get her out of here, no wait. Bring in Hallah. He's young enough to enjoy it."

Hallah came in the door of the room with a cigarette dangling from his mouth. He had not shaved since the takeover. His hair was uncombed.

"Hallah. I have a small job for you. Miss Adamson has been naughty again. She keeps stirring up the hostages and complaining. I think it would be better if she were locked in a different room. Perhaps you could share your locked room with her, yes?"

Hallah grinned. "She must be punished, that is true. I'll sacrifice and keep her in my room. To punish her."

"Yes, yes, now get her out of here. I don't want her bothering me again."

Hallah grabbed Sharon by the wrist and strode toward the door.

He pulled her out the door and down the hall. Two armed guards followed closely. They went along another corridor, up a flight of stairs, and then into a master bedroom that must have belonged to the owner.

It was over thirty feet square, with a huge bed in one corner, exercise equipment in another corner, and a Western-style wooden hot tub in a third. Steam came from the water in the tub.

She heard him say something to the guards on the door, who laughed and walked away. Hallah closed the door, locked it and put the key in his pocket.

She stood in the center of the room. Someone had spent a fortune furnishing this place. It was gorgeous, and she had been brought here to be raped. She had a few tricks she learned in the steady stream of self defense and karate classes her mother insisted she take as soon as she started going out with boys who shaved.

He came up behind her softly, but she heard him. It was where she wanted him. He grabbed her from behind around the waist, missing her arms. She powered her right elbow backward, smashing into his sternum and bringing a shout of pain and surprise. He let go of her but she slammed another elbow behind her, hitting just below his rib cage and bringing a gush of air from his lungs as he bent over.

Sharon spun around, saw his surprise and how he was starting to lift his hands. She kicked with all her might. Her "sensible" shoes for walking whistled upward, grazed his thigh and then jolted into his genitals. The stiff shoe leather blasted one testicle north, smashing it into a shattered pulp against his pelvic bone and bringing a shriek of pain from Hallah.

The youth went down in a writhing mass on the floor. Sharon dove on top of him, searching him for a gun, a knife. She found his knife first, a curved dagger, and just as she had been taught, she struck before she had time to talk herself out of it. She fisted the blade's handle, lifted the knife, and drove it downward into Hallah's chest.

Again and again she pulled the blade free and powered it down into his chest. The first stab grazed his lung and grated against a rib before it penetrated farther. The second time the blade slid between ribs clearly, sliced into Hallah's heart and killed him instantly. The third stab was not needed.

She pushed back from him and saw his eyes staring vacantly. She checked for a pulse beside his Adam's apple but found none.

Hallah was dead.

She almost threw up. She gagged and rolled away. Tears cascaded from her eyes. She had killed him! She had to beat it down. Later she could react.

She searched him thoroughly, found a thirty-eight-caliber revolver and two fast loads, fifteen shots. He also carried a derringer, a small two-shot, smaller-bore weapon that was loaded. She put the derringer and the cleaned-off knife in one of the practical yet concealed pockets of the stewardess skirt she had been wearing when they were hijacked.

The thirty-eight she kept in her hand. She found the key to the door in his pocket and quietly unlocked the panel. When she peered out through a thin slit, she saw that there was no guard on her door, and none down the long hallway. Hallah must have sent them away when he talked to them.

Plan—she had to plan before she did anything. She had a knife and two guns. That should help her get some more weapons. She had fired a submachine gun on the range. She knew how to keep the muzzle down so it didn't climb during a ten-shot burst. She wanted an SMG right now, but first she had to find one, or more. She would work her way to the rooms where the men were held. On the way she hoped she could liberate more weapons.

She had warned Farouk that she had been an Army brat, but that must have meant nothing to him. Hallah had used the most common attack approach on women. For weeks they had been taught how to get free. The course had not instructed her how to kill her attacker. Her army colonel father had taught her that, emphasizing the mental attitude as well as the ability to use a knife and a gun. She was glad he had taken the time to train her.

Sharon peeked out the door again.

It was time to move.

CHAPTER
TWENTY-TWO

Gorman paced up and down in front of a full colonel who leaned back, relaxed, at his desk.

"Why the hell don't they check in?" he demanded, not expecting an answer. "They need to check in and be sure the damn radio net works. Then we'll know if and when we need it."

The Israeli colonel watched his ally, then sipped on ice water. He was a veteran of the Entebbe raid by Israeli air units which had rescued passengers held by Arabs.

The two men were at a moderate-sized Israeli air base near Haifa in the northern part of Israel. The base was only seventy-five miles from Beirut.

"I can't get over how close everything is out here," Gorman said. "I drive a lot in Texas and Montana, and you can race along at eighty miles an hour all day and hardly get out of a county, let alone leave a state. Here a hundred miles and you violate the air space of six sovereign nations."

"Relax, Mr. Gorman. They think they are in control. When terrorists believe that, I always smile, because I know they are not. They are defense, I am offense. Just like in your American football, the offense always has the advantage.''

''Sure as hell hope so.''

''We're covered, Gorman. You have a hundred and thirty personnel to move. I have Chinook helicopters, CH-47s, that can take out forty-four fully armed troopers. That means at least fifty civilians can be loaded on each one. We've fighter escort, no problem there.

''We go in with five Chinooks, just in case we lose one on the way in. We could smash up two Chinooks and still have enough moving power to get our people out. This is not like that thousand-mile-over-the-desert fiasco you people got into before over here.''

''So damn many things can go wrong, Colonel.''

''Your people thought of that. We're sending three Cobra gunships, fully loaded, for support. Those sweethearts have two six-packs in each bird, one out each side door.

''Remember that those babies fire 5.56mm slugs at four thousand rounds a minute out of six rotating barrels. Like the old Gatling gun. They can plough up the damn ground. Besides those, the six pack, each Cobra has an automatic 40mm grenade launcher and a variety of air-to-ground missiles it can fire.''

''Sure, except we don't have a clue where Cody is or even if he's found the hostages!''

''We monitored that radio check he made with Rufe Murphy. He said: 'Moving on target, hope to have your support come daylight.' So he's on-site and getting ready for his daylight attack.''

''Four men against an army? I knew we handled this all wrong. Let's make a radio-net check. Cody's receiver will be off if he's on a silent attack. But has to leave his on to monitor anything from Cody. Let's try it.''

They went to the radio room and sent the call.

''Hunter, this is the Fox. Please respond.''

There was no reply. The colonel took the mike and tried it again. This time an answer came through loud and clear.

''Foxy, what's happening? The hunter is in position,

working into site. Except a call around 04:00. Out, I will relay it on to you. Confirm. Out."

"Confirm, Fox; out," the Israeli colonel said.

Gorman was not convinced. "Yeah, sure, it sounds good. But Murphy is laying back a mile or two with the bird.

He's not even with Cody right now. How do we know Cody's making progress? And the damn time is winding down. We're well into the second twenty-four-hours now. So help me if that bastard Cody fucks up again, I'm gonna kill him for sure!"

The colonel went to the small refrigerator in his office on the air base and took out two cold beers. "Once we get Murphy's or Cody's call for assistance, we can have jet fighters overhead in or around Beirut in six minutes, from scramble to first flyby. The choppers will take a little more time to get there, but it's only seventy-five miles. Closer if the terrorists brought the hostages to the south somewhere."

"Yeah, I know, I know. Why did it have to be Cody leading the operation? I just plain don't trust that sucker." He snapped on a TV set in the office. "Guess I'll have to live with it until I can take care of the matter personally."

"From what I've heard, he's almost a one-man army himself when he gets charged up. He'll probably go through those Palestine Liberation Guerrilla Force fighters like a saber through marshmallow cream."

"Sure," Gorman snarled. "And I'm sitting here with my bare ass hanging out, and the hell of it is, I lose either way!"

Cody and Caine kept well away from the stream light the Shiite guard carried to the shed. Soon they heard the generator fire over and chug along before the doors to the building were closed. Two of the guards remained on the generator, and the big shot marched back to the mansion and went inside. He hadn't noticed any missing guards.

Waiting is often the hardest part of any operation. Caine and Cody stood it until it was a little after 3 A.M. Then they each made a sweep around the area where the exterior guards should have been posted.

Cody found the first leaning against a tree, sleeping.

His razor slashed, and the PLG Force soldier would sleep forever.

He met Caine at the arranged spot just beyond the motor pool. They retreated to their observation post behind the mansion.

"Found only one sentry out there, sleeping like a baby," the Brit reported. "I dispatched the chap with extreme prejudice."

"You have your keyboard for the C-5? I think we'll introduce these bums to real war before they know we're here. Sun should be up about five or so. At four-thirty we start the show by detonating the charges. The barracks first, so we can close out the dance card on half of Farouk's troops. Then blow the office and then the others."

"How do we liberate the mansion? I'd guess you don't want to blow the place apart."

"We eliminate all opposition outside the house, then we figure out how to get inside and rescue our people."

Sharon stepped into the hallway of the second floor of what she figured was the central part of the mansion. She locked the door behind her, since that could slow down anyone finding Hallah's body. She moved down the hallway slowly, but at a normal-appearing walk. She had waited until nearly 3 A.M. to start her move.

Most of the guards should be sleeping by now. She took the knife from her skirt pocket. She would use it if she could. It would do no good to be discovered before she could get to the men's rooms.

She changed tactics and ran lightly down the second-floor hall. Most of the men were in the west wing, the women in the east. She came to the west wing and began trying the doors. All were locked here. Ahead she saw a man sitting in a chair and leaning on a table. His back was to her.

Guard! She moved slower now, making no noise at all on the soft carpet runner.

Directly in back of the man she paused. By the sound of his breathing, she knew he was sleeping. She changed her grip on the knife. It had to be done. She reached her hand around the man's face, lowered the gleaming blade and sliced it twice across his throat.

She felt the steel bite into flesh. On the second stroke, blood spurted onto her hand and she pulled the blade back quickly as the man fell facedown on the table.

She jerked her hand back, saw the hot blood on her hand and gagged. She steeled herself, would not allow herself to throw up. She leaned against the wall while a sudden lightheadedness washed over her. She had killed another human being! Twice! She trembled so she almost dropped the knife.

Slowly she reached back toward the dead man and wiped the blood off the knife and her hand on his shirt. She shuddered again, moved away without looking at him and tried the door. Locked. Her key would not work. She got a key from the dead man's pocket without looking at him. It worked to open the door.

She pushed the door inward quietly and stepped inside. Men lay on the floor, some slept sitting against the wall. Only eight of the older men were on cots. She looked for Jenks the co-pilot. When she found him she shook him awake.

"I have guns! We can get more! We have a chance to break out of here!"

Jenks saw her, recognized the short-haired blonde stew, but ducked under the blanket.

"Go away!" he hissed at her. "I don't want anything to do with any escape!"

She sat there puzzled and furious for a moment. Then a hand touched her shoulder.

One of the young men on the flight, who she figured had been in the military, grinned at her.

"Lady, those are words of music to my ears. You must have wiped out the guard to get in here. He still have this Russian rifle? Come on, Willy is here! We're going to have all the help we need!"

Willy checked the guard in the hall, pushed him down a little more so his bloody throat wouldn't show, then took his AK-47 and his two extra clips and even found a hand grenade in his pocket. Willy hurried back in the room and woke four of his buddies who were traveling on civilian passports but were with the peacekeeping force in the Sinai peninsula.

He organized them, and they quickly slipped away to find and kill any more guards on doors and to alert the other men who were in a big area two doors down.

It was nearly 03:30 hours when Willy and two others huddled with Sharon, who would not give up her thirty-eight, but she did give the derringer to one of the men.

"If we could find all of the passengers, we could get them to the first floor and out windows and into the trees back there," Sharon said.

Willy shook his head. "Sharon, you're our general, but the terrain out there is a bleak, barren desert of hills. The guards would pick us off one at a time or capture us. What we need to do is capture this whole complex and then use the transport and blast our way back over the Green Line into East Beirut."

"Dreaming, man," another soldier from the Sinai said. "They must have forty men down there. We've eliminated three or four, and they have all the firepower. I've been in combat before, in Nam. We've got to know what the hell we're doing or we could be shooting each other."

"We get more weapons," Willy said. "We need to shake down every room in this whole place until we find all the rifles and pistols we can use. A few SMGs would help, too."

"How much time do we have?" Sharon asked.

"Until somebody finds the first dead guard. Then the roof is going to blow off this place. Then we have to be ready to stand and fight."

"Wake up all the men," Sharon ordered. "We at least can be ready to escape when we make our chance. Everyone who wants to help us fight, get them in one room and we'll start collecting weapons. The biggest problem is we don't know how much time we have left."

CHAPTER
TWENTY-THREE

Abdel Khaled turned over again. Damn the bed, damn the mattress! Nothing was right up here in the hills. Almost nothing. He and the team had taken over the plane; they had generated more publicity and mass media notice for their small band than ever before. Even the powerful Kaddoumi could not stop them.

But that didn't help him sleep any better. He went to the bathroom, had a drink of water, but nothing helped. An idea came to him slowly and it made him smile. He pulled on a robe and looked into the dimly lit hallway. Four doors down was Hallah's room.

The girl, the stewardess, she might still be there.

He hurried down the hall, saw no one, and used his master key, which would open any lock in the place. One light was still on in Hallah's room. He turned and closed the door quietly, then locked it before he looked into the luxuriously large bedroom. The bed was empty! It had not been slept in.

He took another two steps into the room. He saw a man's hand extending past the sofa. The large room seemed to crash in on him in the few seconds it took him to rush around the couch.

Hallah lay on his back on the floor. He was fully clothed, his arm thrown out, and his chest a mass of blood. Quickly Abdel beat down his anger, his fury, and touched the man for a pulse.

There was no need. Hallah's body was cold already. He had been killed two hours ago, three, perhaps five or six! Who had done it? The hostages? The woman? The stewardess? Where were the killers now? Was it a threat to their mission here?

Slowly, Abdel slumped on the couch. He felt drained, totally exhausted. How had it happened? Hallah gone in a second. Abdel remembered the wonderful weekend in Damascus and shivered. Never had he felt such understanding, such perfection in another human being. Hallah was young, but quick to learn, ready to give fully of himself.

He stood and stormed back to his bedroom. He checked the clock. It was a little after 4 A.M. He would rouse the troops and start questioning the hostages one by one. He would shoot each one after questioning. That way he would get rid of the killer!

He pulled on his clothes, strapped on his prize .45 Colt automatic and slung a submachine gun around his neck. In his fatigue-jacket pockets he stuffed ten extra loaded magazines for the SMG.

Abdel ran to the control room, where they had set up a radio and a siren. He sounded the siren to wake up everyone.

The siren wailed through the bleak hills.

Farouk charged into the room, turned off the switch on the siren and picked up a loudspeaker microphone.

"Attention; disregard the siren. There is no emergency. Continue with your normal duties. I repeat, there is no emergency."

Farouk put down the heavy mike and stared at Abdel. "Have you lost your mind? We are not going out of our way to attract attention here. We are not trying to tell everyone in northern Lebanon where we are hiding the hostages. How can you live and be as stupid as you are, Abdel?"

"Someone killed Hallah!" Abdel shouted. "I just

found him, his room's door was open. Somebody used a knife."

"And so you were so furious that your lover was dead that you are now going to wake up the troops and have them slaughter the hostages?"

"I want only to question them. We need a complete inspection. There may be others missing. Some guards may be killed. Someone has Hallah's weapons!"

Farouk calmed. "Yes. The weapons. They could be trouble."

A guard rushed into the room.

"Three guards in the hallways! All have been knifed to death!"

"The hostages, are they still in their rooms?"

The guard unslung his SMG and raced up the steps to check.

A handgun fired and the guard stumbled back down the steps, his hands holding his chest, which was splotched with bright red. He looked at Farouk for a second, then fell down the last three steps, dead on the landing.

Tahia rushed up to the steps. She had just dressed and thrown a holster and belt over her shoulder.

"Trouble?"

"Yes. Hallah is dead, also some guards. We're not sure where the hostages are or how long they have been free. We think the stewardess is responsible—Sharon Adamson."

"We must kill them all!" Abdel screamed. "Don't you see? We must kill them all so we can destroy the evil ones who killed Hallah and our guards. None must escape. All of our men will be issued submachine guns. We will kill the hostages wherever they hide, in the mansion, on the grounds, in the garden. They all must die!"

Farouk slapped Abdel sharply on the face. Abdel leaped back, the forty-five coming into his hand quickly. He pointed it at Farouk and then Tahia.

"They all must die! I command it. I am now the leader of the Guerrillas! My word will be obeyed."

"Will you kill us, too, Abdel?" Farouk asked softly. He wore a long robe and slippers. Abdel did not answer him.

"They all must die! It must be done. They killed

Hallah! We must maintain our authority. We must extermi-
nate these infidels and do it before the sun comes up so they
do not despoil another of Allah's perfect days!''

Tahia moved toward him. He swung the gun, pointing it
at her.

''Abdel, we all liked Hallah, but he is a casualty. The
war goes on. We must fight and strive and move forward.''

''Don't try to trick me!'' Abdel screamed. He moved
the weapon's aim back and forth between them.

A guard ran into the room. He began talking before he
saw the situation.

''We have just found two more guards killed outside....''

Abdel shot the guard once in the chest. Farouk lifted
his robe. His hands were still in the pockets. A pistol barked
twice, and the robe smoked a bit around the pocket.

Abdel took one round in his chest and the second
through his heart. He fell.

''Check all guards, all prisoners,'' Farouk commanded.
''Check the grounds. I want Sharon Adamson found and
brought to me. She had to be the one who killed Hallah.
She told me her father was in the U.S. Army. Hurry, hurry!
We have much to do.''

''Do it!'' Cody told Caine.

The explosives expert touched a button on his radio
detonation board and the barracks/dayroom on the grounds
went up in a splintering, quaking roar that showered wood,
shingles and chunks of rocks all over the compound. Twenty-
two militiamen sworn to fight to the death for the Palestine
Liberation Guerrilla Forces did just that. Most died in their
beds.

A few militiamen staggered out of the rubble, backlit
by the resulting fire, when they were picked off by rifle
shots from the second floor of the right wing.

Before the defenders could draw a breath, Caine exploded the motor pool building, the office building and the
shack where the generator purred away contentedly until it
burned itself out in the roaring diesel-fed blaze that billowed
up, feeding on six barrels of fuel.

Below, flames raced through the four structures. A few

confused militiamen staggered about, only to be picked off either by the sharpshooters on the second floor or the heavy machine gun which suddenly opened up from the guard tower manned by Hawkeye. The Texan chopped up anything that moved in the big yard in front of the mansion.

Cody and Caine peered through some light brush from their concealed position above the end of the huge country house. Cody figured the friendly fire from the second-floor window meant some of the hostages had escaped, got weapons, and now were trying to fight their way out.

"We can do the most good inside this end of the mansion," Cody said. "Let's see if we can make contact with the Americans up there."

They came up to the rear entryway of the right wing of the mansion, and found a guard on duty. He aimed his weapon at Cody immediately, but before he could pull the trigger Caine sent three Uzi parabellum rounds into his chest and neck, jolting him backward, his life's blood spilling over his rifle. Cody grabbed the weapon and rushed into the building.

A guard fifty feet down a long hallway vanished to the side, and Cody and Caine ran halfway up the stairs.

"Ahoy, you on the second floor!" Cody bellowed. Nothing happened. They rushed up the rest of the way to the second floor, but found only another long hall, with five doors leading off each side. The downslope rooms faced the courtyard. They were the important ones.

Cody covered Caine as he checked the first two doors. They were locked. Caine shot the lock off the first door and kicked it in. One militiaman inside cowered in the corner. He looked no more than thirteen years old.

The Brit grabbed his weapon and his spare magazines and pushed him back in the corner.

"How can they let kids go fight their wars for them?" he asked. The next room was empty. Cody knocked on the third. They could hear shooting from inside. When a lull came, Cody stood at the side of the door, knocked and bellowed. "Americans out here, damn it!"

After a pause a strong male voice came through the door.

"What sport did Babe Ruth play?"

"Baseball, idiot, we're here to help you. Open up."

A lock clicked open and something was pushed away from the door, then it opened inward. A woman's face looked out. She saw Cody.

"Are you for real?" she asked.

"Real enough. How did you get away? Where did you get your weapons?"

"Come inside quickly, we're trying to figure out where you guys came from," she said. Cody and Caine slipped in the door, and they shut it and pushed back the barricade.

"Sharon Adamson, head stewardess from the flight," she said holding out her hand.

"I'm John Cody and this is Richard Caine. We've come to get you out of here."

"Just two of you?"

"We have help. The outside is pretty well under control. How many more of the terrorist militiamen inside?"

"No idea. We were going to try to get to the buses and get back to East Beirut."

"Can't happen. Farouk and his men have probably killed the buses by now. How many rifles you have up here?"

"Seven, and one thirty-eight-caliber revolver."

"I'm going to give you two more recently acquired rifles. I'll need to take six armed men who have had military training if possible. Three will go with Caine and three with me, so we can start clearing this mansion. We need positive control."

"Be light in another half hour," Caine said.

"I'm going with you," Sharon blurted. "I want to go, to help. I feel responsible for these people."

Cody nodded. She seemed to be the leader, even though five or six of the men with the rifles had to be military men.

"Keep two armed men here, we'll divide the rest. We'll clear the second floor first, all three wings, then work down."

They cleared rooms each way down the second floor corridor. Cody kicked in doors that were locked. They found no one in the first seven rooms. Then two big rooms had women hostages in them, and beyond that they found two militiamen just waking up.

They quickly surrendered.

"We have no way to handle prisoners," Cody said.

Sharon was already tying them up with their own belts and bootlaces. "There has been enough killing. Let these men live."

It came out strongly, not as an order, but as a statement that brooked no rebuttal.

Down the hall two Arabs ran into the corridor, fired two shots and were blasted apart by silent Uzi rounds from Cody's chopper.

He and Sharon stormed down to the next room. Cody heard voices inside. He kicked the door open and covered the room. There were six more women from the plane there. They cried when they saw Sharon.

"It won't be long now, ladies," she told them. "We're going to take care of you. Please stay back from the windows, and lie on the floor until the shooting stops."

Then she was gone into the hall, rushing to catch up with Cody, who had just kicked in the next door.

CHAPTER
TWENTY-FOUR

Cody, Sharon Adamson, and their team of three Marine Corps infantrymen worked down the rest of the second-floor corridor to the end. They found three more Shiite militiamen and quickly dispatched them. But not before one of the Marines had taken a round in the meat of his shoulder.

Cody stared down at the sweep of the yard and the gardens in front of the mansion. The four outbuildings were still burning. Half a dozen dead men lay on the ground in front of him. One of the buses had both front tires flattened.

Dawn was only minutes away.

He took out the radio, lifted his antenna and called to Rufe.

"Rufe, you awake?"

There was a pause.

"Am now. Time to move?"

"Soon. Like to have some of those Israeli jets overhead in about twenty minutes. Then move in the slow birds in another twenty minutes. Our work here going well."

"That's a copy, Mr. C. I'll be there in ten. Over and out."

Cody waited a few moments by the window. Caine and his team were supposed to come back to this end when they finished clearing the second floor all the way to the far end. He took another look at Sharon.

"You seem to be the kingpin here. How did you get it all started?"

"One of the terrorists tried to rape me. I got lucky and killed him and took his weapons. Then I found where the men were and we started working at getting ourselves free. It's downright scary what a person can do when she has to, Mr. Cody. That was the first time I've ever hurt anybody, let alone kill someone. I still shudder when I think about it."

"Forget about it for now."

Caine came a minute later and they sent two men who turned out to be Marine embassy guards down the steps first for their point. When the Marines had a room cleared and safe on the ground floor, the rest of them charged into it and began moving forward to clear the twenty rooms on the ground floor.

They had just left the fourth room and darted into the hall, when a door opened ahead of them and two Arabs jumped out, snapping off shots from handguns.

"Trouble!" Sharon shouted. She dove for the floor, rolled once and came up with the submachine gun she had liberated from a dead Palestinian chattering on full auto. She held the bucking weapon on target for eighteen rounds and the two attackers went down.

Cody tilted his soft cap back on his head and watched the woman in her airline hostess skirt stand, and, without looking at the weapon, eject the spent magazine and slam another one into place. She charged the handle to get a fresh round in the chamber, then looked over at him.

Two Marines began hopscotching from room to room. Most were vacant on this right wing. At the center of the mansion, they held up and waited for a conference.

"Could be trouble ahead, sir," one Marine said. "There's a whole big pile of furniture set up in front of the far door through the little anteroom. Come take a look."

Cody heard the machine gun outside chattering again.

Four bursts of five rounds, then one of ten. Hawkeye must be finding some new targets and living up to his nickname.

He edged up to the hall doorway and looked into the next room. It was twenty feet across, and on the far side big wooden desks had been pushed up against a door leading the other way into the central section of the mansion.

"Have we accounted for all of our passengers and crew?" he asked Sharon.

She had been counting as they moved and had a Marine on the other fire team also keep count.

"All except two. They may have been moved somewhere."

He picked one of the smaller Marines and they darted out a rear door to the back of the mansion, keeping close to the wall as they slid forward toward a window.

"This should be the first room past the barricade," he whispered to the Marine. The window stood five feet off the ground. "I'll give you a leg up and you take a look through the bottom of the window and see what or who is inside."

He laced his fingers together, forming a step, and the Marine lifted himself to the window. A moment later he jumped down.

"Two Arabs in there loading magazines. Whole pot full of ammo."

Cody would have used a grenade, but he wanted it to be a surprise visit when they went through the doorway of this room and into the hall beyond the barricade. He unslung the Uzi, pushed it to full auto and motioned for the Marine to give him a hand-step upward.

He edged up slowly until he could see through the window, then pushed the Uzi against the glass and sprayed a dozen silent rounds into the two men working over ammo cartons.

At once he found the window lock, opened it where the glass was broken in, and lifted the window. He squirmed through, then told the Marine to go bring the others.

In the room, he pushed the bodies to one side, found a fully loaded Uzi and four freshly filled magazines. He put the new Uzi over his shoulder and pocketed the heavy magazines.

Then he went to the window and helped Sharon climb through.

She looked at the ammo, found two more magazines for her SMG and waited. When all nine of them were in the room, Cody checked the door. He turned the knob silently and eased open the panel.

The hallway stretched out a hundred feet, but twenty feet down he saw a machine gun on a tripod aimed in his direction, with heavy sandbags holding it in place.

"Any more grenades?" Cody asked Caine.

The Britisher tossed him two, one at a time. Cody had considered trying to pick off the gunners with the silenced Uzi, but the odds were bad. He jerked the safety pin from the grenade, held it in his right hand and eased open the door. His arm was a blur as it snaked out the door and whipped the grenade down the hallway in a throw and roll that should get the required distance. At once he shut the door and waited the 4.2 seconds.

When the concussion of air hit the door from the blast of the grenade, Cody let it swing open. Ten seconds later, when all the shrapnel had landed, he jumped into the hall and hosed down the gun emplacement with twenty rounds from the unsilenced Uzi.

The grenade had detonated just behind the emplacement, shredded the gunner into an early grave, blasted one MG mount off its spot, and tilted the gun at the ceiling.

He heard shouts beyond, and doors slamming. Two men rushed into the hall, but his Uzi riddled them before they could get off a shot. The unsilenced Uzi had more range and impact, since part of the force normally used to expel the slug out the bore was not being swallowed up by a suppressor.

The Marines and their basic room-to-room combat techniques took over as they cleared a room, covered the next man who moved into the upcoming room, and worked quickly down the hall. They found only one Arab, who had a broken leg, with the white bone showing through his calf. He cried quietly on a bunk. After searching him and the room, they left him there for cleanup time.

Sharon waved Cody forward. "Up here!" she yelled.

He hurried to the room and found what had to be the head man's office. It had a map on the wall with marker pins, a logbook, another list of what could be members or units.

"The most interesting part is back here," she said.

At the side of the room they found Abdel Khaled's body.

"He was number two in command, the one who murdered Captain Ward on that cross."

"If the other terrorists aren't here," Caine wondered aloud from the doorway, "where the bleeding hell are they?"

Daylight. Farouk looked out the window from the central wing of the mansion and knew that his cause was lost. The support buildings were all in rubble and burning, his transport was destroyed, most of his fighting men had been murdered in their beds by the barracks blast.

Now the passengers and crew, with some outside help, had taken over the second floor and released all the prisoners. It was only a matter of time. At least he could get away with Tahia to live to fight another day.

Tahia had tears in her eyes as she fired her automatic rifle at the machine gunner in the tower. How had they been able to take over the whole camp, blow up the buildings? Who had done it?

"We must fight until every one of us is dead!" Tahia barked. "We can hold out in here for days. Help will arrive for us. These people only want to get away. We let them go and they will stop attacking us."

Farouk shook his head sadly. "We are beaten this time, Tahia. A strange combination of factors we did not, or could not, control. Come, we must go. There's a back door here, and a sheltered path downhill. We must hurry."

A grenade went off fifty feet down the hallway.

Tahia knew then that Farouk was right. She took two more clips for a lighter-weight SMG she picked up and followed him to the door.

He opened it slowly and looked out. All clear. He had taken only a dozen steps down a path that led along the back of the center wing, when a rifle round slammed into the stonework over his head.

He caught Tahia and dragged her down.

They crawled toward the base of a raised planter, working slowly along behind that to a small patch of cedars that had been planted but never watered enough, having grown into a stunted hedgerow barely a head high.

For the moment they were safe. They ran slowly in back of the cedar hedge to the far end of the mansion, then turned downhill. Ahead of him, Farouk found three of his soldiers cowering behind some trees.

"Men, move forward, down the hill," he ordered. "You three will lead the way to a victory for our cause!"

Two of the men raised their rifles and hurried forward. The third soldier threw down his rifle.

Farouk shot him in the face.

The machine gun, so intelligently placed, stuttered out a welcome as the two PLGF militiamen tried to cross an open space beyond where the generator shed still burned. The buzzing lead slugs drove them back to the protection of a pair of tall cedars.

Farouk lay where he had dived into the dirt to safety behind the big trees. Tahia sat down beside him.

"We are doomed," she said quietly. "It is over, Farouk. It was over in Athens when Najib informed, when Ali was killed, only we didn't know it. Why has Allah betrayed us?"

Farouk sighed. He rubbed his hand across his tanned and wrinkled face. "They are learning, these Americans."

"And we made mistakes, many mistakes, but we have left our mark. Nations know us now."

"But who are *we*? Just you and I? If so, then Ali died in vain back in Athens."

"No! Never even think that! We will escape from here and we will rise again. We will build a new army of supporters and we will make certain the Palestinian cause will triumph!"

Six sleek, U.S.-made jet fighters slashed over the top of the ridgeline at fifteen hundred miles an hour, only a blur as they blasted through the sky. Then they made a long, easy turn and came back much slower.

"Israeli fighters," Farouk snarled. He watched them. "Now it will be harder than ever to get away."

"Where can we go?" Tahia asked. "It is too far to walk back to Beirut."

"Child, I have a surprise that not even Abdel knew about. Quickly now, follow me!"

CHAPTER
TWENTY-FIVE

Rufe Murphy came in at fence-top height with the captured YZ-24 chopper, took one round in the tail section and lifted up to three hundred feet, where he could get the overall view. He had tried twice to get Cody on the radio but the sarge probably had his receiver turned off.

Caine had done good work with his C-5, Rufe could see by the blackened and still-burning piles of rubble. The main building looked much as it had yesterday. Cody had not wanted it blasted, or it would have been in ruins already. Rufe could see no targets. Disappointed, he tried the radio again.

"Big man, this is the Rufe, on-site."

"Hear you, buddy. Just wait and watch, we're doing some mopping up here. Shouldn't be too long."

Rufe held the chopper in a low hover and checked the grounds around the house again, but he wasn't sure who was who.

The radio rattled again.

He refined the frequency setting and the signal came in clearer.

"Chopper near the deck, do you need assistance?

This is flight seven out of the Fox den doing a bit of recreational flying this morning, several thousand above you.''

"You'd be them jet jockeys from down south. Looks like our team is winning. Too chopped up to know which is the good guys just yet. Where are your slow cousins?''

"ETA is about four minutes. You be ready for them?''

"Double-check, Seven.''

Rufe worked the small radio on his lap.

"Groundlings, this is Rufe. Got your ears on down there? Jet set upstairs says the choppers will be here in about three and a half minutes. Where you want them?''

"Rufe, you might not believe this,'' crackled Cody's dry response, "but the area is not secure yet. We need another ten. Coordinate for me, will you, buddy? Out.''

Cody put down the radio. He stood in the main door-way of the mansion and checked the terrain. They had cleared the big palace. The Marines who had been passengers were doing the clean sweep through brush and gardens inside the wall. So far they had smoked out six healthy Arabs who had thrown away their weapons.

As soon as the buildings were secured, Sharon went to the rooms, where she had told the passengers to remain, and made a final count. She had a hundred and twenty three. There were six U.S. Marines fighting with Cody. She had them all!

Near the back of the group of women someone screamed.

"It's Mrs. Vereen!'' a man shouted. "Come quickly!''

Damn, damn, damn! Sharon raged at herself as she ran. The passenger who was a nurse was beside Mrs. Vereen, who had fallen and lay on the floor. Her head nestled in the nurse's lap as both sat on the floor.

Mrs. Vereen gasped for breath and held her chest a moment, then she saw Sharon and smiled.

"Sharon, most interesting flight I ever took. You are wonderful.''

"Don't talk, Mrs. Vereen. We have military helicopters coming here from Israel; they should be landing in ten minutes. Then it's only seventy-five miles to a good hospital in Haifa. You hang on!''

"Sounds like you're giving me an order," Mrs. Vereen smiled.

"I am, and don't you dare disappoint me. We'll have you out in the first chopper and I'll send the nurse with you and they will just get you fixed up in no time. Your color is looking better."

Mrs. Vereen reached out and took Sharon's hand. "Thank you, Sharon, for what you did for all of us."

"Now you just hush. We're going to have a party tonight. We'll all come to your room at the hospital and make noise and be obnoxious and everything, and you'll be laughing and remembering all of this."

The nurse put her hand on Sharon's shoulder. Sharon looked over. The nurse shook her head sadly.

"Mrs. Vereen won't be able to make it to the party, Sharon. I'm sorry."

Sharon looked at her. The elderly face seemed the same, the lips slightly parted, a faint smile. But something had left the eyes, that wonderful spark of life they had known only a few seconds before.

She lowered her head and cried.

The nurse had put a jacket over Mrs. Vereen's face, and the people around her had unconsciously pulled back from her body.

Sharon turned from the scene. Her eyes found the co-pilot, and she scowled at him.

"Nobody said you had to be a hero, Jenks, but the danger is past, this is strictly routine business. I need you to divide all of the people here into groups of ten. Let men and women be together if they want to be. Groups of ten and bring them all down to the first floor, ten at a time, so we can get ready to load the choppers."

She had checked with Cody. The plan was to bring in one of the Israeli Chinooks at a time and land right in front of the entrance where a parking lot once had been planned. There would be eight or ten Israeli soldiers on board and they would deplane and serve as security around the air-craft. When thirty former hostages were loaded on the craft, the security would pull back inside the chopper and it would lift off.

She still carried the Uzi machine gun. She gripped it tightly, then fastened it across her back on the sling. She wasn't about to give it up to anybody.

She saw the small chopper swing over the compound again, drop down and investigate something on the ground, then swing up. That would be Rufe, from what Cody had said; one of Cody's Army. She heard other choppers then, and in the distance she saw five big twin-top rotor Chinook helicopters swinging around and around in a holding pattern, about a half mile out.

Now all she needed was Cody's go-ahead to bring in the big birds. She ran out the front door of the mansion looking for him. One of the Marines on the steps said he last saw Cody and two of his Marine buddies running toward the far side of the estate.

She started that way, then heard the firing and ducked down and pulled the Uzi around where she could fire it. No hurry bringing in those birds. The entire area had to be cleared and checked, safe for civilians.

Cody had been at the far end of the mansion when he saw movement to the left of the old generator shack. Something didn't seem right.

He saw two of the Marines and yelled at them to follow him, then he ran to the fringe of trees and looked down the slope. At the back side it leveled out more and there had been a try at putting in a golf course below, but it never worked out.

There was a vehicle of some kind under effective camouflage netting at the bottom of the slope, almost to the outer wall.

He scanned the territory between the hidden vehicle and where he thought he saw movement. A man lifted up and darted past an open spot to a stunted row of cedar trees that marched its way almost to the bottom of the hill.

Cody fired six shots into the row of trees where the figures had vanished. He had seen three more dash to the same place. He ran forward to a better firing position, found his spot and dropped down in a prone firing position, looking down to see a man already at the hidden rig, pulling off the protective covering: it was a four-man chopper!

Cody dropped to one knee and brought up the Uzi without the silencer, tracing a pattern of slugs around the bird's engine. Another man ripped off the last of the coverings. Two people ran from the end of the cedars. One looked like a woman. Before he could lift his weapon to fire, Hawkeye's machine gun chattered out a ten-round welcome.

The woman went down.

For a moment the man hesitated, then he dodged down beside her, behind a small hump that hid them both.

Tahia looked at the blood on her blouse.

"I am not hit! As Allah is my witness I am strong and can continue!" She felt hot tears in her eyes. She could not keep up the lie. "Yes, Farouk, I *am* hit. Badly, I fear. I—I can't get to the helicopter, but you must. Go! Go now while there is still time!"

"How can I leave you, Tahia? They will capture you, humiliate you."

"Go, Farouk! You had sense enough to leave your own brother behind in Athens when he would have compromised the mission. You must do the same thing now. I'm hit too bad to get to the helicopter, let alone live long enough to get to a doctor. Go, now!" She could barely force out the words, the pain hurt so.

Farouk looked at her, then nodded, saying nothing. He left her an SMG he had carried and two extra clips. Then he turned and darted toward the chopper.

One of the men he had sent ahead had the engine started and the rotors spinning.

Tahia watched as he dodged, darted, and stumbled his way to the copter. He got through the rifle fire, dove in the chopper door, moved over to the pilots seat and gunned the engine. He had to wait for the engine to become fully warmed up before he could lift off.

She groaned as she tried to move and bit her lip until blood came. She pulled herself up to the top of the small rise, where she could serve as a rear guard. Ahead fifty yards she saw the big American and two men who had joined him. They charged forward.

She triggered two six-round bursts at them, then edged

lower as the return-fire came. She rose and fired again, felt bullets whip past her, and then they were gone.

Two minutes, she told herself. Farouk needed another two minutes to make sure the engine would not quit on takeoff. No one fired at the chopper now. She had pinned down the riflemen!

She fired and ducked and fired again, then she pushed in her last magazine. The Americans were up and moving ahead to another spot of protection. She fired until she had only two rounds left.

Tahia struggled to stand on the rise. She put the submachine gun to her chest and screamed, "For the Glory of Allah!" She pulled the trigger.

Cody saw the Arab woman fall just as the terrorist chopper lifted off the sand like some giant, bloated, metal insect.

He jerked the radio from his pocket, flipping the transmit switch.

"Rufe, come in fast!"

"Yeah, Sarge?"

"Did you see that other chopper, the one here behind the mansion? Come in here and pick me up pronto. I've got to go after whoever is in that bird!"

"Roger that. Give me twenty seconds."

When the chopper came in it kicked up a storm of dust and sand. Cody ran through it and opened the pilot's door.

"Out, Rufe, this one is mine! See you back at the top of the hill."

Rufe bailed out and stood there while Cody jumped in the chopper, fastened his belt, put the two Uzis on the co-pilot's seat beside him and lifted off.

CHAPTER
TWENTY-SIX

It took him almost two minutes to spot the yellow copter among the barren hillsides and steep ravines below, and when he found it, almost at once one of the Israeli jets made a harassing attack on the terrorist chopper, slamming past it at 600 miles an hour, rocking it in the turbulence, giving Cody time to catch up.

He checked the line of flight the yellow bird took, and slanted cross-country to cut him off. The jet made another pass, firing a rocket near the bird, but not hitting it.

When he lifted over the next rise he saw the militia chopper just ahead of him and in range. He found the firing button and tried to line up his sights on the swaying helicopter. His first rocket fired but missed.

That shot let the pilot of the other bird know someone was on his tail, and he took evasive action, dropped into a narrow ravine and slammed along dangerously close to the rocky walls of the canyon.

He took a deep breath and followed, but could not get lined up for another shot. He checked the YZ-24s pods and had only one rocket left.

They came out of the gully into a wide valley, and the other bird climbed rapidly. In thirty seconds of dogfighting, Cody realized the yellow chopper was faster and more maneuverable than his.

Then the yellow bird was gone. He looked around and almost too late saw him coming in from the side for a perfect shot. Cody dumped his bird lower, but felt the impact as the small rocket blasted in the air and rained hot shrapnel through the YZ-24. He held his breath to listen, but the engine sounded the same. No real damage.

He swung upward and away, now the hunted instead of the hunter, wound into a valley, then lifted over a small rise and checked behind him. His radio talked.

"Easy, Cody chopper, he almost nailed you," the jet pilot watching the fight said. "Want me to assist?"

"Only if I can't get him. I owe this guy. If I buy it, you nail the S.O.B."

"Roger. Here he comes again."

Cody worked his controls, bucking the chopper to the left, diving toward the desert hills, sure his landing gear was going to scrape the outcropping before he could pull up, but the maneuver forced the yellow bird off his tail.

He pivoted his chopper and raced head-on at the yellow flyer. For a moment he had a target, then the other pilot, who must have spotted him coming, dove to the side.

Cody went with him and got off his last shot from the rocket pod. The round barely missed, slammed into rocks and acted almost as an air burst on the enemy chopper, less than twenty yards from the rocks. The yellow bird limped away, but Cody was dry; no more rockets, and the machine gun was out of rounds as well.

He saw a trail of smoke from the chopper and toward the other bird. It was plain now that the yellow craft was not operating at full potential. He caught it easily and pulled in behind it. He pushed the Uzi out the open doorway but could not get in the right position to fire. His chopper was a two-handed flyer. At last he got off a five-round burst, but the rounds went wild as his own bird pitched and fell away.

He was tempted to call in the Israeli jet, but he had another idea. He pursued the yellow craft, maneuvering over it, then dropped down and fired a burst of rounds through the top of the other craft.

It fell away to the left, as Cody guessed it would and he stayed right behind, sending another burst into its side, but evidently not hitting anything vital. The chores of wars past enveloped him. Then the yellow chopper wheeled suddenly, and a man showed in the open doorway with a AK-47 aimed directly at Cody, who dumped his chopper to the right and down, but not before he saw the rifle bucking in the man's hands.

Cody felt the rounds hit his craft up front. The marksman had aimed at the engine—and hit it. Cody felt his bird's thrust weaken, then the lift faded away as the rotor began turning slower, losing power.

Cody checked his altitude.

Three hundred feet.

Not high, unless you're falling straight down with no power.

He rammed down the collective pitch-control lever that controlled the pitch of the rotors, flattening the blades, trying for autorotation of the blades from the YZ-24's downward momentum. As the chopper commenced a descending glide, the air from its downward speed rushed up through the blades to keep them spinning. A glance at the tachometer told him the autorotation of the blades was climbing in rpm's, as he worked his chopper's collective pitch-control level and the cyclic control stick. He ripped back on the cyclic lever, with the Yugoslavian chopper descending with stomach-wrenching speed at less than fifty feet from the ground.

The chopper nosed up sharply, then Cody shoved the cyclic forward again, and the YZ-24 slammed into the crash landing with a shuddering crunch, the landing gear buckling powerfully. Then the rotors stopped.

The *choppa-choppa* of the terrorist bird returned overhead, hovering lower and longer than it should have, Cody decided, the pilot probably right in guessing that most of the Israeli air cover was concerned with cleanup at the mansion and had not traced them yet. The terrorist chopper must not have had any more ammunition or rockets either.

Play dead, Cody decided.

He sat there in his pilot's seat with his head back, so he could see the other copter as it circled warily; then he saw it come in closer yet and continue to hover.

When a rifle barrel appeared out that chopper's door, Cody ended his death scene, grabbed the unsilenced Uzi and sent a stream of parabellums at the yellow craft and saw the rifleman lunge out the door and topple in a deadfall to the ground 100 feet below.

Cody used the final rounds in the Uzi to aim into the engine section of that chopper, and was rewarded with an abrupt plume of black smoke and the winding-down sounds of the big rotor blades slowing.

The pilot of that craft knew what he was doing too, though, and he had been low enough so that he coasted his craft into a patch of rocky clearing several hundred yards away from Cody's downed bird.

Two dead choppers.

Now it was one on one.

Cody checked his magazines and found he still had two fresh ones. He took the unsilenced Uzi and slid out the far door opening, away from the other bird. He lay behind the squat chopper and took stock of his ammo supply: sixty-four rounds in the two magazines, plus whatever was left in the one in the weapon. No grenades. One four-inch fighting knife. That was it.

He watched the other downed bird.

It bounced slightly and Cody knew a man had left it. He switched his Uzi to single shot and began crawling through a slight depression in the barren soil toward a deeper ravine.

He was twenty feet from the chopper when a grenade exploded, shattering the fuel tanks on his helicopter, erupting it into an eye-searing fireball.

He hit the gully running, downhill, in the only direction the enemy could have moved, twenty yards to where he paused to lift up to see over the lip of the ravine, to study the landscape in front of him: unrelieved desert hills. Scrub growth of some kind.

He scanned the whole scene, watching for movement,

then he took it in sections, dissecting every bush, every rock. He found the man wearing a gray jacket and brown pants in the fourth section. He was about 150 yards away.

Cody lined up the Uzi, moved the selector to full auto and blasted twenty rounds into the spot where the terrorist lay. When the jarring of the Uzi quieted, he watched the spot again. The man was gone; wounded, he hoped, but not dead. He surged to his feet and raced twenty yards to a new ravine that zigzagged in the direction he wanted to go.

The heavy sound of the AK-47 on automatic fire thundered across the barren hills as Cody dove the last six feet into the ravine and safety.

His enemy was alive.

His enemy had enough ammo to fire fully auto.

He ran hard along the arroyo for two hundred yards to where it leveled out, found a small rise to hide behind and again searched for his prey. This time the man had concealed himself behind a large boulder. It was not quite big enough, and one leg and a foot with a white running shoe on it extended to the side.

Cody worked forward out of the low place, moving swiftly from rock to rock, from cover to concealment. He was halfway across the fifty yards of desert real-estate, when the shoe pulled back. Cody rested behind his own rock now, waiting for the first shot. None came.

He picked out his cover carefully this time. He was not quite thirty yards from the terrorist. Ahead, the best protection he could find was a small boulder fifteen yards out. No sweat. Just like the coach back at Princeton telling him to get fifteen yards on a quarterback draw up the middle on a third and fifteen. He switched the Uzi to full auto again, and lifted up.

Behind the rock ahead, Farouk Hassan had not seen Cody. He knew he was out there somewhere. He massaged his knee, which was on fire with pain. He had not counted on a helicopter pursuit.

He touched his left arm where three bullets had smashed the bones. He could barely lift it.

Firing a heavy AK-47 with one hand was hard. But he had to do it if he wanted to stay alive. He needed to look around the rock, but he wasn't sure if it would be safe. The American would be after him from that side, where the ravine ended. He shouldered the weapon, held it in place and pushed the muzzle around the rock. When he looked out, he saw the American lift away from his hiding spot and charge forward.

Farouk's finger found the trigger and held it back until he saw the barrel begin to overheat and twist in protest. Then the AK-47 jammed. He flung it aside, pulling a knife from his boot sheath.

Cody had seen the muzzle edge around the rock, but by then it was too late; he was committed to charging forward and in the open. He darted to one side, then back and forward as the weapon fired on full auto ahead of him.

Hot lead tore into his upper left thigh. He felt the lead bore through his flesh, tear apart capillaries, cut open small arteries, then slice on through the muscle and continue into the sand. He groaned.

As the terrorist's AK-47 began to overheat, the line of fire changed and the last four rounds out of the muzzle slanted to the right, meeting his movement, slamming into the Uzi's receiver, blasting it apart, killing the weapon, stopping it from ever firing again.

The Uzi spun out of his hands into the sand. Cody reached for his forty-five, but remembered he had used up the last rounds in the room-to-room fighting, and now had only his knife. He pulled it and waited for the terrorist to stand up and try to claim his kill.

Nothing happened.

He lay there in the sand, his thigh bleeding, his mind computing all possible reasons why the enemy had not charged forward. Slowly, he lifted from his prone position, reversed his hold on the knife handle into a fighting one and stood so he could see behind the rock.

Farouk Hassan was binding up his left arm.

"English?" Cody asked.

"Some," Hassan said. He picked up the knife. "I am Farouk Hassan, leader of the liberation of the aircraft two days ago. I will not be taken prisoner."

"Stupid thing to say," Cody growled. "When you die,

you're dead. The only part of you that lives on is memories, and maybe in a history book. Forget the glorious afterlife, forget your religious fantasies of Allah. If you die here, and now, it's like a long dreamless sleep. You simply cease to exist."

"I feel sorry for you, American, if you truly believe that. If so, what is the purpose in life?"

"Not to die for Allah, that's for damn sure. Throw away the knife and I'll call in a chopper."

"No."

Cody took the pocket-size radio and pushed the talk switch. "Rufe, I lost the bird. We have two choppers here with broken wings. Divert one of the Chinooks out here to pick us up and get started loading back there. Copy?"

"Copy. One big banana heading your way. The jets overhead will direct it. Out."

Farouk looked at Cody as he pushed down the antenna on the radio and put it back in his fatigue-jacket breast pocket.

"You think it is so easy, American? We fight for our lives here, like you did in 1776. Eventually we will win! Palestine will have a nation!"

"Never," Cody replied. "Not as long as you bomb airports, kill women and children, execute old men and women on airport runways, and act like animals with no morals."

Farouk shook his head. "We will win, because we are willing to die for our beliefs!"

"Depends how many of you there are to die," Cody barked. He walked closer. At ten feet he stopped. "Chopper should be here soon. Then I want you to put down that knife and act like a human being."

Farouk snorted, looked away to the west, where he heard a chopper coming, then threw the knife like an expert.

The blade came point-first into Cody's shirt front, jolted into the plastic back of the small radio and drove through it into a mass of transistors and silicone chips and two heavy-duty batteries, where the blade stopped.

Cody pulled the blade away from the radio and looked

up as Farouk surged upon him. He tried to knee him in the groin, then his fingers of one hand tore at Cody's eyes.

Half blinded, Cody struck out with his right hand, which held the Arab's own knife. The still-sharp point drove hard into flesh, and Farouk's hand fell away from Cody's eyes. Cody saw the knife driven deep into the Arab's chest. The terrorist fell into the sand on his back.

Farouk Hassan's eyes closed and then opened.

"American, either the long sleep, or Allah's eternal garden, I will know soon which it is to be. You will only wonder." His head rolled to the side and his eyes stared at the sand, but saw nothing.

Sharon Adamson stood with the passenger list she had kept folded in her skirt pocket, checking off each person on the list as he or she entered the Israeli Chinooks. She had never been so glad to see a military helicopter in her life.

The Israeli were sharp, efficient, practical. They left four men from the first three choppers to serve as a backup security force.

The six U.S. Marines had given their weapons to her and went back with the passengers. Two of the Marines were given first-aid by Israeli medical corpsmen. She watched the third chopper lift off with the last of her passengers and crewmen. She said she would come out in the next bird.

She had followed Cody's chase across the desert as best she could by the radio reports. Now she waited for the chopper to come back with Cody.

She hoped that he was still alive. She had set Mrs. Vereen's body to one side. It would go out with the last load, along with any of the terrorists Israel wanted. An officer had set up a small table outside the mansion and had been talking to each of the Shiite captives. They had rounded up fourteen men, some of them so young they did not shave yet.

The Israeli captain came back to Sharon and smiled. He spoke perfect English.

"I'm convinced none of these people were more than backup forces for the hijacking. We don't want to take them as prisoners. It would serve no purpose. We'll take all of their weapons, and any ammunition they had, then release them when we're ready to pull out.''

The *whup-whup-whup* of the big chopper crowded into the conversation and the bird landed on the LZ marked now with a staked-down plastic red X.

Sharon ran to the door and met Cody when he stepped out. The medic on the plane had wrapped up Cody's thigh bullet-hole, and he was walking with only a slight limp.

She introduced Cody to the Israeli captain in charge of the pickup.

''We have the last of the former hostages well on their way to Haifa, with jet fighter protection,'' the Israeli said. ''No one is going to try to interfere. We need another hour or so to clear up everything here, then we'll be moving out.''

''Captain, I'm pleased to see you,'' Cody said. ''Sorry I couldn't save one live terrorist for you. I should have had the leader, Farouk Hassan, but he wanted to die.''

''Many of them are like that.'' The captain paused. ''We have enough sandwiches and coffee and Cokes to feed an army in that next chopper down. Would you and the lady like to have a bite of breakfast?''

Cody suddenly realized that he hadn't eaten in over thirty hours. He nodded, reached down and caught Sharon's hand.

''I think I just heard chow call. Would an Army brat like you like to be served for a change instead of doing the serving?''

Sharon laughed and smiled. ''I could stand a sandwich or two, now that you mention it. And I would die for a good cup of coffee.''

CHAPTER
TWENTY-SEVEN

Pete Lund smiled broadly as the President of the United States put down the phone. The President reached across the desk and held out his hand.

"The last of the hostages is safely in Haifa. Cody's Army pulled it off without losing a man, and the Israeli's report no casualties among their troops, pilots, or machines! Totally a beautiful, successful mission! Congratulations, Pete!"

"Thank you, Mr. President. I knew Cody could do it. He's a valuable man to have around. What happened to General Johnson?"

The President grinned. "Well, I would think that he has found something more important to do than eat crow!"

They both laughed.

This was the first time Lund had ever been alone with the President of the United States, but he could not feel more relaxed or comfortable.

"I'll expect a full report by Cody within two or three days, Pete. From the looks of things now, I'd say that Cody's Army has more than met all proscribed objectives and tests on this mission. We took the hostages out without any more loss of life, we did not get a bloody international nose for overkill, and we worked closely with the Israelis in getting their people out as well. I don't know what else we could ask for.''

"I'm sure John Cody and his men will be pleased, Mr. President. There is only one thing that I might suggest.''

The President looked up, with surprise. "More? What else could we expect of them?''

"It would be my expectation that now that the team has proved itself, that the men would be anxious to have another mission.''

The man smiled tiredly. "You tell Cody there will be more work for him and his men. There are always delicate problem-situations like this where we can't send in a platoon of Marines to do the job, like we did back in the 1920s and 1930s. Yes, indeed there will be more missions.''

"The men will appreciate that, sir. I'll go ahead and set up permanent quarters, then, at Andrews, so they will be close at hand. If they do want to wander, I'd think a twenty-four-hour recall would be sufficient lead time for their reporting at Andrews on future missions.''

"Good, good, Pete,'' the Chief Executive nodded. "You take care of it. I don't think we really need General Johnson in on these discussions after this. He's a fine man and does his job well, but in these cases, we will act without his counsel—but keep him informed.''

"Is there anything else, then, sir?''

"We have some problems shaping up that have me worried, Pete, but we'll discuss that in the future. Talk to my staff and set up a weekly appointment on Monday mornings at ten. You'll be on call through the Agency at any time, I would think, but let's get together here at ten each week on Monday and review hotspots.''

"Yes, sir. I'll take care of the details. Thank you sir, for getting Cody into action. I think we're going to be calling on him more and more.''

Cody watched the slender girl stow away her third tuna-fish sandwich and three cups of coffee. He chuckled.

"Sharon, you were hungry.''

"Pigging out. They never will believe any of this when I get go home to Ft. Lauderdale. Back there they remember me from the high-school annual, where they said I would be the 'girl most likely to succeed as a secretary.' For a while I thought they might be right."

"Bring that coffee, I want you to meet the rest of our crew," Cody said.

They went out of the big chopper to the steps of the mansion, where the Israeli captain was interviewing the last of the new prisoners.

They watched as the stack of rifles, automatic weapons and new boxes of unpacked rifles, SMGs and cartons of ammo were carried to the helicopters.

Rufe and Hawkeye sat on the steps. Caine had heard about the sandwiches and ran for the spread.

"Team, like you to meet Sharon Adamson, the spark plug who got the whole escape operation started by the hostages. She almost had it wrapped up when we got here. Sharon, this ugly guy with the machine-gun finger is Hawkeye Hawkins, handy man to have around."

Hawkeye grinned, shook Sharon's offered hand. "You ever want to change jobs, ma'am, we've got one more enlistment open in our army," the Texan drawled. "Pay is lousy, but the company is good."

"Thank you, Hawkeye. I'm more of a flight attendant than a full-time commando, but thanks for the offer."

"Sharon, this is Rufe Murphy, my entire air force. This guy can fly anything with wings and a motor—except a bumblebee—which we know, scientifically, can't fly anyway."

Sharon held out her hand and it vanished in Rufe's huge paw.

"Happy to meet you, Sharon. Hear tell about what you did to them terrorists. Way to go, gal! Just damn glad you on our side!"

"Thank you, Rufe, I appreciate that from one flyer to another. Have you ever flown four engines?"

"Sure have. Pushed around B-52s for a time, and then some passenger jets for an outfit out of Paris. Not the best for me, though, just being a straight bus driver."

Sharon laughed. "I'm sure all of the passengers and

crew will want to see you and say thanks. All unofficial of course, because we understand you four have not really, officially, been here at all. Still it would be great if you could come to the party tonight in Haifa. You know that we never would have broken out of here by ourselves. We had seven rifles and one pistol, and they had everything else and about sixty armed men.

"They probably would have killed us all before they were done. Abdel was crazy as a loon, blood-crazy. Farouk was a little saner, but still a zealot. Tahia evidently lost her lover in Athens, so she didn't care if she lived or died anymore. The boy, Hallah was just that, a boy."

The Israeli captain walked up and indicated he was finished. They had all the weapons and ammunition. He had sent about twenty Lebanese survivors running down the trail toward the small town.

He brought out two American flags and had them draped over two plain wooden coffins they had brought from Haifa. Captain Ward's body had been found in the brush and cleaned up before he was put on the chopper.

Mrs. Vereen's body was laid carefully in the second temporary coffin and carried on board.

Everyone stepped on the last chopper. Cody and his three men and Sharon stood there a moment more, staring at the huge mansion that had been the site of such trauma in their lives.

Sharon would never forget it. She had grown up here, she had assumed command, become a leader. She would never back down to anyone now.

Cody knew the President would be pleased. He had received a short radio message from Pete Lund expressing the Commander-in-Chief's views.

Sharon held out her hand. "I really don't need any help to get in this bird, but it would be nice. Would you mind?" Cody helped her inside, found her a soft place to sit down on big pads used to cushion fragile loads, and then dropped down beside her.

"We won't be able to come to the party tonight," Cody said. "We can't risk the publicity. Some of the passengers are going to talk. Tell them we were Australians;

we just got caught up in a situation and had to fight our way out of it. Should fool most of them. Remember, there was no official U.S. participation in this strictly Israeli operation.''

Sharon grinned. ''I know that. We'll miss you at the party. Most of our passengers say they will fly out tomorrow for Tel Aviv, their original destination. I'll be staying over a few days in Haifa to rest and get my head together. Will you be going right back to the U.S.?''

''Not sure, Sharon. Don't have any orders yet.''

''Oh. Well, I'll be staying at the Hilton. If you are going to be around a couple of days, maybe we'll see each other.''

''It would be nice to think so.''